PRAISE FOR
We're in Trouble

"I would like to claim that I discovered him, but you can't really discover writers like this: the quality of the work is so blindingly obvious that he was never going to labor in obscurity for any length of time ... Sometimes, when you're reading the stories, you forget to breathe ... They're beautifully written, and they have bottom, but they're never dull and they all contain striking and dramatic narrative ideas ... They're literary in the sense that they're serious, and will probably be nominated for prizes, but they're unliterary in the sense that they could end up mattering to people."   —Nick Hornby, *The Believer*

"Coake's debut collection, *We're in Trouble,* offers psychologically taut stories of people in moments of crisis. It begins at a gallop with the title story, a heart-pounding tale about the menace that sleeps inside us, revealing itself when we are overly curious or just careless."   —*Chicago Tribune*

"Expertly crafted and edited to the bone, they fill us with fear of a very human kind. As Chekhov famously said, if there is a gun hanging on the wall in the first act, it must fire in the last. If a wife washes a glued-together plate at the start of a Coake story, by the end, we will find out how it breaks."
—*The Baltimore Sun*

"Coake's quietly horrifying short stories don't depend on graphic violence or oceans of blood for their effects. They disturb on a deeper level and can't be driven from the mind as easily as more conventional horror stories . . . [Coake] doesn't need to rely on flowery language to engage a reader's attention. Coake's stories have strong plots, the kind in which characters make decisions that matter: They mirror the sharpest of human turning points." —*The Columbus Dispatch*

"These stories grab you by the heart and don't let go. Their reality is mesmerizing, not for the spectacular and horrifying outward circumstances of the stories . . . but for the portrayal of the characters as they struggle to get through the maelstrom of these events." —*Arkansas Democrat-Gazette*

"[These stories] are potentially real-life situations of life meeting death, written with a haunting clarity that makes the reader dread turning the page, not for fear they will find a lunatic covered in sores and seaweed taking a chainsaw to the main character, but because they might find, through the writer's exquisitely rendered characters' emotions, feelings of loss that they have already or might someday experience themselves. They might find themselves hurting for the wounded human spirits that the writer has presented in these pages." —*Recoil* (Grand Rapids, MI)

"Coake's stories are elegant and redolent of an aching form of humanity. Coake deserves praise not just for the studied quality of his work, but for having the courage to unveil the scary visions in his head." —*Star Tribune* (Minneapolis)

We're in Trouble

WE'RE IN TROUBLE

STORIES

Christopher Coake

A HARVEST BOOK • HARCOURT, INC.

Orlando   Austin   New York   San Diego   Toronto   London

www.HarcourtBooks.com

Brenda Hillman, excerpts from "Mighty Forms" in *Bright Existence*
© 1993 by Brenda Hillman, reprinted by permission of Wesleyan University Press.

The Library of Congress has cataloged the hardcover edition as follows:
Coake, Christopher.
We're in trouble: stories/Christopher Coake.
p. cm.
1. Psychological fiction, American. 2. Death—Fiction. I. Title.
PS3603.O14W47 2005
813'.6—dc22 2004017419
ISBN-13: 978-0-15-101094-3 ISBN-10: 0-15-101094-3
ISBN-13: 978-0-15-603277-3 (pbk.) ISBN-10: 0-15-603277-5 (pbk.)

Text set in Garamond MT
Designed by Cathy Riggs

Printed in the United States of America

First Harvest edition 2006
A C E G I K J H F D B

for
Joellen Thomas

Contents

We're in Trouble   1

Cross Country   31

Solos   61

In the Event   107

A Single Awe   143

Abandon   175

All Through the House   245

We're in Trouble

We're in Trouble

A SUITE

I. Back Down to Earth

ERIC AND KRISTEN ARE IN UNFAMILIAR TERRITORY. THEY have only known one another a few weeks, but they have decided they are already deeply, madly in love.

This love, this unexpected boon, has come to them with amazing speed and intensity. And at the right time. They're young—Eric is twenty-four, Kristen twenty-two—but they met as each was concluding a long and tumultuous relationship. Kristen had just left her boyfriend of four years. Eric's divorce, after three years of marriage, has only this week been finalized.

In celebration, they have taken a hotel room downtown, and have barely left it for an entire weekend. And, here in the late hours of their last night in it, they've just finished making love. Now they talk softly, sweetly, in the dark. About their memories, their secrets. This tumble of words excites them as much as the warm, damp shape of the other's body beneath the blankets. Everything they say and do now seems to carry weight, meaning, a symbolism of great and private importance which exalts them, and what, together, they hope to be.

Kristen says, in a whisper, I want you to tell me something. Anything. As long as it's important to you.

Tell me what you want to know, Eric answers. I'll tell you anything. I have no secrets from you.

Something only you could tell me. Something that *is* you.

Anything?

Tell me the most vivid thing you can remember. Then I'll do the same.

Eric is quiet, but she can feel his hand, warm and flat on her belly. His fingers curl and uncurl.

Well, mine's a bad thing, he says.

Mine's good, she says.

Kristen plans on telling him about the first time she saw him, which is not, perhaps, the memory that's most important to her—that would be her mother's death, to which she's only alluded, and about which she tries not to think. But for now, topmost in her mind is the picture of Eric, barely a month ago, in the next line over at the movie theater—the broad wedge of his back and the slow smile on his face, the hesitation which she saw him fighting, as he kept his eyes on hers. He was going to the movies alone; so was she. She saw him and he smiled at her and kept looking, fought his shyness, and she knew—knew it completely—that he would end up with her. She wants him to know this. Kristen approached him—she'd never been so bold before—and after making their halting introductions, they laughed at themselves, the obviousness of their shyness and desire, the pleasure of their bravery, and then they sat together during the movie. And she was *right*. He did end up with her. Here they are, together.

She wants to tell him she was never in doubt.

Mine's exceptionally bad, Eric says. I don't know if I should tell you right now.

Tell me. It's good you're going first. We'll start with the bad and then we can finish with the good.

You're sure?

I feel like we can handle anything, she says. Just like this. Don't you feel that way?

He shifts a bit, kisses her dry lips, and tilts his mouth close to her ear.

I WAS SEVEN when this happened. My family went to a state park down in southern Indiana, and in this park were a bunch of deep ravines and cliffs. It was my mother and my father and my younger sister and our—my—dog. His name was Gale—I named him that because he ran so fast. I was proud of the name, to have thought that one up. Gale, he was a mutt, mostly German shepherd. Maybe a couple of years old, but we'd had him since he was a puppy. I'd raised him. He slept with me at night. I loved that dog. He was one of the great playmate dogs, waiting for me when I got off the bus, protective of me when I was around other kids. Always wanting to do a good job—like dogs do, you know?

He had this ball, a rubber squeaking ball, that was his favorite toy. We brought it with us to the park. At midday my father took us to a picnic area and started up one of the grills. My mother and sister went to wade in the river. Me and Gale climbed a slope, into the woods, to play. I started throwing his ball, and he started chasing it, and we kept going on and on into the woods, away from the trail. Gale kept getting more and more frantic and excited, and he'd catch his ball and run with it, tearing off into the bushes, with me just trying to keep up.

We kept climbing and I got the ball from him finally. We'd climbed high enough to get to the edge of a cliff overlooking the river. So—I don't know why, I know I didn't mean any harm by it—I started tossing the ball close to the edge of the cliff. I wasn't trying to do anything—I mean, nothing *wrong*—I was testing him, you know, to see how fast he was. I was . . . *proud* of him. He'd tear off and get his ball before it got close to the edge, and I guess I thought he knew what we were doing as well as I did.

Then I gave the ball a stronger toss, and it bounced too close to the edge, and I saw I'd messed up; it was going to fall off, Gale was too far away to get to it. But he went for it anyway. The ball went over the edge, and he didn't slow down—he was too keyed up, I'd gotten him too excited. I shouted out, *No,* trying to get him to stop, but he didn't until he was just at the edge. Then he realized where he was, and he skidded in the dirt and went sideways, and then his back paws went off the edge of the cliff, and he was stuck there, hanging on with his front paws and his elbows, trying to push himself back up over the edge.

I ran to him, and when I was close to the edge I saw how far down it was. Maybe a hundred feet, I don't know. A long, long way. I saw it all like I'd taken a picture of it, and I can still see it. The cliff was old, dark, rotten limestone, and it was covered with moss, and I can remember how it smelled, all wet, like turned-up soil, and vines went up and down it, and at the bottom was this dark shadowed bank, covered with old black leaves, and some slimy-looking dead trees. The edge of the cliff was crumbling and covered with gravel, and I felt dizzy looking over it. And instead of grabbing Gale's collar I kind of . . . kind of stared for a minute, you know, I just froze, looking at the drop.

But only for a second, a half a second. It couldn't have been long. Gale was trying his best to get back up, kicking against the rock with his back paws, and scraping at the gravel with his front paws. He almost made it, but then lost it again and started to slide. He was looking at me with his eyes bugging out, and making this . . . this *huffing* sound. That's when I got on my hands and knees and went to him and tried to grab his collar, but a rock must have given or something, because he fell right when I got to him. He made a . . . a yelp. When he knew.

I was at the edge, leaning out over it, to get his collar, and I could see him fall. His paws kept moving, like he was trying to get at the rock still, but he was falling in air. He turned over once or twice. Halfway down he hit an outcrop of limestone, and I think that was what killed him. He bounced off of it, but he didn't move on his own after. And when he hit it, he made . . . this sound, real quick and sharp. Kind of like a scream that got cut off in the middle.

He hit the bottom where the cliff turned into a slope, and slid down it like he was made of rubber. The old wet leaves bunched up in front of him and slowed him down. He left a trail through them, and underneath the leaves was this glossy wet rock. It looked like something had gotten skinned. I looked at Gale just once when he stopped sliding. I was a long way up, but even from there I could see his teeth were bared.

I was on my hands and knees, crouched at the top of the cliff, looking over. I got vertigo—I still can't go near heights. The whole cliff started to tilt forward, like it was trying to dump me off—kind of like the whole world was a wheel and it was turning forward. I thought—I thought I could see the vines start to lean away from the rock. I remember I wanted to scream, but my throat was all closed up.

And . . . I almost jumped. I almost jumped after him.

I can't explain it, not exactly. I mean, of course I was upset—I was seven, and I loved that dog as much as anybody in my family. But it was more than that. I wanted to die, too. I'd done such a horrible thing that I had to. I knew it. I knew even at seven what it was to want to die.

And . . . it was more than that. It wasn't that I wanted to. It was that I *had* to. They took me to church then, my folks did, and it didn't just feel like I'd done something wrong—it felt to me like the world was tilting because God wanted me dead, because I'd done something so wrong that all He could do was sweep me off the top of the cliff, send me down after my poor dog.

It was like I didn't have any choice in the matter at all. My hands were sliding across the gravel and I kept seeing Gale, the way his legs kicked in midair, like I knew mine were going to, any second. Just as soon as I stopped fighting it and gave in.

KRISTEN IS QUIET for long time. Then she says, You didn't fall.

No.

How?

I lay flat against the ground. I put my cheek against the dirt and closed my eyes and grabbed clumps of grass and held on as hard as I could. And after a while the vertigo stopped. When I could make a noise again, I shouted until my parents came.

Then what happened?

I cried for a week, and I had nightmares ... I *still* have nightmares. Maybe once a week my head sends me right back there, and we play it out all over again.

He sighs, a long deep sigh, and says, Except that most of the time I fall.

She turns and puts her arms around him. He can feel her cheek against his bare chest. It's damp. She holds him tightly.

Your turn, he says, after a moment. Tell me the good thing.

She tightens her arms.

Come on, he says, tell me.

He puts his nose into her hair, which smells like strawberries and sweat. He closes his eyes and tries to see her face, but part of him is still somewhere else. He sees the gray wet rock.

Please, he says. Please tell me.

II. All Babies Come from Heaven

NATALIE AND JOAN DO NOT BELIEVE IN GOD. THEY can't abide the thought of one. Nor fate, nor destiny. Things do not happen for a reason. This is one of the ways they love each other: by understanding that their love, in the face of all the order the universe withholds, is also a *belief.*

Because nothing they have seen in their lives can convince them that the world wishes them to do what they do—which is touch one another, make love together, live together. Joan, the child of hippies, has never believed in God, but she has known about herself since she was a teenager, and has had plenty of opportunity to see what the world thinks of her for it. But for Natalie, a lapsed Catholic, lapsed hetero, this understanding has been more difficult—Joan had no understanding to turn from, but Natalie did. She misses Mass, the comfort of ritual and answer. And, sometimes, she misses her past loves. She was engaged once, to a nice enough man, and it was never his fault that she began to understand—to believe—what she has always felt for women. They'd planned a baby, she and this man, and when she came out—and a year later, when she began to live with Joan—she couldn't help thinking she'd abandoned motherhood, probably forever.

Until this morning, when motherhood has returned to her, when Joan said to her, Okay, let's do this. Let's have a baby.

For the entire second year of their relationship Natalie and Joan have argued about a child. When the issue first arose, Joan told Nat she didn't want to give up any part of her career to child-raising. She's a medical researcher, and a good one; she likes her job and works long, long hours. Natalie, on the other hand, works for an accounting firm she dislikes. She has never felt particularly tied to work—none of her jobs has ever seemed like the point of her life. She told this to Joan: I don't have anything to want other than you. Do you want me to be like that?

And besides, Nat said, it's a baby. A *baby*.

Joan told her, You say that word like some people say *Bible*.

For months, they were tense, awkward—until Natalie had begun to think her first great love was ending. Of course they loved each other, of course they meant to stay together. But the want of a baby—this was intractable. Natalie couldn't hide her disappointment, and Joan's way was to be annoyed with her for it.

But then—almost miraculously—things began to change. A month ago Joan said, I can see what this is doing to you. So let's talk. I love you too much to go on like this.

And so they talked. They started in the abstract: They're not too old. Nat's just twenty-nine. Joan's a bit older, but it's Nat who wants to carry the baby, to be pregnant. They feel permanent. They've bought the house—and the house has been perfect. They are financially secure. And, even after all the argument and tension, they feel, now, more in love—if such a thing is possible—than when they began.

But despite all the positives laid out before them, Joan stopped short of agreement. She said, Well, it's possible, that's for sure. Let me think, okay?

For a week or so after their talk Natalie felt light on her feet, almost giddy. A year from now, she kept thinking, and it will have already happened. She went to a store that sold baby clothes, found herself picking things out, fondling tiny shoes. But more and more days passed, and Joan kept silent, and Natalie understood that she was taking too long. Joan was either pretending to decide, or deciding against it. Nat prepared herself to leave—because she would have to; the pain and longing she felt had taught her too much about her life. She loved Joan, but that love alone just was not going to be enough.

But then came this morning. As they lay curled together, Joan told her—from nowhere, and after a short, loud stutter—that sometimes she sees children in the mall, along the sidewalk, and she feels pulled to them, feels that she could, maybe, see herself as a mother.

Joan—Joan, of all people—blushed when she said it.

Nat, seeing this, began to weep.

Are you all right? Joan asked.

Yes, Nat said from behind her hand.

So you want to have a baby?

I love you, Nat told her.

That afternoon they go for a run. Joan runs every day; she has been a fanatic about it since high school. On weekends in the warm months Nat goes with her. They run at a public park not far from their house, where a paved track circles a lake almost exactly a mile in circumference. Joan runs several circuits, and Nat keeps pace with her for the first, then jogs and strolls as it suits her after that. Nat has learned to like these excursions together, but even so she remains unathletic, soft. They go to clubs sometimes, she and Joan, where Nat is still uncomfortable. There she sees other couples—all the dykes who have so obviously split up into hard and soft, masculine and feminine—and though she and Joan have laughed about the obviousness of this, Nat wonders sometimes if that is in fact how *they're* seen: Joan with her lean body and short hair, Nat still with her love for long skirts and her ponytail and her need for a baby and her shyness at these places, where she falls behind Joan's smiles and greetings until all she can do is nod and flutter like a wallflower at the prom. Be brave, she tells herself, and sometimes she thinks this to make herself run faster, to catch Joan, to bring more air to her lungs.

The lake is next to a divided highway; to reach it they drive down from the road and park in a small lot on the other side, and then walk underneath the highway on a wide concrete footpath. Natalie has never liked the path, because from beneath, the bridge seems too flimsy, the highway and the cars too near overhead. The concrete shakes and echoes, and she's aware of the tons of steel zipping along just a few yards above, and when she walks through the sunlit, open space between the north- and southbound lanes she winces, expecting some automotive horror to spill over onto the steady traffic of runners and cyclists and children and dogs underneath.

But she doesn't think of this today, when she and Joan walk beneath the bridge. It's a beautiful June day, not too hot, not too humid, and Natalie is looking forward to the run. She's keyed up, almost jumpy—all she can think of is waking to Joan's kisses on her shoulder, Joan's cool palm on her belly, and the merry and secretive look in Joan's eyes just before she spoke.

Nat says to her, as they walk under the bridge, You're chasing *me* today.

Joan touches her lower back and says, I'd chase you anywhere.

And that's when it happens.

From above they hear the shriek of tires against pavement, and then a crash that thunders and reverberates through the open space underneath the road. Maybe fifteen people are under the bridge; Nat ducks, sees everyone wince and duck. Then they hear a second squeal, two more hideous crashes and booms, and Nat, looking a few steps ahead to the sunny gap between the lanes, sees a doll fall suddenly down from the highway; it strikes a concrete pillar supporting the north lane, bounces off, and drops heavily to rest in the grass and trash, off to the side of the path, not twenty feet from her.

For a moment everything is quiet, and then a murmur passes through the people under the bridge. All of them are looking at the roadway over their heads. Joan says, Holy shit.

Nat is looking at the doll. No one else seems to have seen it. She glances at the concrete post again, because something is different there; she wants to make sure she's really seen it. And so she has. Where the doll struck, high up, there's a small, rusty smear, like—

Her fingertips go numb. She has a moment to wonder at herself—why isn't she screaming? Shouldn't someone scream?

But no one else has seen. The others are moving now. Someone even laughs, nervously; a man pantomimes a heart attack, staggering backward with his hands at his chest. Joan's jogging ahead, emerging into sunlight and shading her eyes upward, trying to see what happened. Nat turns away from them, smelling smoke.

She leaves the path, stepping across old rainwater puddles and hummocks of grass. She can hear her own breath. She doesn't want to look, doesn't want to walk another step, but she knows too that she must, because if she opens her mouth—to tell Joan, to tell anyone—she will scream, and she can't allow that. Perhaps there is something to be done, some help to give, and she is the only one who knows.

It's a girl. She's wearing a small blue dress. She has thin blond hair, silky child's hair, tufting in the breeze. She can't be more than a year or a year and a half old. Natalie can see this from a few steps away; the child is too small to be any older. She lies on her stomach in the grass, her head turned to the side, away from Natalie. Her blue dress is torn, and much of her hip and rear are exposed and pale. She is wearing a tangled diaper. One of the her legs is bent, and points away from the other. Nat circles her, stumbling a bit on the uneven ground. She puts a hand over her mouth—she's aware of a thin noise in her throat—because she can see that the fine blond hair is speckled with glass, can see—Nat's throat aches—part of the girl's face, her eye staring out, white and blue and a blossom of deep red, can see that her head is lopsided, falling in on itself like a beach ball losing air.

Now there's screaming. Nat sits down, heavily, in the damp grass, and it takes her a moment to understand she hasn't yet made a sound; the scream she hears now comes from up above on the road, and it is a woman's scream—of course it is—ragged and panicked and angry; it is the sound of loss, wrapped around a name.

Nat keeps hers in. Hers is nothing. Only one scream means anything, *can* mean anything, and she listens to it rising and falling, this scream which can only be a mother's.

FOR A WEEK after the accident at the bridge Nat and Joan barely speak about it.

This means, of course, that they also do not talk about the baby they have agreed to conceive. Nat sees that Joan would like to; Joan meets Nat's eyes whenever she can, and Nat knows she can barely keep her questions in—Joan's method has always been to bring things up, to put them out in the open. And, too, Nat knows that Joan is suffering, suffering for *her*, knowing she can't say anything that will make things right. Natalie would like to make this easier for her somehow, to ease the tension, but she doesn't know a way. Whenever she thinks of the dead child—or the one she might have—she feels sick. Her head hurts.

Nat has surprised herself by talking, instead, with God.

She doesn't consider this prayer. She has always been uneasy with prayer—which seemed to her, when she was younger, when she fully believed in God, as greediness: asking for things she could not have. She always told herself, back then, not to be ungrateful—that if she were God she would be overwhelmed, and maybe even made angry, by the millions of requests the world must heave skyward.

And besides, if she *could* pray, she wouldn't know what to ask for. Nat can barely frame the questions. But she needs answers to them anyway, and she knows these answers reside somewhere far away from her, and from Joan, and so Nat throws her voice up to the heaven that isn't there, to the God in whom she doesn't—not really—believe.

She's not after the big question—why a baby has to die—but the personal one: Why has this happened to *them,* to Nat and Joan, on the very day Nat's wish for a baby was granted? (And—if she is being honest with herself—she should say that all along, as she's dreamed of a baby, she has always hoped, most fervently, for a girl.) Why, of all the people under the bridge, was Nat the one who saw the girl die? Why did *she* have to walk to the girl and see what death had done to her?

Because these events, put together, seem far too ... well, *meaningful.* Too full of portent. At first she's just wondering—but then, she's asking. She's not requesting a boon. Only an explanation of the symbols. Is she being warned not to have a child of her own? Or urged to hurry? Urged back to church, to God? Away from her lover? Any statement, any possible answer, seems too complex, however she puts it together in her head.

Finally she wonders if what she needs is in fact much simpler, if her many questions are really one question; if in fact she's asking the big one after all: Are You there? Or aren't You?

In her mind, the only answer she receives is the same one, repeating over and over: the child dropping down from the sky.

Two weeks after the accident she surprises herself once more. After they have climbed beneath the covers, late at night, Nat says to Joan, I don't think I want a baby anymore.

Joan props herself up on one arm. She speaks too quickly, and Nat knows she's been preparing for this.

I don't think you mean that, Joan says. Do you?

Nat crosses her elbows on her knees and says, I do.

Why?

Because the baby will die.

You don't know that. You can't *possibly* know that. It was a freak accident—

No, Nat says calmly. The baby will die. Maybe at four, maybe at seventy-nine, maybe it'll be stillborn. But every baby dies.

Nat sees the look on her lover's face. She smiles and touches Joan's cheek, and adds, I know how that sounds. Really, I do. But don't you see? A baby decides nothing. We choose to bring it into the world, and the world, or God, or whoever, chooses when it leaves, and all the baby does is get tugged along.

You're scaring me.

Nat says, She was one year old. She hadn't even started talking yet. What do you suppose she thought about when she died?

Joan clasps her hands in front of her mouth.

Nat says, Shouldn't you at least get to form a thought about it, when you go?

I don't know, Joan says, grimacing and reaching for a cigarette. Here we are, thinking about it. Do you think this is better?

What I mean is, I think I've been selfish.

Having a baby isn't selfish.

The world doesn't need any more babies.

Maybe not. But we're free to have one.

Joan starts to explain, to go over again the things they've discussed. At some level, Nat is proud of her for trying. For doing what she thinks is right, to make Nat's own arguments for her. Natalie hears now the things she's said, sometimes tearfully, cast again in Joan's strong voice: How they will be excellent parents, how the world, the way it is, thinking the way it thinks, needs the child they will raise. That problems— all that troubles them about the world—can only be changed by people who raise children not to hate, not to fear.

How can I teach a child not to fear? Nat says. Every time I looked at her I would be terrified. She would know I was lying.

Nat turns off the light. Joan tries to talk some more, but Nat says, Please, no more tonight.

Joan waits a while, then stubs out her cigarette, and sighs, and settles under the covers.

Nat has been calm, but now, with the lights out, her breath shudders, and she begins to sob.

Joan says, Come here, honey. And Nat, without turning, rounds her back, and Joan molds herself to it and slips her warm hand under Nat's breasts. Joan kisses her at the nape of her neck, at the line where her hair begins. Her breath is warm on Nat's neck, on her shoulder blades. Her hands are soft; she rubs Nat's shoulders and back, along the curve of her spine.

It's okay, Joan says. We can do this. We love each other too much not to do this. You have to believe that.

Nat closes her eyes. Inside her head she sees the car, and inside it the little girl and the girl's mother. The papers said they were driving to the park, too, headed down the highway to the next exit. (Had everything gone well, Nat and Joan might have seen the mother and the girl in her stroller as they ran, the little girl watching them goggle-eyed; smiling, maybe, in response to Nat's waving hand.) The mother had the girl out of her car seat, on her lap, because the girl would not stop fussing. Silly—insane—but to the mother, perhaps, it was more bearable to think of the girl on her lap than to listen to that crying, to let her daughter be so troubled. The papers and the news have been unkind to her, but of course the mother could not have predicted what would happen next.

Natalie hopes it worked, this plan of the mother's. She hopes the little girl was asleep, as the cars began to slide and cross and collide in front of them.

Or better: Natalie hopes the girl was awake, smiling, looking into her mother's face. She hopes the girl's last thoughts weren't thoughts at all, but feelings: the wordless surges she must surely feel, staring up at the loveliest face she knows, and seeing all well within it; the swelling of a perfect contentment, a perfect love, before the sky opened up and the baby flew up and out, into a moment of perfect fear.

III. We've Come to This

AT THE AGE OF SEVENTY-NINE, ALBERT IS DYING.

A month ago he was diagnosed with cancer, and after much consultation with his doctors, he has chosen to refuse treatment. This is, he thinks, the right thing to do, the only choice. What he has is extensive cancer of the bowel, and treatment would require chemotherapy, and surgery, and a colostomy bag. As a result of these efforts his life might be extended, but—everyone takes pains to be clear about this—it will most assuredly not be saved.

His oncologist talks to him slowly, with a lot of eye contact, using phrases like *quality of life,* and *tough decisions.* But, to Albert, the decisions aren't tough at all. A man his age, he knows, is going to get caught by something. No one can guarantee he'll even survive the surgery, and chemo, they say, is hard on the heart and liver; the treatments are as likely to do him in as the cancer. He'd suffer horribly for what—a year? A year and a half? His wife, Elise, would be forced to watch. Albert knows that if he were a younger man, more forces might be marshaling in his defense, but he is not young. They can call it cancer, but this is what they mean by dying of old age.

So Albert—a man so healthy and hale it's been joked about all his life—can see his own end. He's a goner, and soon—a month, they say, maybe two. He'll be given medication for pain, and, if the pain is severe enough, he'll be given an epidural, like pregnant women have.

I won't lie to you, the oncologist says to him, when Albert tells him of his decision. There's no easy way to talk about these things, but I feel you should know what's ahead of you.

And here the oncologist looks at both Albert and Elise— Elise who sits straight and grips Albert's arthritic knee with enough strength to make him grimace.

The oncologist says, This is a bad way to go, Albert. It gets, progressively, worse and worse. We might be able to keep ahead of the pain, if you work with us, but the methods we use will affect your ability to think and reason, and to act on your own behalf. These are serious narcotics we're talking about. If you take anything out of this meeting today, make it this: See the people you want to see, and soon. Say your good-byes now, while you can. Don't put off signing documents that need to be signed. The decline is faster than you'll think it can be. I'm sorry—but that needs to be said, and you need to accept it as quickly as you can.

Albert's already on codeine—there's a live animal in his belly, most days—but the oncologist, before Albert and Elise leave, hands him a prescription for oral morphine. This will get you started, he says. The oncologist looks at Albert, his eyebrows raised, and says, in a low voice, Follow the instructions on the bottle. You don't want to mess around with this stuff. Understand?

At first Albert thinks the man is being condescending, but as he drives home—Elise can't; she's weeping, almost wailing—he understands what the doctor has really told him.

During the next two days, when he sits in the study with his papers and his records, doing as the doctor instructed, he keeps the bottle of morphine pills nearby. Sometimes he reclines in his easy chair and turns the bottle around in his hands. There's not much to go over, not much to weigh, but all the same he gives the possibilities a knock or two in his head, and then decides.

He has never kept a secret from Elise in his life, and cannot do it now.

I have had a choice to make, he says, standing in the doorway to the kitchen. And I have to tell you what I've chosen. I need you to be strong about it.

Elise, making him potato soup, stops stirring. The phone rings, and they say nothing until the machine picks up. The damn thing rings off the hook these days, since they put the word out. While it rings they stare at each other, and by the time they're done Albert can see that she knows what he's going to tell her. Her eyes widen, and her mouth opens a little, and then she covers it with her hand.

He says, I want to have a few people over. A dinner party. This weekend, I guess. The old boys, and Mark and Danielle.

Al, she says, please don't.

After the party, if I can, I'd like to make love to you. We may not have much longer to try.

She's shaking her head, and the wooden spoon rattles slightly against the rim of the pot.

He says, After that, I'm going to do it. In the meantime, we'll get the will in order.

She says, whispering, I can't let you.

I have to be able to say my goodbyes, he says. I want you to think about what it means, if I just let this goddamn thing take me. Think about what you'll have to do. The way you'll have to see me, and to take care of me—

I will do anything, she says. You know I will.

I know it, he tells her. Oh yes I do. But, Elise. There's no way—he licks his lips, which are dry now, almost always—I know there's no way to keep you from seeing me dead. But I love you, and I don't want you to see me *dying*. I want to say the things to you that ought to be said. I don't want to go like your father did. Do you want me to have to do that?

She winces, and this hurts Albert to see, but he had to say it. He knows she's been thinking of her father all along, just as he has.

And Elise *has* been thinking of her father. She thought of him as Albert complained of his stomachaches, and one day, when he came home from his daily walk around the park, clutching at his gut, she saw for the first time how pale he was, his skin nearly translucent. She urged him, calmly, to go to the doctor, but she knew full well what the doctor would find. She'd only seen that color once before.

Her father had died of prostate cancer. Near the end, drowning in morphine, he'd somehow, in his head, gone back to Parris Island, and even though she sat with him every day at his bedside, he didn't recognize her at all. He called her awful names, spat and hissed, and sullenly said Yessir and

Nosir when she asked him if he wanted more juice. Albert was with her. He saw everything.

No—almost everything. She'd shooed Albert from her father's room when she had to tend to his diaper, and to his bedsore. The bedsore, as wide and deep as her fist, which every day she cleaned and packed and swabbed and dressed— while her father lay on his stomach and howled in pain, cursing her and telling her to hurry, hurry—all the while holding her throat against the slipperiness of the dressings and the heavy soaked packing cotton she pulled from the wound, and the sight that made her clamp her jaws together and pray for strength: the spot at the bottom of the sore, like a blind eye half-closed, that was the white knob of her father's tailbone.

And Al, her Albert, still handsome, still *there*—standing with a hand on the door frame—is telling her what must be said. His eyes are very blue, and lately his eyebrows have gone white and tufted, and this makes him look even merrier than he did when he was younger. His shirt is neatly tucked in, and the buttons are lined up with his belt buckle. Why *these* things? Why does she think of these things? She knows: because they will soon be gone. These things she loves about her husband will vanish, one by one. Without warning. His mind, sharp and funny and chiding, will dull, become childlike. She will transform from wife to mother to nurse. She has never heard her Albert scream, but that is coming. They can talk about pain control all they like, the doctors, but this is cancer, this is an enemy she knows.

I've thought of Dad, she tells him. Of course I have.

I have thought about all of this, Albert tells her. And of the things that are precious to me— He breaks off, and pinches his lips together with his hand. But he composes himself.

I have always loved to talk with you, he says. I don't want to say anything to you I do not mean.

She nods.

I won't ask you to help me, he says. But I'll want you to be there. If you can't I'll understand, but . . . but Elise, if I have to die—he shakes his head—let me die with your arms around me. If you love me you can do this.

She manages, barely, to turn the heat off beneath the soup. She goes to her husband, and, for the ten thousandth time—the hundred thousandth?—she pledges to him, as fervently as she can, clutching at his shoulders and his arms (they're thinner now; she can feel it) her love.

THEY HOLD the dinner party that weekend. Elise cooks a roast and red potatoes: Albert's favorite. Their children come (but not the grandchildren), and two of Albert's old friends, fellow engineers, and their wives. The engineers have brought cigars and a preposterously expensive bottle of scotch, and seem to have agreed amongst themselves to be cheerful. The children sit, tight-mouthed and pale, shocked at their father's happy mood. He and Elise have agreed that they must not know what he has planned. But his friends don't have to be told; they are old men as well, and believe, as Albert does, in dignity, and even if they can't guess exactly what he aims to do, they will have guessed that this party will be the last time they'll ever see him. Albert stands with them out on the back deck after dinner, all of them holding tumblers of the good scotch, and the lit cigars, and after a lull in their talk, Albert tells them, Gentlemen, it has been my pleasure. I hope you know how I think of you.

The two men, misty-eyed, clutch at his shoulders.

Please look in on Elise, Albert says. I know your wives will—but you, too. Make sure nothing needs fixing; she's no good with tools. But you must—please don't let her be alone. She hates to be alone. This will be more difficult for her than she's letting on.

How could it be easy? one of his friends says, husky-voiced.

That woman's been a fool for you for fifty years, the other says. Since the very first.

Albert sighs and takes a drink. This will hurt his stomach, but not unbearably; he has loved his friends too much not to drink their scotch now.

The first friend starts to chuckle, and behind it is the same nervous shake with which they've all been speaking.

What is it? Albert asks.

I was about to tell you how lucky you are, the man says.

They laugh, and it is as Albert had hoped. Laughter! He's a dead man, but on this night, with these men, he drinks in eagerly one of the last laughs he'll ever have, savors it as the rare and fine thing it is, and above it the rareness and fineness of them all.

LATER THAT NIGHT, he and Elise lie together in their wide, soft bed. He aches; the ache is everywhere now, not just in his belly, and he can start to feel pain in the bones of his hips and thighs. Even the simple act of sitting has become difficult. Soon, if he lets it happen, he will be unable to sit still, and he will have to call the hospital for stronger meds. It's not bad now, but in a day, or two, he will surely have to pick up the phone.

Sometimes he tries to convince himself that the hospital and the doctors have made a horrible mistake, that he will, in the end, be well. He was tempted into thinking it again tonight, out on the deck with his friends. But in a moment of quiet and repose, like this one, he can feel the cancer inside of him with a still certainty, can almost trace its outlines under the soft loose skin of his belly. On other nights he has felt fear, but tonight, Elise warm and soft next to him, lovemaking done—they could not finish, but he managed, heart racing, to fit himself inside her, for a while, and thank God, thank God for that—he feels no fear.

He spends a moment alone, in his head, where he makes a brief statement, informing the Lord of his plans. When he says a prayer afterward, it is for Elise.

My love, he says, it's time.

She takes a breath.

I knew you'd say it now, she says.

She kisses his forehead and sits up, and looks at him. Her face is bleary, her hair a silvery mist.

Please, she says. Wait a day.

He touches her face. No, he says. It should be now. I have everything I wanted. It won't get any better.

He tries to stand, swinging his knees off the edge of the bed, but when he sits up the pain in his belly catches fire, and he moans.

Settle back, she says. I'll get you a pill.

They're here, he says. On the nightstand.

She takes the bottle, quickly, and walks into the bathroom. She fills a glass with water from the tap and shakes out a morphine tablet into her palm. She returns to the bedroom. Albert switches on the bedside lamp.

Here, she says. Take this.

Not yet, he says. I'll take them all at the same time. I can bear it. Honey? Could I trouble you for milk?

She sucks in a breath. Albert has always loved milk—when he sets down an empty glass at the table his eyes are as satisfied as a sleepy cat's. She walks down the hallway to the kitchen and pours him a tall glass. She'll never see his eyes look like that again. Her father's were glassy—turned up, slightly, to show the whites. In a few minutes Albert's will look that way, too.

She returns to the bedroom. He takes a sip, and sighs, and says, May I have the pills, love?

The bottle is in the pocket of her robe. She takes it out and holds it.

Albert, please, she says. Another day. Give me one more day.

He stares at her, his mouth tight.

Elise, I can't. No.

Please.

We both know this is better.

I can't—I can't watch you do this.

You'd prefer the alternative?

She shakes her head. She knows there's nothing she can argue. Of course she doesn't want to see him lessened, suffering. But this? This? She holds in her hands the instrument of his death. She can't be expected to . . . to just hand it to him, can she?

She kneels in front of the bed. Albert, she says.

He puts the glass of milk on the bedside table. He takes

her hands, with the bottle of morphine enclosed between them.

He says, You can keep the lights off until . . . until it's over. It won't take long. Just hold on to me, and when it's done, call Mark and tell him something's wrong. He'll be here in fifteen minutes. I have written a letter. It's on the desk in the hallway, right now, with your name on it. Pretend you don't know about it. No one will ever know you helped me.

Al, I can't.

He tries to pry the bottle of pills from her hands, his broad fingers jimmying open her thin, cold ones. He tries to do this slowly, persuasively, while he talks. When she realizes what he's doing, she doesn't even think—she pulls quickly away. Her hands slip from his, and his elbow strikes the bedside table. The glass of milk wobbles and then falls. They both watch it fall. It strikes the dark hardwood floor and shatters. Glass and milk and froth slide coldly past Elise's knees.

Damn it all! Albert says, sharply.

I'll clean it, she says, rising.

Elise—the glass—

She steps away from the bed, still holding the bottle of pills, stepping over the milk. She puts on a pair of flat shoes from the closet. In the bathroom she takes a towel from the rack, and picks up the wastebasket. Then she returns and begins to clean up the mess, kneeling carefully again.

I'm sorry, she says thickly.

This is what I didn't want, he tells her. His voice creaks a little. This is what I mean. See what it does to us?

And as she kneels, swabbing at milk and shards of glass, her knees aching, her throat aching, she thinks, It? *It?* All he's done is ask her to help him . . . to help him kill himself. And when she can't, when all she can do is tell him she cannot bear it, when all she can do is ask for one more day, one span of hours, for mercy, for another hour in the dark without having to worry about his next breath, or the one after it—this is what *it* does to *us*? Not once did he ask her what she thought of this. Not once did he give her a say in how things between them are to end. And this—this is all he can think to say?

She scrubs harder at the floor.

Albert's stomach hurts. He leans back against the headboard and kneads his belly. He's sorry he shouted. His poor wife sops up the spilled milk. He sees a shard of glass near her hand, and points to it, and he is ready to tell her about it when she sees it herself, and plucks it from the milk. The tenderness of the gesture, the delicacy of her hands, makes him want to pick her up. If only he could! To clutch her to him and explain. Can't she understand? He knows his love for her. This—this end—is the only gift he has left to give her. He wants to tell her the sentences he's prepared. He wants to tell her the last things he'll ever say, for her, only for her. If she'd just look up at him.

He puts a hand on her shoulder.

How dare you, she thinks, biting her lip, scrubbing.

He repeats the words, carefully, in his head, waiting for her to raise her eyes:

Elise, I am a lucky man. I have never loved you more. You are my life.

Cross Country

This is the evidence:

I was nine, traveling cross-country with my father from Colorado back to Illinois. My family had lived in Colorado for all of my childhood, and our move to the Midwest was fraught and unhappy—what would turn out to be my father's last concession to my mother, a return to her home in Chicago. A love of the mountains was one of the only things my father and I had in common; when he learned he'd have to stay a week longer in Colorado to complete the sale of our cabin, he allowed me to stay with him. My father was a distant and silent man, but during that last week we hiked and fished companionably, never mentioning the city. Then, reluctantly, we headed east.

My father didn't like to stop at hotels, so we were on the interstate late at night, late in the way that it can be only on the road, far away from any home—as though we were separate from real things and real time. And it was then, while we ate at a truck stop in Kansas, that I saw them: a boy and a man.

The boy was my age, or a little younger. We looked at each other from booths across the diner while my father napped, head on his arms. The boy seemed odd, somehow: pale, upset. The man with him—large and unshaven—sat with his arm stretched out across the seat behind the boy's shoulders. He smoked cigarettes and watched the boy eat. They left before us.

As my father drove us out of the truck stop, our headlights flashed on a pickup truck in the parking lot. Inside, his face glowing in the bright light, was the boy. He looked, to me, as if he had just finished crying, or was just beginning. He looked frightened. The man was in shadow next to him, with his hand on the boy's neck. I thought—and I thought it more, the more I thought— that I saw the man's head pulling back from the boy's. Then they slipped into darkness. Their truck pulled onto the road behind us, and vanished down the westbound ramp, while we headed east. My father seemed to have seen nothing out of the ordinary, yet I didn't tell him what I saw. What could I have said? I wasn't sure of what I'd seen, and my father did not have the patience for my imaginative leaps.

But as we drove on to Chicago and home, I tried to imagine where the little boy could be going, and what was between him and the man. I knew it could have been nothing. I'd been yelled at by my father plenty of times, with tears as a result; all boys have. But I couldn't shake my dread. I was nine, given to nervous flights of fancy, nightmares. I began to imagine I'd witnessed something awful. What if the man *wasn't* the boy's father? Throughout the rest of the trip, my mind returned to that truck, to the man and the boy driving away from us. With every mile I was sure the boy traveled into danger. Or did he? It seemed to me a puzzle I ought to be able to solve, and yet the more I turned it over in my head, the less certain I was of what I'd seen.

My parents divorced a year later, and my father moved away. As I'd feared—as I'd known—he receded from us, until he became a stranger, nothing more than terse notes at holidays. I spent the rest of my boyhood self-absorbed, dreamy, lost. But the boy's face, shocked, frightened in the headlights—that bit of the real world had reached me. That meant something. I looked at milk cartons and wondered if the boys' faces were that boy's face. But I couldn't remember his features with any certainty. He could have been any boy. The man could have been any man. They could have been going anywhere, doing anything. I saw the boy's body at the side of a mountain stream, white as a snowbank, facedown. Then he sat next to me, doodling, in algebra.

Maybe, I thought, I could help him. Maybe I could take him someplace. Maybe I could get him out of my head. But I've been hesitant. Would it be better to know? Or better not to?

I keep thinking and thinking: My boy. What's happening to my boy?

I.

The boy is excited at first, leaving Chicago; he chatters for a solid hour. The man smokes cigarettes and drives the pickup one-handed, smiling, listening to the boy's voice. The boy lives in a suburb to the north, and doesn't get to see the buildings downtown much; he cranes his head out the window to see the Sears Tower as they pass it.

It's one thousand four hundred feet, the boy says. He has pale circles around his eyes; his cheeks are burned a bright red. Last weekend he and his mother went to the beach. The boy is towheaded and pale, and on the lakeshore his skin burned badly enough to blister. The man can almost see him at the beach: Looking at the lake for a while, though it's not rare enough to hold his interest. Staring at people while he staggers across the sand—the boy's inexhaustibly curious, and less tactful than most kids. Tripping, probably, once or twice, and sprawling onto his chest. (He's grown a lot in the last year, and his coordination's left him; the man guesses it won't come back until the poor kid's in his teens. That's the way it was for him, anyway.) He can picture the boy swimming: dog-paddling a bit, holding his chin high out of the water, pleased and terrified all at once.

The kid doesn't quite fit, wherever he goes. The man loves him for that, for the ease with which these little pictures suggest themselves. The boy stays in the man's mind.

The man puts his hand on the boy's shoulder, then quickly removes it: almost a tap. The boy turns, looks at him, says, What? When the man just smiles and shrugs, the boy goes back to his sightseeing.

The man keeps smiling at the back of the boy's head, the

way the wind lifts his hair, light and inconsequential as a bird's down. About as irresistible, too. The man wants to twine his fingers into it. He puts his hands on the wheel and tells himself to be calm, to keep his eyes on his driving. They have a long way to go. They have time.

ARE YOU SURE it's okay? the boy asks.

They're out of town now, moving southwest past late-summer corn. The city vanishes quickly here; everything recedes. A Midwestern haze rubs out every sign of the world beyond two miles' distance; the sunlight comes from nowhere. A few cars float along ahead of them. No police, either—the interstate rushes along at eighty.

The man turns down the radio and pretends not to have heard the boy's question. This worked a half hour earlier; the boy lost interest. The boy's mother thinks the little guy has attention-deficit disorder, but the man disputes it—the boy's smart and wide-eyed, and his mind always looks to the next thing, but to say that's a disorder seems to do the boy no favors. Still, the man is never sure what questions to anticipate from him. He's a little afraid of what the boy might do—but he looks forward, in a way, to whatever it is the kid will throw at him.

He thinks, not for the first time, how the boy is wasted on his mother.

Is it? the boy insists.

Is what?

This trip, the boy says. I'm sort of thirsty.

A little while more. We'll need gas, then we can stop. There's pop under the seat, I told you—

It's kind of warm. I mean the last one was.

No problem, cold pop at the next stop. The man thinks about playing further with the rhyme, but that's not the boy's sense of humor.

What are those? the boy asks.

They're passing a small pasture fenced by split-wood rails. Behind the fence two llamas graze. A third watches the traffic, dewy-eyed and bemused.

Can you tell me? the man says. I bet you know.

They look familiar. The boy pronounces it *fer-mill-yer*.

Here's a hint. They don't usually live in this country.

I remember the word. It's got two L's.

Yeah.

Llavas?

Close. Llamas.

The boy turns his head for a last look.

They're pretty, don't you think? the man asks.

Yeah, the boy says. I wish I brought my dictionary.

I bet we can find you one.

Mine's got my notes in it.

The boy annotates things he reads with a weird mix of symbols and codes: stars and wavy lines and exclamation points. The man has asked what they mean, but the boy won't tell him.

At the next exit the man pulls the truck into a busy tangle of off-ramp fast-food restaurants and truck stops. The largest truck stop advertises itself as a "stopping center," and at least a hundred cars are parked in a lot which can hold many more. He asks the boy if he needs to go to the bathroom; the boy says no. The man asks if he wants to go inside, and the boy says no again. He seems sleepy. The man tells him to keep the truck locked.

The man walks across the baking blacktop, pulling his shirt away from his chest, and into the little convenience store attached to the gas station and diner. No one looks at him. He knows he's not much to look at, and here on the side of the road the men who come and go around him seem, to his eyes, rougher than him, more worthy of notice. Heavy-bellied truckers, dead-eyed cross-country travelers. A couple of college-aged kids with unwashed hair and tie-dyed shirts play video games, swaying and ducking. The man takes two bottles of cold pop from a cooler, and then sees a rack displaying magazines and a few books. There he finds a small paperback dictionary, next to stacked collections of crossword puzzles. He picks up the dictionary and several of the crossword books— they seem like something the boy might like. He takes a package of pens and a blank pad, too. The clerk is a teenaged girl, stationed on her own, away from the staff at the diner; she seems bored and disinterested, and sure enough, when he checks through she doesn't glance up. He pays cash.

In the parking lot, just outside the shop, two state police cars have pulled next to each other, facing opposite directions. The cops inside seem like mirror images of each other: young mustachioed men starting to thicken in the neck. Their haircuts are short, and they wear sunglasses. They're laughing, and as the man passes by they reach out and slap palms between their windows. The man keeps his head down and goes to his pickup, parked at the edge of the lot, getting his key out and at the ready.

The boy isn't in the truck. The man can see this from several feet away, but keeps his pace steady—the kid might be asleep, that's got to be it. But when he draws near the window he sees that the seat is empty. The boy's door is unlocked.

The man sets his purchases inside and, calmly, looks around the lot. He sees only parked cars, and people getting in and out of them. The policemen still laugh with each other in their cruisers. He circles the truck, looks into the bed. Nothing. The parking lot ends at a strip of grassy land which rises up to the edge of the interstate; there's been a drought so far this summer, and the grass is gray-green, tinder dry, as far as the man can see. He takes a breath. Beyond the diner and the shop are long rows of self-storage sheds. Across the street there's an ice-cream place. They all seem, at the moment, places a boy might want to go.

He calls the boy's name—not a shout, but loud enough for him to hear if he's wandering nearby, down between the cars. There's no answer.

He walks two rows over and calls again, hearing nothing.

The man locks the truck and walks slowly back to the convenience store. One of the cops glances up. The man gives him a thin law-abiding smile and pushes through the doors, into the air-conditioning.

He looks in the adjoining diner and sees nothing. The college kids are still playing video games. He scans the rows of groceries. He walks into the men's room and calls the boy's name. So far he hasn't panicked, but he starts to when he goes back into the shop. He swallows and asks the clerk if she's seen a little boy come in. She says, Yeah, little blond guy? I gave him quarters.

The man sees him this time. Behind the college kids. The boy is sitting in a race-car game, one of the machines with a closed cockpit and a steering wheel. The man stands next to the machine and watches the boy race to thumping drums and guitars. The kid swerves—his head and shoulders move—

and his little video car hits a cow on the roadside, which explodes into chunks of red meat; the car keeps going, and the whole machine bucks and shudders.

Watch out! the machine booms.

You scared me, the man says softly, and the boy jumps.

Just a second, the kid says.

All right, finish your game, then we have to go.

Yeah, the boy says, halfheartedly.

The man and the boy walk back to the truck. The police look at them and the man smiles again, sheepishly. He tries not to glance back at them, but the boy does, giving them a good look at his face. He even waves.

When they're on the interstate, the man says, You can't do that. I need to know where you are when you leave the truck. I told your mother I'd keep you out of trouble. Would you do that to her?

I waved at you. I thought you saw.

This is a lie, but the man ignores it. He puts his hand on the boy's shoulder and squeezes until the kid's looking up at him.

The next time you do that, I'll have to do something about it. Do you want me to have to do that? Punish you? We're supposed to be having fun.

The boy looks at him for a moment, then down at his hands.

No.

All right. The man glances into the rearview mirror. Well. I got you a dictionary and some games. They're in the bag there.

The boy doesn't move for the bag, but the man expects this. The boy is an expert sulker.

They're quiet for a while, driving.

I want to be a policeman, the boy says abruptly, looking out the window at the passing fields.

TOWARD EVENING they cross a river. They've turned to the west now, driving into slanting, dazzling light that comes from just above the horizon and gives the man a headache. The man thought maybe he'd drive the night through, but wonders now if that was too ambitious a plan.

He pulls the pickup into a fast-food place on the other side of the river, at the foot of the off-ramp. They order dinner inside. The man keeps watch outside the restroom door, waiting for the boy to finish his business. The restaurant has an outdoor play area, currently empty of children; he offers the boy a chance to stretch in it. The boy refuses. His face is slack and shiny.

They eat in the truck. Through the windshield they can see the bridge they've just crossed, and the tops of cars and trucks passing over. The river beneath is brown and thick. Westbound windshields glint orange as the sun lowers. The man massages his temples.

Can I call Mom? the boy asks.

No, not tonight. She knows where we are.

I want to talk to her.

The boy's voice is tight. The man looks up. He starts the truck, and says, Do you want anything else before we get moving?

There's a phone. Over by the door.

There's phones everywhere. Do you *need* to talk to her?

The boy shrugs.

Aren't you having a good time? the man asks.

It's boring.

Trips are like that sometimes. It's more fun at night. The wind gets cool and better songs play on the radio. And before too long we'll be in the mountains.

I don't want to go.

Now, you told me it sounded fun. The man puts the truck in gear and begins to pull out of the parking space. The boy's watching him. Maybe that's it: he's tired enough to stay on one topic. The man says, You want to put a tape in? You can pick.

I don't like any of that stuff you listen to.

A radio station?

She doesn't know we're doing this, does she?

The boy's still staring at him with his dull, sleepy eyes.

The man says, carefully, watching the road, Well, I didn't want to have to tell you this right away, but you won't let me get away with it, will you? Keeping a secret?

The man noses the truck onto the ramp and picks up speed.

Well, the man says, Your mother's . . . your mother's been having some problems lately. You know she's been tired, right? Not feeling so hot at night?

The boy nods, and there's something different in his eyes now.

She's going to the doctor. It's not a big thing, but she's been worried, and they're going to keep her for a few nights, and even though it's, you know, a little different for us, she wanted me to take you on a trip. You've been talking about the mountains, and so she wanted me to take you out there while she does the tests. She told me not to tell you for a while so you wouldn't worry. She wants you to have a good time.

I want to call her.

Well, that's the problem. She's not home right now.

The boy swallows.

The . . . the hospital?

The man nods.

We could call her there, the boy says.

The boy's voice is shaking—but just a little bit; he's hiding his worry. The man wants to hug him. He's a brave kid; his mother never sees it. Just says how much of a handful he is, how much he fights her. But he's a kid, and in trouble, and look at how he takes it. How he digs in. The man knows it's no big thing to beat up, or be beaten up by, another kid on the playground. Or to trip over your own feet. The man knows that, for boys and adults both, it's really about taking it, seeing the world as it reveals itself and then being able to stand up to it all. Some people can't—the boy's mother, for instance, always complaining. But, somehow, not the kid. The boy pushes his hair back away from his eyes, a false gesture; he's acting. The man knows: the boy's going to fight him, too, more and more before the trip is over.

Today she needs to rest, the man says, quietly. Can I give you a message? What she told me to say?

The boy nods and looks away from the man, out the windshield. They both watch the road as the man says the boy's name, and then:

Don't worry, honey, she said. Be brave and we'll talk soon. I want you to have a good time. I want you to be good. Try and relax and I'll give you a call in Colorado. Just think of this as a vacation. I love you, honey, very much.

The man looks sideways, a little, when he says the last

part. The boy keeps his head turned toward his window. His cheek is red, colored by sunburn, sunset.

You okay?

Yeah.

I can stop, if you want.

No.

LATER, AFTER MIDNIGHT, they're parked at a rest stop. The man tries to doze, to get an hour or so in; he has a sweatshirt bundled behind his head. The boy napped for an hour on the road, and now he holds a flashlight over his lap.

A waterfall, the boy says. Seven letters. Second one's an A.

The man thinks, groggily.

Do you know it? he asks. Or are you just testing me?

The boy grins at him. Oh, I know it. Do you?

No. You should get some sleep.

Nah. I'm all awake now.

But the boy does, eventually, get sleepy; he turns the flashlight off half an hour later. He curls into himself against his door. After another minute he reaches under the seat, rustles around, and then spreads his jacket over his chest and arms.

Cold? the man asks.

Yeah.

You can lean on me if you want.

The boy hasn't slept against him since he was a toddler. The man tries to keep his eyes half closed, play it cool—has he given it away? How much he wants the boy to say yes? But the boy just shakes his head.

I'm fine like this.

All right, the man says.

Do you know it yet? the boy asks.

Know what?

Cascade, the boy says, almost cruelly. It's cascade.

II.

The boy, curled on his side on the soft motel bed, watches through slit eyes as the man sleeps. The boy lies still for quite a while, listening to the air conditioner rattle, making sure of the depth of the man's breathing. When he's sure, the boy sits up on the bed, hoping it won't squeak, though if it does he'll just say he's going to the bathroom. But the man keeps snoring. The man's hair is wet; he's sweating in his sleep; the air conditioner doesn't work that well. Hot sunlight seeps in past the blinds.

The man had told him they'd drive straight through, if they could, but at noon he said he was too tired, that they should get a room and try to sleep. But the boy slept already; he's not tired now. His whole life he's only managed to sleep in short spurts. At home his mother is used to him slipping into the living room at night to watch television. But the man made him turn the TV off before they went to bed.

The boy puts his feet over the side of the bed, and then stands, shifting his weight over to the arm he has leaning on the bed table. The man asked the desk clerk for a wake-up call at five; it's only two now. Three hours in here listening to snores will be forever.

The boy sits on the floor and ties his shoes. Now, if he's asked, he'll say he wanted to go downstairs to the big lounge and watch TV. The man will tell him no, but it's a nice story and won't make him feel bad. The man has tried hard to keep the boy happy—the boy knows that, and even if this feels strange to him, even if sometimes he thinks the man is lying, he knows the man wants him not to be sad.

When his shoes are tied the boy walks carefully to the door. The room's carpeting is thick and muffles his sounds. The man has left a chair near the door, with his pants draped across it. The boy knows why. The man's keys and change are in the pants; the man thinks that if the boy tries to leave the room he might make noise. Tricky. The boy scoots the chair back, inch by inch. The change jingles a bit, but not much, and the snores never stop.

The door is the real trick. The boy tells himself to be patient, and, moving just a few inches at a time, he unhooks the door chain and turns the dead bolt as slowly and quietly as he can. He reads the instructions on the back of the door to distract himself, about where the motel guests are supposed to go if there's a fire. There's a diagram of the rooms; theirs is blacked in. The boy tries to imagine a fire, dying in a fire. When he was six his best friend up the street died in a fire. Someone set it, but they never caught whoever it was. His mother won't tell him about it, even though he's asked; he wants to explain to her that it's worse not to know, even if she is trying to protect him from things she thinks he's too young to understand. The boy dislikes her sometimes, when she gets like that. He's deliberately burned his fingers twice on the burners of the stove, trying to imagine. He holds his breath sometimes, too, trying to figure out what it's like to breathe smoke—but that's harder; he gets too dizzy.

His mother wouldn't let him go to the funeral.

The man, though, told him a little; he was around for a while then. The man has always tried to answer the boy's questions, which is why, when he doesn't answer now, the boy knows he's lying.

Either that, or his mother really *is* very sick; it's not a lie; it's worse than the boy supposes, than the man is telling. The boy can't figure it out.

He hears the door latch click, and then the door swings in toward him. He opens it just enough to slip out into the cool hallway, smelling of cleaner and the weird burned odor of vac-uumed carpet. Outside, he pulls the door shut, slowly, and he thinks the latch isn't so loud when it catches.

No one is in the hallway. He hears the television playing in a couple of rooms as he passes. One room's door is open. A fat woman is inside, pulling bedsheets tight.

He descends an open stairwell into the lobby of the motel. It's not a very good motel. The plants are plastic and dusty, and the carpet's worn. Two kids are running around the lobby, both younger than the boy; their weary parents are checking in at the desk, and the mother shouts at the young ones in such a tone that even the boy, watching, snaps to. They come to her side and begin whining. The boy fights an urge to go over and pinch them. He does that at school a lot, to younger kids.

He doesn't like kids much. He has two friends his age who read comic books with him, but he doesn't go over to their houses if he can avoid it. They all sit together at lunch, at school, and they try not to attract the attention of older kids, who do more than pinch. His mother doesn't know that the three of them have the nicknames Faggot One, Faggot Two, and Faggot Three. The boy is F2. F1 has it the worst: he's fat. F3 is a coward: he runs away, but he usually gets caught and tripped. The boy just tries to be invisible, and for the most part the strategy works. He wouldn't want to be either of his friends.

When the couple has left the desk, the boy asks the girl behind the counter if there's a pay phone, and she points across the lobby, to a dark niche next to the restrooms.

He puts a quarter into the phone and picks up the receiver, but there's no dial tone.

It's broken, he tells the girl at the counter.

Oh, I'm sorry, I forgot. I was supposed to put a sign up, but it got all busy there for a while. Can't you just call from your room?

He shakes his head.

I need my quarter back, he says, and she gives it to him, clucking her tongue. She then goes back to reading a novel— a mystery, it looks like.

The boy walks out the motel's front doors, and stands in the misty heat. The motel is maybe a half mile away from the interstate, but the boy can still see it, off in the hazy distance; he can hear the big trucks moaning. He's not sure where this place is exactly. He napped and read almost until the man pulled into the parking lot, and then they went to their room without talking much. Up and down the street he can see restaurants and strip malls, a big water tower, and some houses. Most of the license plates on the cars say Missouri.

Finally, across the street, next to a stone building at the center of a small, grassy park, he sees a pay phone. No one's at the park, as far as he can tell. There's a basketball hoop, a couple of horses mounted on thick, rusty springs—and a jungle gym, which he likes. He slips between the cars of the parking lot and then crosses the street, running through a gap in the traffic. It's very hot; even that bit of running makes him sweat. The stone building holds restrooms, which smell foul as he passes their open doorways. On the wall between the restroom doors is a drinking fountain; the boy tries it, but the water is warm and tastes a little bit like dirt.

Then the boy puts his quarter in the phone and dials his number in Chicago. An automated voice comes on the line and asks for more money.

For a few minutes he searches the sidewalk and the grass for more change, but only finds a penny. He could go back into the room and get the change from the man's pants, but he's not sure that's enough. Really, he's relieved. He's breathing fast—was he really afraid? Of what? Why wouldn't he want to know? Is he afraid of what happens next, if it turns out the man's lying?

A lot of what the boy feels is a surprise to him. He wonders, not for the first time, if he's crazy. He says a few cuss words under his breath, then looks around to see if anyone is near. He's still alone.

He checks his watch, but it's only been a few minutes since he left the motel. He walks to the jungle gym, then climbs to the top. After a few minutes he starts to imagine it's a skyscraper that he's working on, that the drop beneath him is many hundreds of feet. This makes his palms agreeably sweaty. He talks to himself, acting out a conversation between two workers. He hangs from both hands, and says, It's okay, while the other worker says, Hang on! Don't look down! Grab my hand!

He loses himself at this, wobbling on the edge of the bars. It's an hour later when he feels the need to pee. He climbs off the jungle gym, then looks back and forth between the motel across the street and the restroom in the park. The traffic has picked up on the street. He takes a breath, then walks into the stinking bathroom.

The restroom doesn't have a door; the entrance is just a U-turn around a concrete wall. The boy hates that kind; anyone could lean in and see him. He doesn't like to be seen while he pees—he can't pee, actually, when someone's in a bathroom with him. This one has a urinal inside, and two stalls. The urinal is out of the question. The toilet in the stall nearest the urinal looks and smells like it's been clogged for days; the one in the corner, next to the wall, seems all right. He walks in and latches the door behind him.

He's halfway through peeing when he hears footsteps. Then someone clears his throat, outside the stall door. The boy reddens; he feels the heat in his face, even behind his sunburn. His pee stops.

He doesn't want to go back out into the bathroom past whoever's there, so he pulls his shorts down and sits on the toilet, prepared to wait it out.

The man outside the stall whistles for a bit. He walks back and forth, and the boy sees a scuffed pair of brown shoes, and white sockless ankles, one of them scabbed over.

Whew-eee, says the man outside. His voice is deep and graveled. That's one shitty mess, ain't it? Stinks to heaven.

The boy doesn't say anything. He's still blushing. Outside, beyond the stone wall, he can hear the traffic on the road, the wind in the trees that line the park.

I know you're in there, says the man. It's all right. You can answer me.

I'll be done in a minute, the boy says, too loud. His voice cracks.

Yeah. That's what I figure.

The boy looks at the door, terrified for a second that he forgot to latch it. But it's latched. As he looks up from the latch he sees a sliver of the man's face. An eye. The man's looking through the crack in the door frame at him. The boy wants to moan; he bends over himself instead.

You going? the man asks. Or you just hiding?

My dad's outside, the boy says. The lie comes out as a half whisper.

The man laughs. I watched you for a while, playing. I didn't see your poppa.

He's coming. Any minute.

How old are you? the man asks, but the boy doesn't answer.

I guess about eight, the man says. Am I right?

The boy hears his feet shuffle, and then, suddenly, the man jerks on the door of the stall. It rattles against the latch; the stall walls shake. The man chuckles again.

I want to show you something, the man says. The boy, who's been watching the shoes under the door, looks up and sees the man's eye pressed close to the crack again. His eye is brown; the white looks yellow.

Look, the man says.

Lower down the crack, the boy sees a knife blade, poking into the stall. He blinks, wondering if he can really be seeing it. It looks like a kitchen steak knife, with a jagged bottom edge. The metal is dirty and stained. The man rattles it back and forth between the door and the frame, then pulls it out with a rasp.

You know what that is? the man asks.

The boy doesn't answer. He wants to run, to try and sneak out, under the side of the stall. But first he has to pull up his shorts; it would take too much time. There's a window over his head, in the stone wall, but it's too small even for him, and the glass is behind chicken wire, and the man would just reach over the stall and get him, and could do it anyway, any time he wants—

That's my dick, the man says. You want to see my knife?

The boy hears a zipper opening. He closes his eyes. His hands and feet are numb.

Look here, the man says. The boy glances up, without meaning to, for only a second. He can just see it, pressed against the crack, pink and brown.

Now you tell me, kiddo, the man says, which one you want me to put in you.

Go away, the boy whispers.

No. I want you to answer me. Tell me which one. You just say.

No.

The man rattles the door again, and then, as the boy watches, he kneels. Dirty fingers grip the underside of the door. The man's bearded face bends low, into sight. He grunts, his mouth twisted. He smiles, showing brown teeth, lifts his head out of sight, then looks again, smiles again.

Peekaboo.

That's when the boy hears his name called.

Here! he shrieks. I'm in here!

The man outside the door growls and jerks upright.

Jesus fucking Christ.

The man, somewhere outside, calls the boy's name again.

Next time, you little piece of shit, says the man with the knife. The boy sees the scuffed shoes turning, hears rapid steps, hears the silence come back into the bathroom.

The boy quickly stands and pulls up his shorts. His hands and arms are trembling. He hears his name again, hears the man's panting as he enters the restroom. The boy opens the door and flings himself out of the stall, and there's a moment where the man's back is turned, and the boy nearly screams; he thinks for a second it's the man with the knife, waiting for him. But then he sees it isn't; this man is *his,* and without thinking about it the boy throws his arms around him, and is sobbing, his face pressed into the man's belly.

THE MAN PACKS their things quickly. He tells the boy to stay next to him. They don't have much, between them; the man throws it all back into a duffel bag, and they walk out the side door to where the truck is parked. The boy has tried not to cry, but he can't help it. Since the bathroom, whenever he's tried to say anything, he's snuffled in giant sobs, and the words don't come.

Finally, by the truck, he stammers, Are we going to call the police?

The man doesn't say anything. He shoves the duffel behind the seat of the pickup. When he's done he lifts his head and glances around the parking lot.

Aren't we? the boy says.

They'll make us stay in town, the man says, and then looks at the boy. We need to get going.

Don't you think they ought to catch him?

Yeah, the man says. Come on, get in.

But—

The man sighs and then puts his arm around the boy's shoulders.

I don't want you near him again. I don't want to worry

your mother. I know, I know. I *know*. He was a bad man. But your mother—

The man's face looks strange now, an odd gray color.

Let's not frighten her, okay? the man says.

The boy stares up at him.

You'd have to stay here, the man says. You'd have to testify, and pick him out of a lineup. Do you really want to have to do that?

The boy looks down at his hands. He sees a man out of the corner of his eye, and turns. It's an older man, getting into a car, just a gray-haired old man, but he still feels his heart hammering.

Come on, the man says. Let's get out of here. Okay?

Okay, says the boy. He gets in the truck. The man clips in his seat belt for him. The man smells sweaty, and he's breathing hard. And, the boy realizes, so is he, until they're on the road and the city and the motel and the park all fall away behind them.

III.

Long after dark, the man pulls into a truck stop, somewhere deep in Kansas. They've come most of the way now. Since he rescued the boy from the park toilet the two of them have driven nonstop, barely speaking. The boy hasn't slept. He tries to read, but the man sees that he's faking it; the boy looks bleary-eyed, nearly shell-shocked. He nods off every once in a while, but he always snaps back awake. Though he won't say anything, the boy often looks around him, as though he sees, has thought to see, a threat nearby.

The foul-smelling vagrant in the bathroom. The man can still see him, pushing past him and running away, into the trees on the other side of the park. He smelled awful, like a dog that's been living on garbage. The man can barely stand the thought of it. He still sees the boy's tear-stained face, can still hear his hiccuping sobs. The man wishes he'd stopped the vagrant, leaped at him, wrestled him to the dirt, and choked him dead. The boy won't say exactly what happened in there, but the man can guess well enough.

The truck stop is huge; at the center of it, behind the pumps, there's a diner and a gift shop—even a twenty-four-hour garage, with mechanics for the big trucks. It's like a small city; it glitters in the dark and is crawling with people. The man parks at the edge of the lot, next to the road.

Are you hungry? he asks the boy.

The boy shakes his head.

Are you all right?

The boy nods, automatically.

I'd like to try and get some sleep, the man says. Will you be all right if I do?

I guess, the boy says.

The man locks the doors. He rolls up a shirt under his head and leans against his door. He feels the boy sitting, still, on the other side of the truck.

You miss your mother, don't you?

Mm-hm.

The man can't help it. You'll see her soon, he says. He can't tell the future, despite his plans for it. He wonders if he's lied or told the truth.

The boy looks out the side window.

Is she really sick? the boy asks.

Yes, the man says.

You're lying.

No, the man says tenderly.

The boy sniffles.

I just want to say, the man says and pauses, clearing his throat. He can't bear it, if the boy cries. He could never bear that. He can barely stand to be in his own skin, knowing that something he's done has made the boy cry. Knowing that this whole enterprise can only lead to the boy crying, the boy saddened, the boy less a boy than when this all began. He puts his hand on the boy's shoulder.

I just mean. I know it's been a while, but—

The man's vision blurs with tears, surprising him.

But you've always been important to me.

The boy nods.

You have to believe me. I don't want to hurt you. I love you.

The boy looks at his hands, curled on his bare thighs, fingers gripping thumbs to palms.

Will you come over here? the man asks softly.

He lifts his arm. The man can't say how he knows the boy will come, but the boy does, sliding across the seat and under his arm. The boy puts his face against the man's chest. The man lowers his face into the boy's hair and smells it, smells his scalp, beautiful even through the smell of the boy's sweat and fear, beautiful in the same way the boy's face, even beneath its dirt and shine and sunburn, is beautiful and white and pure. He takes the boy's slim, light hand.

The boy sleeps for a while, like that. The man stays awake longer, treasuring the closeness. The boy jerks awake, maybe a half hour later; when he sees where he is, he pulls quickly away and sits against the door, his face tight and offended.

Hey, the man says. The boy folds his arms against his chest and looks out the window.

It's all right, the man says. You used to sleep against me like that, when you were young. Do you remember?

The boy shakes his head.

BUT HE DOES remember. He hadn't, until the man said it. He remembers the man coming home at night, kissing the boy's mother, sitting with them on the couch in front of the television. He remembers the three of them eating dinner, watching TV. He remembers sitting between his mother and the man. He hears the adults laughing. Remembers the weight of the man's arm. Remembers being carried upstairs, his head bumping against the man's chest.

The man squeezes him.

He remembers a kiss good night.

Always know I love you, the man says now. It sounds like he's crying.

THEY EAT INSIDE the diner, very late. The boy orders pancakes, and the man sits and smokes and watches the boy eat. The boy wishes he wouldn't: he'd like to do something without the man staring. But he has, hasn't he? He went to the park without being watched, and look what happened.

He shivers and feels his stomach try to force his dinner back up into his throat.

He's tired. He wants to sleep, to sleep in a bed. In his own bed back home. He'd like to sleep now, or just eat his meal, but every once in a while he looks up and thinks he sees the man with the knife, across the diner in a booth or coming in the door. And then there's the man sitting next to him, staring and staring. The man's worried about him, the boy knows that, but he still doesn't like it. So he tries to keep his eyes on his plate.

Across the diner another boy eats breakfast, too. A man's with him, sleeping with his head on his curled arms. The other boy stares at him, and they watch each other until the man says, You'd better finish on up. We have to hit the road.

The boy across the diner drops his eyes, as though he saw something he didn't like.

IN THE TRUCK the man kisses him. The boy is putting on his seat belt when the man leans over and kisses him on the cheek. He does it with a loud showy smacking of his lips; the sound is startling, popping through the fuzzy insides of the boy's head.

The boy draws back from the kiss and looks up to see the man smiling at him, his face inches away, smelling of coffee and cigarettes and the gum he chews to cover up the smell. The boy leans away, but the man puts his heavy arm across his shoulders.

Well, he says. By noon I think we'll be there.

The boy, despite himself, begins to cry. It just spills out. He hates himself for doing it, but he can't help it, not anymore. He hates the sounds that squeak out of him, hates the way his nose runs into the hand he cups over his mouth.

Hey, the man says, rubbing his back. Hey, hey, hey.

The man leans forward and touches his forehead against the boy's. His breath comes very quickly.

It's okay. You're with me. I'll take care of it. Leave it to me, okay?

The boy can only keep crying, feeling his arms quiver. He's never cried like this.

Hey hey hey.

Headlights wash over them, and the man pulls back, quickly, with an intake of breath. The boy squints against the light and curls up on his seat. The man starts the truck, begins to drive. The boy hopes for sleep, anything to end his tears; he curls into himself and tries to will himself away from it all, into the deepest blackness he can find.

It's morning, a little past dawn. The man drives; the boy is asleep. He watches the boy's curled shape, warily. He squints at the new sunlight in the rearview mirror. Sometime just before sunrise they passed the Colorado state line.

After the sun rises fully the boy wakes up, yawning and tousled. For a moment he looks befuddled, unaware, but then his face sets itself; he remembers.

The man says, Guess what? We're in Colorado.

The boy looks out the windows; the man keeps an eye on him, trying to judge the state of the poor kid's mind.

I thought there were mountains, the boy says after a minute. This looks like Kansas.

This half does. Only the west side has mountains.

How far are we?

An hour or so.

The boy looks forward, out the window, craning his neck.

I used to play a game with my father when we came out here, the man says. We'd try to be the first one to spot Pikes Peak. You can see it from pretty far off.

The boy looks through the windshield with more intent.

Tell you what, the man says. See it before I do and I'll get you an ice cream.

What if I don't?

We'll think of something, the man says, and laughs. He pokes the boy in the ribs.

The boy draws away, unsmiling, and then watches the distance.

You'd better keep an eye peeled, the man says. I'm pretty good at this.

The man turns on the radio and smiles to himself as they drive. Both of them look forward, to where the mountains will be; the truck buzzes, rattles, hums. It's hard to see the actual shape of the horizon; the edge never quite comes into focus. A bump might be a mountain, or a cloud, or a bug on the windshield.

The boy is watching carefully, almost forgetting to blink. The man can't help himself. He reaches over and puts his hand on the back of the boy's neck. The boy glances over, then resumes his watch, tight-lipped, owlish behind his glasses.

It's something, touching the boy. The man wants to weep that he can. It feels to him as if all his nerves are now concentrated in his palm. It's . . . it's as if the boy's neck is rippling, like the road, jumping up, falling away, shocking the man's hand— and through it, his whole body—with every movement.

Does the boy know what's happening to them? All that *could* happen? The man doubts it. You have to be older, he thinks, even to guess. Or do you? Maybe before yesterday this was true for the boy, but today the poor little guy could be thinking anything.

Love and pity swell up in the man. *My boy.* He rubs his thumb carefully across the downy space between the boy's jaw and throat, and the boy makes a movement, almost a shiver, or—what? The man can't see; he doesn't want to turn and stare.

He tightens his grip on the wheel, and concentrates instead on what he knows: The flat horizon stretched out ahead. The soft warmth of the boy's neck. His hand resting on it. The way his fingers curl, to fit its shape.

Solos

I.

IN THE LATE AFTERNOON OF MY HUSBAND'S FOURTH DAY of climbing, his base camp calls me via satellite phone. The news is not so good. After climbing straight through the night, Jozef is now two-thirds of the way up the west face of Shipton's Peak. He has come farther on the face than anyone ever has. But now his radio is malfunctioning.

Jozef's friend Hugo says to me, We were talking, and then it just cut off. He says, Of course we worried. But there were no avalanches on the face, and then we spotted him through the binoculars. When the sun set he flashed down with his headlamp that he was all right.

I tell myself, over and over, until my heart doesn't pound so much: Jozef is still alive.

What now? I ask.

Hugo tells me Jozef's options, and I write them down. I always answer these calls in my studio, away from Stane, our son, who is eight. This is a superstition of mine; in case the news is bad, I want to compose myself before I have to face our boy. And when Hugo and I hang up, I sit for a while, thinking of what I will say. Then I take the manila folder full of pictures and walk into the living room. Stane is sitting on the sofa with Jozef's brother Karel, playing on Karel's laptop computer. As soon as Stane sees me he wriggles out from under Karel's arm.

Was that Hugo? he asks. Can I talk to him? You hung up?

I give Karel a look, and he puts his hand on Stane's head.

Hush for now, Karel says.

I sit down on the sofa, a little ways from Karel. I pat the space between us and Stane sits. Karel puts his arm around Stane; his arms are so long that his fingertips nearly brush my shoulder.

Papa's all right, I say. But his radio is broken.

Did he get hurt? Stane's face is more curious than frightened.

No. It just broke. Once it got dark, he used his headlamp to signal he's all right. But it's not very good news.

Stane is watching me carefully. Karel is twisting the beard over his chin with his thumb and forefinger. He knows right away what losing the radio means. But it is as if both of them are waiting for me to tell them how *I* feel about this, about Jozef having his chances reduced, when they were so low to begin with already. I tell myself not to be angry. If I do not know what to feel, how can I expect anything from them?

Is Papa in trouble? Stane asks, his voice quieter now.

I say, Yes. They use the radio to tell your papa where he ought to climb next. It's hard for him to know, when he's in the middle of the face. And he can't climb back down the pillar. He doesn't have the right equipment. He's going to have to change his route.

I open the folder and we look at pictures of the west face, all 3,900 meters of it. Before he left for Nepal, Jozef printed this picture for us, overlaid with a grid. Hugo has the same photo in base camp, with the same grid. Every time he calls he gives me Jozef's coordinates; and afterward Stane and I make a line with a wax pencil: the day's progress. My husband's life, like a stock on the market.

I point out a square in the center of the face, at the foot of a sloping field of ice a kilometer high and wide.

Papa's here, I say. He can't go straight up, like he wanted. So instead he has to go this way up the ice field, here to the ridge. From there he could come home, or go on to the summit. Either way it is very dangerous for him now. It won't be easy for him to make the ridge.

Stane asks, Could he die?

This question takes me by surprise. Jozef sat down with Stane before leaving and talked to him about the west face, about how no one has ever climbed it before. He told Stane it was dangerous, that he could get hurt. We have always talked to our son in terms of danger, and not death. He sees death on the television, of course, and he knows about animals that die to make meat. He knows his uncle Gaspar died and went to heaven before he was born, that he fell on a big mountain while climbing with Papa. But who knows what all of this means to him? Now he has asked me the very thing I am trying to say to Karel between my words.

He could, I say, and I keep my eyes on Stane's. This is a very dangerous place for Papa to be. That was true even before he lost the radio, and now it's even more true. Going to the ridge is risky, and if he gets hurt he can't call for anyone.

Stane thinks this over, his mouth screwed up. This is his thinking face, which at other times has made me smile behind my hand. Not now.

He should come home then, Stane says. By the ridge.

That's what I think, too.

Can I see the picture?

Stane holds the photo on his lap, and Karel looks at it over Stane's other shoulder, as Stane traces his papa's route with his small square finger.

The radio was all he lost? Karel asks me now, his voice husky.

I don't know. He didn't signal much to Hugo.

Did he signal anything for *us*? Stane asks.

Jozef has been passing along messages to us, both through Hugo and through the website Hugo and his team have been updating from base camp. These messages are only a few lines long, but all the same they are what Stane lives for—and why not? His papa might as well be calling from a rocket ship. I would like to lie to him here, but I don't have the heart to do it.

No, I say, he didn't. I don't think he had time.

Stane's pink fingertip moves across the photo, the black triangular cliffs of the headwall, the little icy smears that maybe—or maybe not—will provide a route. Stane looks up at me and Karel, and talks like he has information we do not, like it is in little boy's heads that these issues are decided.

Papa will be okay, he says. He's good on ice.

Karel runs his fingers through his hair, and over the top of Stane's head gives me a look full of fear and relief. He has no children of his own to ask him questions like this. To him, parents are magicians: keeping Stane peaceful is the same as pulling a coin from his ear.

Yes, he is, I tell my son, and kiss his forehead, trying my best to sound as sure as he does: calm, hopeful, as though he and I have not just discussed his father's death.

As though I do not want to scream, to call Jozef the callous bastard that, in my heart right now, he is.

LATER STANE GOES outside to play with his plastic toy men; he has been fighting a war across the complicated terrain of the yard and the drive, and even onto the low and crumbling Roman wall that follows the road for the length of our valley, halfway to Kamnik. Casualties are heavy in this war; many of his men die, only to be resurrected the following morning. I hear him sometimes, making explosions under his breath, mimicking screams. I'm being naïve. All little boys are eager to know about death, and the ways it happens.

I should remember, too — such things are not just the domain of boys. When I was a girl not much older than Stane I became obsessed with the Holocaust. I had just begun painting: I filled canvas upon canvas with skulls and bones and gray swirls of smoke, until my mother told me I would have to see a doctor if I continued.

Karel is sitting at the kitchen table, drinking coffee, student essays at his elbow. I can see he is only pretending to read them.

I'll make dinner, if you'd like, he says.

No, you sit right there.

Really, Ani, you've been running all day. Rest and let me pull my weight.

Karel has been with us all week; he arrived from Ljubljana Saturday, the day before Jozef began his solo. Jozef had been in Nepal almost six weeks by then, acclimatizing, and talking to me and Karel both from base camp at night. It was Jozef who asked Karel to come and stay with us.

I tried to argue—I did not think I wanted company for the week of a climb. But Jozef said, *It will be good for both of you. Don't tell Karel I said so, but he and Marja have been fighting. You two can worry about each other instead of me.*

Karel and I are good friends, we always have been. He is a professor of art history, and even though he and I both know I will never be a great painter, Karel is one of the few people who understands that what I do carries value. He used to paint when he was young. We are the only artists in Jozef's family, and we have always spoken to each other with something like relief.

And in the end Jozef was right—having Karel here has been good for us. Stane loves him. Karel brought his laptop so we can look at the expedition website, and he has been teaching Stane how to use some other programs. He has offered every other second to do housework. In a strange way our house has been more alive since Jozef left; we pay attention to who goes where, to do what. *I'm going to paint,* I always say now. When Jozef is here? I just go.

Karel has been so concerned for me and Stane that he has not spoken of Marja, not yet. I have not asked—other than simple courtesies—but I think Jozef is right about this, too. Karel has been subdued, above and beyond worry for his brother. His shoulders slump, and he sighs heavily, like a much older man. It looks like a long time since he has slept or eaten well. I try to put good food in him, but aside from this I don't know what to do.

I have to admit, in a small way, that I have enjoyed worrying about Karel. He is so much easier to worry over than Jozef.

Does Stane ever want to climb himself? Karel asks suddenly.

I start washing potatoes for zlikrofi. I think about how Jozef and I have had this discussion before. Stane is just old enough to want to do what his father does, to be a famous mountain climber, to be on commercials. I have forbidden it. Jozef knows to agree with me, but he also says, *You have to let him make his own decisions. You can say no, but you might just mother him right onto the rock.*

I tell Karel, He asks sometimes. But we don't allow it.

Jozef goes along with this?

Jozef loves his son. He doesn't want him risking his life.

Karel seems about to say something more, but we are interrupted by Stane, who opens the door and shouts in that someone is here. Just as he says this I hear the sound of an automobile coming down the road. We live deep in the country; we have neighbors here—mostly people from the city in summer homes—but we do not hear cars very often. I look out the kitchen window and see a van slow in front of our house, a cloud of dust from the dirt road billowing slowly behind it. On the side of the van is the 24ur insignia.

Reporters, I say.

Karel drops his cup to the table in disgust. I'll talk to them, he says.

I can do it.

Let me. Please. You're too rude.

The news people have come every other day since Jozef's climb began: 24ur especially. Jozef's last four climbs, all solo, have made him a celebrity—the best climber not just in Slovenia but maybe in the world. One of Hugo's jobs is sending out press releases. I'm sure the news people know about the broken radio.

Giving in to Karel is a relief this time. Thank you, I say.

He smiles at me, very quickly, and then he goes outside to tell the whole country that Jozef's family would appreciate privacy now, in this very serious time.

AFTER DINNER we play games; Karel is teaching Stane chess, and the three of us trade matches for a while until I reach my limit. The boys want to stay at it, so I go to my studio and paint for an hour or two—fussing, mostly. Then Stane comes in to tell me I have been relieved of my bedtime reading duties. Uncle Karel will read, he announces.

My studio is next to Stane's bedroom, and I listen to them while I work. Karel sits and talks with Stane for a few minutes after the bedtime story is over. They have been like this all week: very serious with each other, Karel treating Stane like a little man, and Stane acting like one for his uncle.

I open a window and, standing near it, I smoke the one cigarette I am allowed per day when Jozef is on a climb. I try to send my mind out to Jozef—he will be climbing now—but I keep losing myself in the smoke and the sounds of the voices in the next room.

Then Karel is at the doorway. Stane would like to say good night, he says.

Stane is curled on his side. A toy soldier hangs off one of

the big posts of Stane's bed, attached by a length of string to the knob at the top. Its feet are against the headboard, and it leans back on the rope just like a resting climber, considering the tricky knob up ahead, the best approach.

When did your man go climbing? I ask.

Today. Uncle Karel found some rope and we put him up on it.

Is he careful?

He's very careful.

That's good, I say. I would like to know how the climb goes.

He'll make it, Stane says.

I kiss his forehead and say, I think so, too.

Karel is in the studio, smoking one of my cigarettes, when I return.

I hope you don't mind, he says, turning the cigarette in his hand with obvious relish.

I quit last year, I say.

Me, too. He offers one out of the pack to me.

I lean forward and he fumbles with my lighter and I keep leaning. We are both laughing guilty laughs by the time I take a drag.

You're good with Stane, I say.

He's a smart boy. I hope I don't bore him.

Be serious. He loves you.

He loves his papa, that's for certain. Karel grins. You know, he asked me about the college for a while yesterday, and I still don't think he understands what it is I do there. Finally I told him I look at paintings like yours, and this he understood. Then he said when he grows up *he* will work outside, not sit indoors all day.

I have heard this opinion myself.

I say, Stane's eight. Tomorrow he'll tell you he wants to start a restaurant on the moon.

Karel chuckles, and we sit for a while. With him here I surpass my cigarette limit, and then some. I look out the window and try not to notice that Karel watches me. He is content to do this, I think, and I am content to smoke and be watched. We are quiet and calm.

Well, Karel says, finally, after a showy yawn, good night. Then he hugs me, quickly, from the side, squeezing my waist. He says, Wake me if there's news, all right? Or if you need anything.

Then he moves away from me, out into the hall, not looking at my eyes.

LATER, WHEN I am in the dark of my bedroom, I wonder: What, exactly, would I need from Karel?

If anything, when Jozef is on a climb I feel I have too *much*. I am lying in a soft bed in a warm house, with food and drink only a few steps away. This is safety, after all, the thing we build houses for, what we sleep together in beds to receive. Where is Jozef now? It is early morning in Nepal, the coldest hours, when the west face is frozen; right now he is climbing across the ice field by moonlight. He is at almost seven thousand meters; he will barely be able to take a breath.

Or he is dead. He has slipped and fallen, and no one will know until the morning, when Hugo trains his binoculars on the face and sees nothing.

Jozef chooses this. Alive or dead, he does not have to be where he is.

And I have chosen it, too.

Karel sleeps down the hall, in our bedroom; I have, despite his protests, taken the guest bed. It's better this way; the bed is smaller, and I do not feel the space where Jozef ought to be. The bed Jozef and I use is old—we still have the cheap mattress from our flat in the city, before Stane was born, before we had money. I can hear the frame squeak every time Karel shifts. It occurs to me now that maybe the guest bed is better. I should have let him take it.

Maybe that is what he meant, a little voice says. Maybe what you *need* is to invite Karel to it now.

Karel and I have always flirted; that is the way Karel is, and he does it with the safety of a man who is not often taken seriously by women. It has always been better for us if I pretend not to notice.

But more and more Karel reminds me of someone I knew many years ago. A young man who was in love with me before I ever met Jozef.

This man, Peter, was a student in mathematics at the University of Ljubljana. I worked in a café then. And every day for months Peter came in and made his single coffee last for a long time, as the students do. He kept his books open in front of him, but mostly he made sad eyes at the girls who came and went. I liked him well enough—he always tipped me, and never complained—but I never thought of him otherwise. He was too timid. I was twenty-one, and I had not lost my taste for wildness in men.

But then one day, cleaning Peter's table, I found a folded slip of paper with my name on it. *Anica,* it said, *I can't stand silence anymore. I have been in love with you for months. Here is my number; if you call me I will be happy. But I will understand if you don't, and if so, I will never appear in here to trouble you again. All my love, Peter.*

I thought the note was sweet, and I saved it because of what it said about me. But I did not call Peter. He kept his word; I never saw him again. And then, not too much later, Jozef came into the café, and I didn't think of any other men at all, not for a long while.

Three years later I came across Peter's note in my things— I was packing to move into this house. I was not much older, but something had changed in me. When I read the note again, I was filled with shame. All I could think was how Peter must have sat by the phone that night, and maybe the next, his stomach in knots. How he must have seen, more and more clearly, that he had failed. I should have called him, if even to tell him no thank you. Or let him take me out, just to see, just to be kind. I read his note again and again, and I hoped he was married, and happy.

And soon, after enough of Jozef's climbing, I thought of Peter another way. As the husband I could have had. When Jozef has left me and Stane alone, waiting to hear if he lives or dies, I wonder if I wouldn't be happier in the thin arms of Peter the mathematician, now thirty-five and balding, with a soft paunchy stomach next to mine in the bed.

Wherever he is, he would not be so different from Karel. They are men who live in their minds more than their bodies. They value safety in their lives. Is it awful of me to think of Karel like this—as another kind of life for me? I don't know. But here he is in my house, and it is not my fault that my husband is not. It is not my fault that I have to think of myself: what I would have to do, if Jozef does not come home.

We spoke for the last time just before Jozef left for the face; he called me from base camp to say goodbye. This is our habit, before one of his solos. Five years ago we would have spoken at the airport in Ljubljana, but now technology has made things more immediate. I stood in my studio, the phone to my ear, and looked out my window across our valley. The sun was setting and the peaks to the east glowed a deep orange, like they were burning. In Nepal Jozef stood under a full bright moon.

I'm looking at the face right now, Jozef told me. *You should see it. It's unbelievable.*

I have seen it, I said. Jozef had kept its pictures strewn across our house for a year. I didn't need to be in its presence to fear it. *You should turn around,* I said.

Ani, he said. *Please don't do this.*

We were quiet for a while then, listening to the hum of energy in our phones. I tried to see him where he was: on a glacier, the ice blue in the moonlight, that horrible black face blotting out half the sky. Jozef does not carry phones on his climbs. He will take a radio, for route finding and emergencies. But a phone, he says, violates the spirit of the mountain. After we hung up, I would have no more chances to speak with him. Maybe not ever. But even so I did not know what to say to him.

Tell me you love me, Jozef said. *I have to go now.*

We have an understanding, Jozef and I. He must focus himself for a climb. He needs to know that I love him, that all is right with us. If he is to survive, he cannot go to the mountain angry, or distracted.

But I said, *Please don't do this. There is no shame in turning around. Come home to me.*

Ani, he said, *tell me.*

Even over our little phones I could hear the anguish in his voice. Once he had told me, *Do you know how I make it up the mountains? I pretend they are between you and me. I pull myself to you with my hands.* But I was twenty-one when he told me that. Back then I believed we had magic powers, the two of us.

If it keeps you from going, I said, *I won't tell you.*

I'm going. We've talked about this.

I knew he would. He is still alive only because of his stubbornness.

I was crying. I told him, *I love you,* and the words felt like a defeat.

I love you, too, he said. And then he said what he always must, our mantra, *Ani, as long as you love me I will be all right.*

I was supposed to say, *See you soon.* I wanted to scream at him, to smash the phone against the wall.

Jozef, I said, *this is the last time.*

I held the phone to my side and walked into the living room, where Stane was waiting for me to be finished.

Tell your papa you love him, I said. *Say goodbye.*

Four days ago I was so angry I felt I might shake apart. Now I can barely shut away the shame, the awful shame. He might die—no matter the reason—and I am too selfish to tell him that I love him?

I used to think Jozef and I were made for one another.

Now, for very different reasons, I see that we still are.

II.

When Karel first arrived at our house, he and I made plans to visit his and Jozef's father. Karel has been calling him all along with updates about Jozef's climb—but Papa is a difficult man, and we are never sure what he hears and what he doesn't. It's only proper to make a visit.

Papa lives an hour from here, outside of Maribor, and we leave in the early morning. I am in a foul mood as I direct us around the house. My head aches; if I slept at all I do not know it. Stane whines about taking a bath, and I am harsh with him, which only puts him in more of a sulk. Karel, ever helpful, offers to drive. We are just walking out of the door when Hugo calls.

He's at the ridge, Hugo tells me. We saw him when the sun came up. He's made a camp.

A camp? Is he climbing on?

You know what I do, Hugo says. But listen, he climbed all through the night to get there. He's going to need rest no matter what he does, especially now that he's on level ground. If he makes a move up or down, we won't see his lamp till evening.

I tell Stane and Karel all of this in the car. Karel nods as he listens.

I bet he's going to the top, Stane says.

Why do you think that?

I don't know. He'd have come down already if he wasn't.

Well, I say, maybe he's tired.

Maybe, says Stane. I have a feeling.

Stane likes to say he has feelings; he wants badly to believe he has supernatural powers. We have tried to discourage this; the last feeling he got was that he was going to get a bicycle for his birthday, when he had already gotten one the year before.

Both Stane and I sleep through most of the drive to Papa's. I do not even dream, and then Karel is touching my arm. Ani, we're here, he says.

Papa's house is small and dark, a cottage on a road that used to be lonely, but now is lined with houses. Jozef told me the city came to Papa, not the other way around.

Papa meets us at the door and gives us all bear hugs, making bear sounds. He smells like cigarettes and too much cologne. He is almost eighty years old, completely bald. He has Jozef's eyes, which are icy blue—but in Papa's head they are hard, frightening. Maybe this is because I know how growing up with him was. Papa seems to like me, but sometimes he looks at me, and I shiver, because he knows what I must know.

Inside we sit at the dining-room table, and Papa putters between us and the kitchen. Coffee? he asks. You must be tired.

That sounds wonderful, I say.

How about you, Stane? You want some coffee, too?

He's not allowed coffee unless it's weak, I say.

Oh no no, *strong* coffee, says Papa. Strong coffee makes a strong man. Papa ruffles Stane's hair. Stane looks to me in a way that is half hopeful, half frightened. We can put a little sugar in it, Papa says to him. Sugar for my sugar!

Okay, says Stane.

Papa, Karel says. You're not his mother.

Papa frowns at Karel, then glances my way, a dark look, and for a second or two I can see it, I can see something of what Jozef must have seen so often when he was a boy. But Papa is an old man, and much has changed for him, and so his face softens. He nods at Karel.

He says, Yes, yes. Boys today are not like they used to be. Milk, then? You want milk, Stane?

Stane does not know how to answer, and he looks at me again, imploring.

I say, Milk would be fine, Papa. Say thank you, Stane.

Thank you, Grandpapa.

Karel says, Let me help you, Papa.

Mama, can I have some of yours? Stane whispers, when they're in the kitchen.

I tell him just a sip, but I'm watching Karel and Papa through the doorway. Karel is helping with dishes and cups, moving as he moves in my kitchen—with an eagerness, like a waiter moves around a table. Papa grumbles and sometimes glances back and forth, confused. Karel guides him with touches on the shoulder, little jokes about what health nuts Jozef and I are, about how old Papa is getting, how he'll have to go to a home any day now. What a bad son you are, Papa growls.

I whisper to Stane that his grandpapa is only kidding.

If Jozef was here we would never have gotten past the offer of coffee. We would be listening to an argument, or maybe we would be staring at Jozef refusing to drink the cup in front of him, all of us quiet before the battle of wills.

I can see so much of these men they cannot see themselves. Jozef and Gaspar both fought Papa. They left home the moment they could, each of them a teenager. Karel is the youngest; he was still at home when their mother died. Karel and Papa went through her dying together. I did not know her, but I know Karel takes after her. He knows Papa must be flattered and cajoled, not fought. Through the doorway Papa laughs and rubs his hand along Karel's back. I have never seen Jozef and his father do anything more than shake hands, each looking off in different directions.

The coffee comes, and since Karel made it, it is drinkable. I mix some with Stane's milk, careful to keep the grounds out, and he is happy, though he works to keep his face from crinkling when he sips. Then Papa insists we take our cups outside to the back patio. Today the air is fine and warm, and the patio is a good place to be. The backyard, though, is unkempt, especially compared to the one next door, which we can see through a line of pine trees that acts as a fence. Two children are playing in that yard, the oldest a boy Stane's age. They have a sandbox and a complicated wooden fort and colorful toys. They see us and call out a greeting to Papa, and he waves them over.

This is my grandson Stane, he says to them. The one I told you about—he's a good boy. You three can play, yes? Stane would like your fort.

This decided, he crosses his arms and nods for the children to leave.

Stane looks at me—he does not have many playmates when school is out, not where we live, and he is shy with strangers. I wish that he would be more forceful in front of Papa. It's all right, I tell him. Go on.

The children from next door, thankfully, are friendly. Come on, Stane, they say. Come see.

Papa says to me, when they are in the other yard, You treat that boy like a baby.

Karel says, Papa.

Papa pushes out his lips.

You're right, he says. What do I know of raising boys? Eh? Two lunatics and a teacher.

He says *teacher,* not professor, and he says it with a sneer.

Papa, I say—I cut off Karel to do it. If you'd like us to leave you alone today, we will.

Again, the look, but I'm ready for it. I hold his eyes, and, surprised, he grows old again. His shoulders slump and he stares out across his yard, the piles of stone and the flower beds that in twenty years have produced nothing but weeds. The children are playing on the wooden fort. A nice, happy family, it seems from here. Papa must sit on his patio and watch them every day, the two children, the two parents I am sure are there inside the house. He hears all the laughter.

Well then, he says. How is my Jozef? He is still alive?

I tell Papa the story of Jozef's climb so far. I have brought the file folder of photographs, and he asks to see them. I stand behind Papa's chair—ignoring his too sweet, too smoky smell—and point out the route up the face, the places where Jozef has camped, the ridge which, if Jozef is sane, he will use today to abandon the climb. Papa puts on reading glasses and looks at the photographs over and over, his lips pushed out.

It's as if he reads my thoughts. He points to the photograph and asks, He's here?

Yes.

He won't come down the ridge, Papa says.

Maybe, I say, maybe not—

Papa takes my hand and stares at me. Then he says, Karel, leave us alone for a minute.

Papa, I really—

Karel! Mind me, for once. Do me this one favor and then I promise I'll die and leave you in peace.

Karel's face clouds, but he comes closer, as if to pry the old man's hand off mine.

It's all right, I say.

Karel meets my eyes, then says, All right, all right. He walks off into the yard, halfway between us and the children, and pretends to be interested in the weeds.

Sit, Papa says to me. You sit and we'll talk.

I pull up a chair.

Listen, Papa says. You are a good strong woman. I have always seen this. When Jozef brought you home, I knew you were a woman to love and to marry. You are good for him, the way my Sara was good for me. But the men of my family, we are good for no one.

Papa—

No! Listen. This is important. I have been a bad father, a bad husband. All of my life I've been bad. My sons were good boys but I've ruined them. I know. Sara told me when she was dying. I saw it when it was too late. I have lost Gaspar, and soon I will lose Jozef. This is God's punishment for me. I keep living and my sons will keep dying.

Papa, I say, please don't say that. Because as he speaks I feel a chill up and down my arms. His eyes are red-rimmed and his voice a rasp. He sounds to me both crazy and very sane, all at once.

I taught him everything, Papa says. Jozef will not turn away. He wants to go to the top. He wants to prove himself. You know why I know? All his boyhood I told him he was nothing. I know what he thinks. *Look at me now, Papa. Look at what I have done.* And if he was a banker or a doctor he would be right to do it. But I made him crazy, and look at how he tries to prove himself!

Papa thumps the file folder on my knee.

I thought maybe you were the one to stop him, Papa says. I thought: Here is a woman who will keep him on the ground. And then you had your wonderful son. Such a good boy! You are right to be cautious with him, I should learn this. I am leaving Stane everything, you know.

Papa shakes his head, and I am trying not to cry.

He says, his voice trembling, Jozef is wasting you, and the boy. I have tried to tell him. But he won't listen, no one listens.

I try, I say to Papa. I try to tell him.

Papa gives me a look, both pained and shrewd.

Maybe. But maybe you spoil him, eh? Maybe you spoil both your little men.

Stane is in the yard, calling Papa's name and laughing. He has something in his hand—I can't see what it is. Papa calls to him and Stane runs toward us, loose-limbed, cheeks red.

You listen to me, Ani, Papa says, and then Stane is in front of him. Papa seizes him under one arm, and tickles him with his free hand and says, You love Grandpapa? Say it, say you love your grandpapa, say it, say it, yes?

I love my grandpapa! Stane shrieks.

This is good, Papa says, holding Stane between his big hands, kissing his hair. His eyes flicker to mine and then back again, and he says, Because your grandpapa loves *you*.

WE LEAVE Papa's house at dusk. Stane is already drowsy, and we are not on the road twenty minutes before he is asleep in the backseat. Karel drives without speaking, and I do not break the silence either.

Papa is right. If Shipton's Peak doesn't kill Jozef, some other mountain will. So much is random, up there. Jozef tells me Gaspar was the better climber, after all—and Gaspar is gone, vanished, without even a body to bury.

He died just after Jozef and I were married. Even while we dated, he and Gaspar were planning an expedition: the southeast pillar of Annapurna III, knife-edged and vertical. He and Gaspar would go up quick and light, succeeding where everyone else had failed. And in any event they did well—so well that, near the top, on mixed ground, they followed two solo lines, unroped. *We were racing,* Jozef told me.

Jozef reached the mountain's shoulder. He waited and waited for Gaspar, but Gaspar never arrived. The weather they'd enjoyed all week began to turn. Jozef's base camp told him to come down. But he could not bring himself to abandon Gaspar.

He told me, soon after, shame-faced, *Finally they told me that if I didn't come down, you'd end up a widow.*

Jozef spent the night abseiling down, struggling for hours through the blizzard. By the time he reached the camp he was frostbitten and delirious. He told me that he had heard my voice in the coldest parts of the storm. I told him, he said, to keep going, that I loved him.

I have learned now not to be shocked, when I see Jozef after a climb. Even one that has gone well leaves him emaciated, windburned, covered with cracks and sores. His hands are always rough—he maintains them that way, for friction on the rocks—but by the end of a climb they are almost always bandaged, swollen into stiff mitts.

But I was not prepared for what I saw after Annapurna III. The Jozef I had married was ruddy, bearded, bulging with muscle. The man in the hospital bed in Kathmandu was too thin, his weak chin shaved bare, his eyes heavy-lidded and dull from painkillers and grief. The corners of his mouth turned down like an old man's. Flaps of skin hung from his cheeks, and from his nose. His hands were wrapped in gauze.

He could barely lift his arms to hold me. When I put my cheek next to him he started to moan and sob.

I listened, he kept saying. And, *Gaspar's gone, he's gone.*

I love you so much, I told him. *I'm here. You're home now.*

Only then did he smile—and when he did, his lips cracked and began to bleed down his chin.

WELL INTO THE DRIVE home from Papa's, the cell phone rings. Karel looks at me and pulls the car over to the side of the road while I answer.

He's going to the summit, Hugo says into my ear. He reached the ridge and then a few hours later he flashed his light. He's traversing back to the headwall. He must have seen a route.

I suppose I should have known, I say.

Listen, Ani, he climbed beautifully today. Just beautifully. I think he'll be fine.

Hugo is a fool, and I don't care very much what he thinks. I know too that he is in love with Jozef, that to him any decision Jozef makes is the right one. He has made his bargain like I have.

I hope you're right, I say. Give me a call when you know something.

I will. Don't worry, all right? This is Jozef. He doesn't make mistakes.

I can't say anything to this. I turn off the phone. Stane has not stirred in the backseat. I hide my face so that Karel can't see it. I look into the reflection of my own eyes in the passenger window, and the sight is enough to make me stop. In the window I am a ghost, just an outline of a woman, not anyone who feels anything.

At the house Karel carries Stane inside. Stane puts his arms around Karel's neck but never really wakes. In his bedroom I take off Stane's clothes; he's a rag doll. I kiss his damp fore-head and then walk into the kitchen. Karel is sitting at the table, drumming his fingertips.

Are you all right? Karel asks.

We had the conversation earlier this week, about what a terribly stupid question this is, but all the same he still asks it of me, and with him I am not angry. No, I say.

I'll leave you alone if—

No, I say, and sit down next to him. No. I'm too worked up. I haven't been sleeping anyway.

Me neither. Are you sad or angry?

I say, Both. And terrified. All three and none at all. I don't know.

I look at Karel, then tell him what Papa told me tonight.

Karel says, The old man sees more than he used to.

Then a look crosses his face. Papa and Karel spoke alone for a while, too. I wonder what it was Papa said to him. Did Papa spot Karel watching me, or me watching him?

May I tell you something? Karel asks.

My stomach goes in a knot, but I nod anyway.

Papa guessed a secret, Karel says. Marja has left me. It happened two weeks ago. We are going ahead with a divorce.

Karel. You should have told me.

No. Karel twines his fingers together and stares at them. No, I didn't want to distract you with it.

You think about others too much. I pat his hands and say, Really, I want to know.

There's a half bottle of wine in the refrigerator, and I set it on the table, then fetch glasses. Karel pours.

He says, Marja has taken a lover—she has had him for a year. A friend told me two months ago. I shouldn't have been surprised—we have been sleeping in different beds for longer than that. I never confronted her—maybe I didn't want to believe it. Then last month Marja went away for the weekend, on a trip with this man, and told me lies to my face about what she was doing. Contemptuous lies, and I realized, finally—all this time she has been taunting me. Certainly she has not been discreet.

Karel tips the wineglass one way, then the other. Then he says, The first night she was gone I went to a bar and met a student of mine. I took her home. We used Marja's bed, and I left it messy for her to find.

He smiles, in a sick way.

He says, I didn't do this to make Marja confront me. I know men who cheat for that reason—not just sex, you know, but because there's something wrong, something they can't name, and so they force their wives to name it for them. But this is not why I did it. I did it to *hurt* her.

He glances at me, just for a second. Now we are divorcing, he says. So I suppose I did.

I don't blame you, I say.

I don't feel guilty, Ani. Saddened, yes. But to feel bad for Marja I have to think back many years.

What he says disturbs me, but I don't want to tell him why.

I don't want to tell him how sometimes I lie in the bathtub while Jozef is gone and imagine him coming home from a solo to find us killed. He returns with that calm in him, the Zen thing he says he feels, and then he opens the door to blood and corpses.

You see, my ghost will say to him, *you were not the only one in danger.*

I tell Karel, Terrible thoughts come and go. We cannot help ourselves.

You're a saint, Anica.

I think: Would a saint wish her husband an accident in the mountains? Because sometimes *I* do. I love Jozef, I do. But sometimes the thought rises in me that if he would only die, I would be free of this love. That I can suffer widowhood—I am prepared for it, after all—but not this torture, year after year. I wish for the avalanche to come, for the rope to part, and not only so I can live my life but so I can be *right,* so I can say that all this suffering and worry was for a reason.

Karel puts his hands over mine, and his thumb curls under to stroke my palm. His fingertips are soft; his hand feels like Stane's, like mine. This gesture, this picture of the two hands, must be painful for him, because he stares for a while out the window, even though it is the darkest part of the night.

But he does not remove his hands.

Jozef's a good man, Karel says.

I say, When he isn't climbing, there's no one better.

Karel's thumb keeps making its little circle. I think of the softness of his palms on the bare skin of my belly, sliding along the inside of my thigh.

Karel says, I admire him. Not just because he can do something I can't. I know one thing for certain about Jozef: he would never cheat on you. His vows are his vows.

But he *does,* I say, my throat catching. At least another woman wouldn't *kill* him. I would rather him have affairs.

This is self-pity, but Karel is kind enough not to say so. Unburdening himself seems to have made him calm, light. He has a little smile.

He says, I have always tried to tell myself that Jozef is an artist, that what he does makes the world bigger, the way a painting does. Or maybe he is like an astronaut. I suppose when I think about it I would rather the moon have been walked on, than not.

I tell myself the same things, I say, but what do the astronaut's wives and brothers think, when the rocket goes up?

I imagine, Karel says squeezing my hand, they are like us. Helpless in who they love.

He lifts my hand with his and kisses the backs of my fingers.

I could stop him here. The gesture, we could tell ourselves, was sweet and consoling, nothing more. But I uncurl my thumb and brush it across Karel's lips, and he kisses it, too.

There, I have done it—for the first time in my marriage I have made an advance toward another man.

I am not angry at Karel, but all the same I pull my hand away, amazed at myself. It drops to the tabletop like someone else's. Karel's face changes from tender to shocked. I can almost see his mind retreating from what he has done. I am no adoring student, no silly girl drunk in a bar. I am his brother's wife.

I cannot apologize enough, he says, and leaves the room.

I sit at the table for a long while. My hand is flat on the table. I can still feel his touch on my hand, like water evaporating off my skin, leaving only a tingle behind.

FOR A LONG TIME after I retreat to bed, I wait for the sounds of Karel leaving, for the rumble of his car retreating down the road. I won't blame him if he goes. Will I try to stop him? Tell him it was a mistake? Just because we imagine something does not mean it has to happen. But as I tell myself this I imagine rising up and slipping into Karel's room. I kneel beside his bed and whisper his name, and then tell him, *Tonight, I would like to feel safe.*

But that is self-pity, too. Sleeping with my brother-in-law might do many things, but it would never make me safer. There is no safety in the love I have. I knew from the very beginning, when I told myself Jozef was an artist, too.

For the first few weeks I knew him, Jozef never told me he climbed. I saw he was muscular, I knew from his tanned skin he liked to be outside, but he told me he worked construction, pouring cement—and this explained why his hands were so rough, too. He was very good at asking me questions then, and not so good at answering them, but I thought this was because he was shy. I was used to men pulling at my clothes the moment we were alone (and in truth I liked it) but Jozef had not even kissed me yet. At heart I was a romantic girl, and so his shyness built itself in my head. I imagined all kinds of histories for him while we drank our coffees, while I held his rough hands in the darkness of cinemas.

But then one night, as we walked together, not too far from the university, he said, in an offhand way, that we were near his flat. I asked to see it, and his eyes grew big. He said it was a mess, that there was nothing in it worth seeing anyway.

But I felt bold that night—I told him it was time we saw one another's flats, and held his eyes after I said it.

Jozef took me up a long flight of steps, where the lights were bad, the floors and walls stained. As I climbed I thought about how little I knew of him, how seedy this place was, how I might be walking into danger. I followed his trim shape past the flickering bare bulbs on the landings, and listened to him jingle his keys, and I felt a thrill.

But that was the girl I was then.

When he unlocked the door and turned on the lights, I didn't understand at first what I saw. His flat was an attic room, with a sloped ceiling. A very small place. And all the walls and the ceiling were covered in naked plywood, and jutting everywhere from the wood were small, oddly shaped protrusions, in many different colors. Here and there, hanging from clips, were straps, loops of rope, collections of odd metal implements and tools. In one corner was a weight bench, and in the center of the floor was a mattress and a grimy tangle of sheets. It all smelled strongly of wood and sweat. I had never seen a climbing wall—I could only think that Jozef was a pervert, a sadist. My stomach did loops.

But Jozef looked chagrined, and said, Now you know my secret.

What is all this? I asked him.

He looked at me strangely.

I am a climber, he said. A mountaineer. My brother and I climb in the Himalayas. I train here. He smiled. These are my rocks.

I walked into the room and touched the walls, the plywood and the smooth nylon straps, the knobby holds. Some were rough and felt like stone; some seemed polished down by use.

I said, Why didn't you tell me?

He looked at his feet, and said, Women are sometimes strange about it. I like you, and didn't want anything to change between us. It was stupid of me.

I wish you'd told me.

He blushed, and said, I know. I've been a coward.

I liked that he blushed.

I asked, Are you afraid of me?

He nodded and then looked me in the eye.

You put me in knots, he said.

Jozef, I told him, I can't see how a man who climbs mountains can be afraid of a woman.

His face clouded. On a mountain, I know what I'm doing.

I kissed him. Our kiss didn't last long, but it could have; the moment I moved to him I saw his eyes soften, and I knew he would kiss me for as long as I let him, that he didn't want to be shy anymore. I put my hands on his chest and was shocked at the feel of him. Even muscular men have a bit of softness. Jozef didn't; under his shirt was warm stone.

Show me something, I said. Show me how you climb.

He blushed. I don't practice in front of people. My brother, but not—

Not a girl? I said, still giddy from the kiss. Well, this is your punishment for keeping a secret. You owe me another one.

I'm not dressed for it, he said. This is my nice shirt and pants.

He meant it honestly enough, and I laughed. I went to him and unbuttoned his shirt and slid it from him. His eyes went wide, but he did not stop me. His chest and arms were almost frightening. They still are. His muscles are so distinct, he sometimes looks like a man without skin. I touched his shoulders and he shivered.

He was very rare, I thought, and maybe then I fell in love with him.

You can unbutton your own trousers, I said to him.

I'll change in the bathroom.

A few minutes later, dressed only in spandex shorts, he climbed for me. He climbed a wall in two or three quick moves, his arms lifting him like he weighed nothing, like all that muscle was only a shell filled with feathers.

The ceiling, I said, when he was on the ground again.

He wasn't even flushed.

All right, he said. But you have to keep the mattress under me.

He climbed from the lowest part of the ceiling to the highest, his back rippling near the level of my chin. I scooted the mattress along with my foot. And I could not take my eyes from him. Watching him was like seeing pornography; his movements were strangely intimate. The muscles in his neck and face strained. He made small grunts and moans. A bright lamp in the corner threw odd shadows, and his shoulders began to gleam with sweat.

And he was good. You do not have to understand the particulars of an art to know when an artist performs well. I knew, watching Jozef, that his artistry surpassed mine by orders of magnitude.

He defied gravity, just because I asked him to do it—and when he dropped off the last hold onto the floor, I was ready to make love to him, I was ready to do anything he asked.

His soul had lifted, too—when he turned to me, in an instant before he grew embarrassed and flushed again, I saw triumph, I saw passion. A muscle in his chest pulsed with blood, and it was all I could do not to press my lips against him there, to feel that fluttering, that life under my tongue.

You should take me out again, I said to him. Tomorrow night.

He smiled at me, slyly, and buttoned his shirt across his chest.

III.

The sun is up high outside the bedroom window. For a while I lie still, trying to remember the night before, and when I must have slept. I hear laughter from the kitchen—Stane's—and Karel's deep voice answering. And I remember, with a flood of shame.

And, still, disappointment underneath it all.

I cannot hide from them. I put on my robe and walk into the living room, my feet numb on the cold wood floors. Stane and Karel are looking at the laptop in the kitchen. The whole house smells of coffee and bacon; Karel has been cooking what he knows to cook.

Good morning, lazy, Stane says giggling.

Aren't we clever, I say and ruffle his hair.

Karel glances up from the computer and says, Coffee's on. He gives me a brief look—like a dog that is sorry for something and expects to be hit.

Any news? I ask.

Papa's almost at the top, Stane says. The line's only this far away. He holds his thumb and forefinger apart.

The weather's good, Karel says. He should make it.

Well, that's good. I sit down; I have no idea what else to say.

Now that I am with them, we eat breakfast, though the clock says it is almost noon. Again I feel that strange disconnect—I eat strips of bacon, and thousands of kilometers away my husband is struggling up the headwall of Shipton's Peak. He is, right now, doing what no one in the world has ever done. He writes his name in history as I sip my coffee.

I was thinking, Karel says, that after lunch we could all go for a walk. I've wanted to take a look at the Roman wall. I have Stane's support for this plan, don't I?

He does, Stane says eagerly. Can we go?

This sounds like a grand idea to me, too—far better than sitting inside the house waiting for the phone to ring. And I am grateful to the point of tears that Karel is still here, that he is trying to pretend we did not do what we did.

I shower and dress after breakfast, and I dawdle in the house for a moment while Stane and Karel wait for me in the yard. This is when I decide to forget the cell phone. The weather outside is beautiful, and, one way or another, I would like to be in that world, not inside my head, imagining asphyxiation, frostbite, a four-kilometer drop.

Then we walk. Across the valley the sun turns the limestone Alps from gray to a warm blond, and down lower the blankets of pine are rich and green. The river at the valley floor is not so much a color as a collection of lights and reflections of the land. We stay close alongside the Roman wall, which is really not much to see—it is mostly low and crumbling, with occasional tall pillars, overhung by trees, in places collapsed by growing roots.

Stane ranges ahead of Karel and me, like a shepherd dog looping around to see that his flock is safe, before returning to scout the road ahead. He has a bagful of his toy men with him, what looks like a whole regiment, and whenever he returns he has one or another clutched in his fist. He talks to them, sometimes.

Karel walks next to me with his hands in the pockets of his jacket, looking from side to side across the valley—anywhere but at me. His face is perfectly composed, and this is how I know he is still troubled. Our footsteps rasp too loud, maybe because Stane is now too far ahead of us to make much noise—or maybe because Karel and I have not yet said ten words to each other.

I feel sixteen again, walking with a boy and not knowing whether to take his hand.

No. I feel twenty, waking hungover in a man's bed and wondering how I am to make my exit.

But this is not right either. Maybe it is time to say to myself what is true: that I am a married woman of thirty-two who has come close to her first affair, who wants maybe to fall in love with another man. That it feels like nothing else feels. I blush. A strange gravity keeps pulling Karel and I to each other. Every once in a while our hips bump, and we quickly move apart.

I try to think about Jozef, the difficulties of the summit headwall. Right now he is almost certainly in agony, gasping, starving—a hair's width from his death. And whether he has reached the top, or is still struggling up—even if he is on the way down—he is thinking, surely, of me, of Stane. *I will pull myself to you with my hands.* This is happening, right now, out to the east beyond the curve of the earth.

Then we are next to an opening in the wall, one that leads upward, to a trail.

I am not in control of my words. I say to Karel, We should go through. That path goes up to a nice meadow. From there you can see most of the valley.

Karel thinks for longer than he should. He says, All right.

I call Stane back. He arrives out of breath. I tell him we're going up to the meadow.

He surprises me, though, by asking if he can stay down by the road.

I brought my men, he says. I want to play down here.

You don't want to come up with us?

He shrugs and looks off into the distance. This gesture he has learned from his father. I cannot imagine what plans he really has—or maybe he doesn't have any; maybe he is just tired of hearing grown-ups speak of art and Romans. If he and I were by ourselves, I might tell him to come anyway. But the guilty joy rises up in me, knowing Karel and I will be alone. Stane plays by himself in the woods all the time, he'll be fine—this is what I tell myself.

We won't be long, I say. Don't go too far from the path here, okay?

Sure, Mama.

The walk up to the meadow takes only ten minutes or so. The path between the trees is shaded and cool, and I am pleased to find that my worries recede here a little, as they always have. I love the pine forests in the summer, the thick padding of fallen dry needles under my feet, the clean smell. Here and there chunks of rock break out of the humus, like mountains in bud, patched by moss. Several of them are marred by chalk marks—where Jozef works on holds and problems. I have helped him before, making sure a mat is always positioned beneath him. Lately Stane comes out here to help him, too.

Karel's face is less clouded; he appreciates this place, even if his gravity won't let him say so.

And then we are in the meadow. It is on a slope, and at the upper end of it we stop and lean against a rock and look out over our swath of valley. The river curves and gleams. Our house is just visible off to the left, the sun winking from a skylight. The highest peak across the valley has caught a wisp of cloud in the corrie just beneath its summit—from here it seems no larger than the house, but it must be a hundred meters wide. Jozef has said the mountains make their own weather, that sometimes it will rain up there when all the rest of the valley is in bright dry light. The earth and the sky turn independently of each other, Jozef says, and they sometimes grind and catch. As I think this a breeze picks up and the trees on the slope beneath us hiss and sway. The same air my husband climbs in.

But this is not true. Jozef is climbing at 8,000 meters. We are at 1,200 meters now. I look above the peaks of the Alps, into the deep clear blue. My husband is a madman, halfway to space.

I shift on the rock and my hand brushes Karel's.

This is beautiful, I say. Isn't it?

Listen, Karel says, abruptly enough that he has to cough after saying it. Listen, Ani. I think today I'll go back home.

The thought fills me with even more sadness than I would have guessed. He says these words, and the valley seems less beautiful, the blue of the sky heavier.

You don't have to go, I say.

No, he says. But I should. I've overstepped my place, and I feel miserable. My life is enough of a shambles without this on my conscience.

His hand has still not moved away from mine.

When I was twenty I would have insisted, I would have grabbed him in my arms—back then I thought that was the answer to everything.

If I tell you I agree, I say to him, I don't want you to think that it's because I'm sorry.

His eyes now are soft and brown and a little wet.

I mean it, Karel. Whether you know it or not, you've made this week bearable for me.

I hope that's true, he says and pats my hand. His soft palm rests on my fingers.

Then he closes his eyes and says, Jozef and Gaspar tried to teach me to climb once. Have I told you that? We all went to the Dolomites one summer. It was a disaster. I got up on the rock, and I couldn't move. I almost died, just twelve meters off the ground on the easiest crag in Italy, because my arms and legs began to shake. They had to lower me down on a rope, with Gaspar holding me around my waist. I cried. Eighteen years old and I cried like a baby. They were kind about it, they always were, but I knew I was different from them. We all knew it.

He looks at the sheer cliffs across the valley, maybe thinking, as I am, about how there's not a single one Jozef hasn't scampered up and down and sideways.

I grip his hand and tell him something I have never told anyone. Not even Jozef. It is a secret I keep so close I rarely admit it to myself. Why shouldn't I tell Karel now? I have been ready to give him much more of myself, and this time here, in our meadow—the last of our time together—seems right for secrets.

I did a terrible thing, I say. You remember after Gaspar died? What an awful state Jozef was in?

I remember, Karel says.

And so I tell him.

The year after Gaspar died, Jozef and I moved to a tiny flat in the middle of Ljubljana. I taught art, and Jozef took a job as an instructor at the Alpine Club. He hated it. But that year nothing made him happy. He had lost several toes to frostbite; he could only walk with a cane at first, and he could not hold the construction jobs he loved. And of course he missed Gaspar—Gaspar who had taught him to climb, who had taken him in when Jozef fled their father. But more than anything he missed the mountains, and what he did there. Every night he wept. Some weekends he could not rouse himself from bed.

I was gentle with him. I told him always how glad I was that he was alive. I told him we could live a happy life together. I even told him he might climb again—it seemed an easy lie, a way to pacify him. I believed—I knew—that in the end, Jozef would come to the same conclusion I already had: that climbing was too dangerous, the cost of failure there too high.

But then he met Hugo, who worships him, and made him want to love himself again. Jozef bought special shoes; he taught himself to lose the cane. Then he and Hugo started hiking together. One day I came home and found Jozef putting up his climbing holds on the wall of our living room.

I have to try, he told me.

I told myself that, surely, physically, he wasn't ready.

But one weekend, not two months later, he told me: he and Hugo were going to try an easy route on Triglav. The north wall of Triglav is 1,200 meters high, and sheer. No route there is easy.

I went hysterical. Jozef, in his way, tried to calm me by reassuring me of his prowess, his belief. This is when he told me how my love keeps him alive. How he climbs *to* me.

Finally I made him angry. He shouted, *Do you only want to love half a man? Because that is what I am. You knew who I was when you fell in love with me.*

I didn't understand, I said. *I didn't* know.

You decide, he said, walking out the door. *You can have me as the man I am, or not at all.*

We barely spoke, and that weekend he and Hugo packed their gear and drove to the mountains. And he survived Triglav—not only that, he and Hugo did *well,* putting up a new variation. When Jozef came home I embraced him, told him I was sorry. I was—I couldn't be without him, as miserable and frightened as he made me. And anyway Jozef was jubilant, his old self again.

I can't help who I am, he told me. *I can't, Ani.*

We made love again and again that night, and it was when we lay together afterward that he told me he was thinking again about the Himalayas.

Now I tell Karel, That was when I started poking holes in his condoms.

Karel looks at me, and then again out over the meadow, doing math.

He says, You were pregnant when Jozef left for Makalu.

Yes.

He squeezes my hand. I'm sorry, he whispers.

I thought he would stop, I say. But then the solos started. The baby only made things worse.

I am crying now, and can't say any more. Karel rubs my hand. I pull him into an embrace.

And it happens, it happens.

After a few minutes in his arms, I stop my crying. I look at Karel's face. The way his mouth doesn't know quite how to hold itself, the way his mind is torn between concern and wanting. He is such a good man—like his brother would be, if his brother was not crazy.

Karel's hands slide to my hips, and we hold each other. I take one of his hands in between both of mine and press it between our bodies. I caress his palm with my thumbs. I am used to rough skin, like sandpaper, to bandages and chalk and torn nails. Not this hand which seems to join with mine.

And then I am closer, and Karel is closer, and he is touching my face with all the wonder and sweetness that I have wished for. He bends forward and kisses my forehead; his beard is soft on the bridge of my nose. I close my eyes and listen for Stane's footsteps coming up the path, but the air is still, the whole valley silent.

The thought of my son should stop me, but no: I am putting my arms around Karel's waist, lifting my face to his. I am a woman, it seems, who can kiss a man not her husband while within earshot of her son.

Karel's face is large in front of mine, his hips pushing in close. I take off his glasses and tuck them into the pocket of his jacket. My hands slip underneath the jacket, and I feel his back, smooth under his thin shirt. He kisses well, more forcefully than I would have guessed. He places one large, warm hand flat on my belly. I am making sounds in my throat, the way I do when I kiss Jozef.

Because it is what I must do, I try to stop myself, to think of my husband:

Jozef walks into the meadow. He retreated from the climb after all, they helicoptered him out, and here he is, just home.

He sees us. Karel's hands are under my blouse, at the small of my back. Jozef's face falls into shock, then pain, and I can see that he thinks: I fought for *this*. I stayed alive to see *this*. Karel is kissing my jaw, under my ear. Jozef shouts, *My wife, my brother—*

But this seems too much like vengeance, too much like I am kissing Karel in anger, which is not what I feel at all.

So I imagine my husband in love with me: Jozef, ten years younger, walks into the café. His beard is too big for his face, and the corners of his eyes crinkle up when he smiles at me— as though he recognizes me, as though he is surprised to see such an old friend in a place like this.

Karel's arms are tightening around my waist, pulling me close to him, and up on the balls of my feet. I am stretching my mouth wide against his.

Jozef. I wake in the night after giving birth to Stane, only to see Jozef sitting awake in the corner; he smiles tenderly at me and asks if I would like some water. He holds the glass to my lips and then kisses me and strokes my hair. *I love you,* he whispers, runs his rough finger across my cheek. *I love our son.*

Karel puts his hands under my bottom and lifts me onto the rock. I curl my calves around his legs. He nuzzles the space where my blouse is open.

Love me, Jozef says. *As long as you love me I will be all right.*

Right now his hands are on rock, his lungs ache, he tastes blood.

Death, then. Think of death—death, after all, has given us permission. So here: Jozef moaning into my neck in the hospital. Papa's eyes red with loss and rage. And here: Gaspar's casket, my shocked husband hobbling to it with a cane, putting his hand on the lid, as though something is inside it.

Here is Gaspar's wispy blond girlfriend, arriving suddenly from Dresden, knowing no one and latching on to me in her grief. *We were engaged,* she says to me, her voice so thin it must hurt her to say any words at all. She says, *We hadn't told anyone, we were waiting till he came back to announce it.* There's Papa in a chair, head in his hand, Karel's hands on his shoulders. Across the room Jozef embraces other climbers, some flown in from Russia and America. Two Sherpas are here from Nepal. None of the wives or girlfriends look at each other except in sideways glances, mistaken turns. We listen to the men we love so much say over and over, *At least he died doing what he loved.* I keep my arm around Gaspar's German girl, knowing what she thinks, what all the women think: if Gaspar died doing what he loved, he would have died at home, he would have died inside her. These brave men are cowards, that is what I think. I look around the room, a little drunk from a flask Karel brought, the girl snuffling into my shoulder, and I know—for the first time I know—tonight is only a rehearsal.

My husband, alive, does not stop me. But Jozef dead and gone—this is what makes me pull away from Karel.

Love does not keep me faithful.

But shame does.

I'm sorry, Karel says, breath rasping.

I shake my head and slide away from him. No, I say, angry now. No. We both did this.

He nods twice, quickly, and rubs his jaw as though I have hurt it.

We have both agreed on a course, but there is still wildness in the air, that thing which is so easily called up between us but so difficult to dispel. I walk to the edge of the meadow and back again, to calm myself more than anything else. Karel stands next to the rocks, hands in his pockets, shoulders slumped. I want to tell him not to feel bad, but for now I cannot go closer.

Over the curve of the hill, a curl of dust rises: a car driving slowly toward the house. I look at Karel. We stand side by side on the hilltop and try to see who it could be—we can barely see the road from the meadow, only glimpses through gaps in the trees. The trail of dust slows and begins to billow, and then for a moment we see a van, marked on the side with the 24ur emblem.

Something has happened, I say.

We hurry back down the path. I try to prepare myself. Today is summit day, and that is all the news people care about: they don't ever think about how, if Jozef makes the top, he still has to climb down, half dead. But maybe something else has happened. I tell myself: Hugo wouldn't inform the media before me. But I have been gone for an hour, and there are many people at base camp, all with satellite phones.

I do not believe it, but of course in my heart I do: I broke my promise. I kissed Karel and Jozef has died.

I am almost running when I emerge from the woods onto the road. The van is parked twenty or thirty meters away. I walk to it, and this is what I see:

A cameraman and a newswoman are standing next to the Roman wall, right in front of one of the tall crumbling pillars, three meters high. And clinging to the stone, at the level of their heads, is Stane. I hear one of the newspeople say, loudly, so Stane can hear too, He's his father's boy, look at that.

Stane is climbing. Not the clambering up tree trunks I've seen him do. The newswoman was right.

He has been *taught*.

Stane grips the rock the right way, locking his thumbs over the tops of his fingers, keeping his balance out away from the rock, suddenly lying sideways, leaning away from a crevice while his feet push the other way. By the time I reach him he has touched the top of the pillar, and when he does this he emits a laugh, the squeak of delight I know so well.

The newspeople applaud, and the cameraman moves in, and Stane takes one hand off the rock to wave.

The newswoman is saying something about a new generation, and that's when I force my way past her. I put my hands on Stane's waist and pull him off the pillar. He's heavier than he used to be, but I catch most of his weight, even though it nearly knocks me over.

Turn the cameras off, I say. Get out of here.

The camera swivels to me. The newswoman asks if I have any words about Jozef's success today. All of the nation is watching, she says. We're all very proud.

I turn and walk back to the house, Stane shocked in my arms. I am so angry I can barely see. I pass Karel, just coming out of the trees, and I say, Get rid of them.

Mama, put me down, Stane says. Put me *down*.

I set him down and then swat him twice on the behind, hard. The newspeople can see us, but I don't care. I pull Stane along by the arm. He's wriggling and trying to escape, without knowing why or where to go. I can't help it. I tug him off the road, down the slope, into the trees out of sight. There I swat him again, and again, enough so that he stops struggling and begins to cry. Enough so that he *knows*.

Then I kneel and put my arms around him. Stane smells of little-boy sweat and pine needles. He tries once again to pull away, but then he sees me crying, and this hurts him more than the spanking. I hold him to me, my quivering son.

He is a man, eyes crinkling like his father's, smiling at a girl in a café. He is calling a name into swirling snow, screaming wind, alone.

Mama, he says. It's okay, I was only climbing.

I tell him, You mustn't, Stane.

I am holding him as an infant, handing him for the first time to Jozef. Jozef's face falls into pieces when he takes his newborn son—when he looks up again at me, for the first time as a father. And I know: my husband will never climb again, he will never risk anything, now that he has seen his darling boy. I shake and throb inside and think I might die from love. I watch Stane in his father's arms and I think, *My sweet boy, do you know what you have done? You have given me your father back. You've saved us. You've saved me.*

You mustn't, I say into Stane's ear. I shake him with each word.

You mustn't *ever.*

In the Event

AT A LITTLE PAST ONE IN THE MORNING, AN HOUR AFTER identifying their bodies at the morgue downtown, Danny pulled his truck into the drive at Tom and Brynn's house. Their narrow Victorian was dark except for the glowing living-room window—a babysitter was inside, watching Colin, their three-year-old son. Danny had talked to the babysitter for a few minutes from the morgue, told her he'd be right there—but then he'd taken the longest route from downtown he could find. He'd stopped twice at gas station pay phones, trying to raise his girlfriend Kim, to tell her the news, but Kim had never answered.

Danny shut off the truck. The poor babysitter had started sobbing during his call; by now she was probably freaked out of her mind. Danny's hands on the wheel seemed to weigh tons. He thought about circling the block a couple more times—he was pretty damn well freaked out himself, wasn't he? Or he could just drive off—he wasn't far from the I-70 on-ramp. He could drive from Columbus to fucking Alaska without letting up on the gas.

Then a shadow pushed aside the living room curtain, looking out at the drive. He was caught.

A woman maybe ten years older than Danny met him at the door—the babysitter's mother. She wore a short hairdo that might look good on a movie star, but which made her look just like what she was: a parent of a teenager, thick and square and gray at the temples, trying too hard. Behind her mother the babysitter huddled on the couch, holding herself as if her stomach hurt, her eyes so red Danny's started to burn in sympathy. After he'd introduced himself both mother and daughter gave him the once-over. He'd been rehearsing with the band when the police called—he was wearing week-old clothes and reeked of cigarette smoke. His hair was out of its ponytail.

I'm so sorry, the woman told him.

I'll be all right, he said, surprised that his voice was even working—or that he would say something so bizarre as *that*.

Do you need someone here?

I'm going to call a friend now, he said.

The woman looked relieved.

The babysitter said, thickly, Can I look at him one more time?

So the three of them stood in the doorway to Colin's room. Just last week Brynn had glued glow-in-the-dark stars and moons across the ceiling and walls; they barely picked up a shine from the streetlight outside. The room seemed vast this way, without walls.

Colin was asleep, his covers kicked off his bare legs, his face turned to the wall. He was practically naked, sleeping in tiny underpants. Danny forced himself not to look away—as he'd always done when Brynn laid Colin out on the floor for a diaper change. Or like he'd done last week, when Tom had made a big production of *Show Danny what a big boy you are, show him you can use the potty,* and they'd all crowded into the bathroom to watch Colin do his thing, his face screwed tight, like he was threading a needle. *You did a good job,* Danny told him afterward, and Colin had looked up from washing his hands and said, *Yes, I did,* as though he didn't have pants with cartoon bears on them still drooping around his ankles.

Danny thought about walking into the room, pulling the boy's covers back up, but he didn't. Colin was almost three; three-year-olds were messy, and a lot of the times naked. He had no more place for shame, not now.

The babysitter started to whimper.

Shh, Danny said, and quickly motioned them back to the living room.

There he assured them once again that they could leave—and they did, but only after Danny fumbled for his wallet, and both mother and daughter said No! in unison, almost angrily.

When they were gone, Danny stood for a little while in the kitchen, on the opposite side of the house from Colin's room. It was the only place in the house that wasn't filled with the too-sweet odor of a small child—instead he could smell chili, pancakes, the omelets Tom cooked for everyone on weekends. The smell reminded Danny he hadn't eaten since lunchtime—that he was so hungry he was dizzy. But the thought of rooting through Tom and Brynn's leftovers made him feel like the most horrible piece of shit on earth.

Tom's bottle of Maker's Mark in the pantry, however, was another thing entirely. Danny cut through the wax and then poured himself a shot. And another. The whiskey brought tears to his eyes; these threatened to build on themselves. He took a couple of deep breaths and then picked up the kitchen phone to call Kim again.

Her phone rang four, five times. Danny wondered if, just maybe, he was catching her. They had been tense lately, and though Danny was pretty sure she wouldn't cheat on him, this new hesitance in her, left to turn itself over and over in his head, had mutated into all kinds of horrible pictures. He felt a kind of lunatic gladness as the phone kept ringing. When things were this bad, why *shouldn't* they get worse?

But then—finally—Kim answered, rasping out a hello.

It's me, he said. It's an emergency.

Danny.

Yeah. Kim, listen. I need you to wake up. Go to the kitchen and pour yourself a drink, okay?

She laughed throatily. Too late, she said. I was out with Amanda all night. She coughed. Um. Why?

Danny figured that was good enough.

Baby, he said, listen. I'm at Tom and Brynn's. They're dead.

What?

Tom and Brynn. They wrecked their car.

Kim didn't say anything, so Danny kept going.

My name was in Tom's wallet. I had to ID their bodies.

The words were falling apart, and Danny was starting to shudder; he took another drink and let the whiskey rest burning in his mouth and nose before unclenching his jaws. He heard Kim breathing quickly, maybe crying. He wanted her to cry—if she did, *he* could. He leaned his forehead against the cool yellow wall. He'd helped Tom paint the kitchen, last year, on a weekend when Brynn and Colin were out of town at her parents' place. That was last time he and Tom had had the good old times they used to—drinking beer and barbecuing and watching sports and the violent movies they weren't allowed when Colin was in the house. *Gluttony,* they'd kept saying, painting late into Friday night in order to free up the rest of the weekend. It got to be a chant: *Glut-ton-y. Glut-ton-y.* They'd smoked ribs at four in the morning, eaten them for breakfast. That was right here, in *this* kitchen.

Danny told Kim, Tom made me promise. I have to take care of Colin now.

And she finally understood. Oh God, she said.

I need you to come over. Please.

Umm, Kim said, and he could hear her fumbling, probably trying to find her little cat's-eye glasses. You're at their *house?*

Yeah.

He heard her light a cigarette. She'd been trying to quit. But then Danny had been trying not to drink so much these days either.

Okay, she said. Okay. Let me throw on some clothes.

Do you remember how to get—

Jesus. A car crash? What *happened*?

No one knows. They crossed the center line somehow. Hit a semi head-on.

Were they drinking?

He wanted to be angry—what sort of question was that? But Tom and Brynn had been driving home from a dinner out. They'd both probably had wine. Danny had asked the police what happened, and no one had said anything about booze.

I don't know, he said. Probably not.

Kim asked, Is Colin awake?

Not yet.

What are you going to tell him?

Look, he said, starting to cry for real. Just come over, okay?

Yeah. It—yeah. I'm leaving right now.

Okay. I love you.

He said it just as he heard her hang up the phone.

Then he let go; he spent a good gut-wracking fifteen minutes sitting on the floor, all around him little bits of cereal and—he could see under the microwave cart—two red blocks, some Lincoln Logs. He couldn't remember ever crying like this, except maybe when he used to get stoned and lonely in college. But not—never over people dying, never in *grief.* He shoved his hands in his mouth. Anything to keep those awful noises in.

Anything to keep Colin from waking up.

Tom HAD PUT the question to Danny back when Colin was still an infant. They'd even joked about it.

You must really hate that kid, Danny had said, if I'm the best godfather you can come up with.

Tom smirked and turned their steaks over on the barbecue, then stood back, one hand in the pocket of his baggy shorts, belly jutting. Up until the last year he'd kept himself trim, but his stomach had swollen in the same span of time as Brynn's. Danny saw something different in Tom's stance, too: a looseness—a satisfaction, maybe. He'd had a son: his great accomplishment, the one he'd always wanted.

Tom said, deadpan, I don't have any other options, really. He drank a swallow of beer and looked across the yard at the back patio, where Brynn sat on a wooden chair, lifting her rusty hair from her neck and saying, I know, I know, into the phone. Colin was invisible next to her, somewhere inside a bassinette she rocked with her foot.

Tom said, Mom and Dad are in Africa—and, let's face it, they're not an option. Walt's got four of his own. It's all Brynn's mother can do to take care of her dad—and her sister's a fucking mess. Something happens to us, I want someone to take care of Colin who could actually do it.

You must know something I don't.

As a matter of fact, Tom said grinning, I do.

They had been like this since third grade. From the first moments of their friendship Tom had been steadfast, certain, optimistic; Danny had been troubled, foot-dragging, complicated. Danny had always found their friendship—that they fit together—cosmically mysterious. They were both smart and talented people, but Tom had a grand path to follow, and Danny—Danny just followed Tom. And his life had been happier because of it. He could make a long list of things he might never have done, without Tom telling him he ought to quit his bitching and give them a shot. *Ask her out, you coward. Go back to guitar practice, you're good at it. What are you worrying about? I have to stand in front of everyone and dance a waltz, and all you have to do is tell two or three shitty jokes.* And he couldn't think of a week in the last ten years when he hadn't spent at least one day with Tom, and now with Tom and Brynn—who was, face it, Tom, if Tom were a beautiful woman. That had been the gist of his best man's toast, anyway.

In days of old, Danny told Tom, the purpose of a godfather was really to provide spiritual instruction.

Well, yeah, that too. Tom poked a steak. But if a child's parents were slaughtered by, like, the Visigoths, then the god-father was still bound to take over. I'm not so concerned what you tell the kid about God—

Maybe you ought to be.

Danny, come on. This isn't supposed to put you on the damn roof.

I know, Danny said. I'm honored, all right?

You're a pal, Tom said. He glanced at Brynn in her chair and gave her a thumbs-up. Brynn waved her hands over her head, like a cheerleader with pom-poms, then pointed to the phone and made a face.

God, Danny said. I need another beer.

Wait till you have your own kid. You'll want your bases covered, too.

I swear upon my honor, Danny said, that unless the both of you die in a freak accident, I will never have children. You hear me?

Tom opened the cooler and took out two beers. What honor?

Really. I swear it. The only child I could ever have is yours.

Well, Tom said, we only ever want the best for you.

Months later, when Colin was almost one, Tom and Brynn took Danny into Tom's study. Brynn had Colin on her hip; he goggled at Danny, drooling around a fistful of Danny's keys.

We finished all the paperwork, Tom said.

What paperwork?

You know. The in-the-event-of-our-untimely-passage paperwork. It's in here.

Tom opened a drawer in his antique rolltop desk and took out a metal lockbox the dimensions of a sheet of legal paper, and maybe three inches deep. He said, All my emergency paperwork is in here. The key's taped inside the drawer. Okay? Just in case.

Good God, Danny said. You people are unbelievable.

Brynn said, I promise: on Colin's eighteenth birthday we'll have a big Danny's-off-the-hook party.

Colin squirmed, so she set him down. He immediately crawled off into the hall; Tom chased after him.

Brynn put her arm around Danny's waist. Thanks for doing this, she said.

Danny nearly jumped; Brynn was a hugger, but that didn't mean he wasn't alarmed by it—by her—even after three years.

Hey, he said. It's no big deal.

Sure it is. She kissed his cheek, then rubbed lipstick off the spot she'd kissed. Don't worry about it, okay? We're not going anywhere.

Danny's cheek grew hot. Listen, you're—you're okay with this? With me doing this?

She laughed. Why wouldn't I be?

I don't know. Because I'm a mess, maybe? Like I can't even balance my checkbook?

Brynn gave him a look, then patted his shoulder. We talked it over, she said. You're a good person.

Danny groaned and glanced out into the hallway, where Tom lay on his back, lifting Colin up and down above his chest like a weightlifter with a heavy bar.

Brynn said, You're like a brother to Tom. That means a lot in my book. And you can play beautiful music. You're nice to girls. You worry. Bad people don't worry.

Hitler worried about lots of stuff.

Be serious. I just have this feeling about you. We both do. You'd do fine, if.

Danny wished he had a drink. Well, he said, just make sure we never find out, okay? I couldn't do this without you guys.

Do what? Colin? She frowned, gave him that look again.

Jesus, Danny said. Anything.

WHEN HE WAS DONE crying Danny sat propped against the kitchen wall, trying to keep himself in the drained state of calm that had settled over him when he finally caught his breath. Trying not to think about how Kim had turned a fifteen-minute trip into one a half-hour long and counting.

And here was a distraction: The metal lockbox in the study. The key, taped inside the drawer.

He stood up, wincing. Remembering the lockbox reminded him of the twenty or thirty problems that had been flashing in front of him all night, ever since the police had called. The ones he had to think about sooner or later: a whole fucking avalanche of problems.

He poured himself another shot.

For instance. The band had gigs this weekend that would have to be canceled. He'd have to take a hiatus for a while— there was no way around it. A couple of guitarists in town might be able to play his parts; the other guys could make those calls, but they'd need to start right away. Like tomorrow; they had a gig at the coffee shop on Thursday—

The coffee shop! True Brew—Brynn's business, Danny's job. It was due to open at six; the morning crew showed up at five, in just—Danny checked his watch as he walked into the living room—three and a half hours.

Brynn had started up the shop last year, in an empty storefront a few blocks away from the house. It could have been a lark. Tom made enough money to support the family on his own, but Brynn had a business degree and was not, generally, the kind of woman to half-ass anything she did. And so the shop had been a big success almost from the moment it opened, with Brynn as owner and store manager, pulling twelve-hour days in split shifts, taking care of Colin when day care and Tom weren't able to. Her only questionable move in the whole process had been hiring Danny as her assistant manager.

No. He was being pathetic. The deal had worked out for both of them. Danny had thought Brynn was joking when she first suggested it; his only experience (aside from drinking obscene amounts of coffee; he played bluegrass, and it helped to be a little wired) was running a register, which he had done at video stores, record stores, bookstores. He'd majored in music, for Christ's sake; he had no skills.

But when she explained the details he could see the pride in her face—Danny got a job that suited him, with gig nights off, and Brynn got extra help she could stand. She told him she'd even sign up the band to play Thursday nights.

(*Jesus,* he'd said, stunned. *Sure, Brynnie.*

She smiled and called into the study, *Hey, Tom—Danny just told me I could boss him around.*

Tom leaned into the living room and said, *Then I'd say both of you got exactly what you wanted.*)

Brynn had always worked the morning shifts; Tom took Colin to day care on his way in to work. Danny closed. When Kim showed up—and when the fuck was that going to be, anyway?—he'd have to send her over to True Brew with a sign. The shop would have to stay closed, for what—a week? He and Brynn were the only managers. Danny would have to promote one of the kids. But who'd take the place over for good? Maybe one of Brynn's family—

Brynn's family. *Tom's* family. He was such a fucking idiot.

The police had found Danny's number in Tom's wallet, and called him into the morgue, after he told them the families were all in other cities or countries. *I suppose I* am *family,* he'd said. Now he had to call the real people: Brynn's mother, who was in Colorado Springs, caring for Brynn's father—he'd suffered a bad stroke two years ago. And Tom's parents, who were on missionary work in Sierra Leone. He didn't even know *how* to reach them. Even Tom only talked to them a couple of times a year. And then there was Brynn's sister in Pittsburgh, and Tom's brother Walt in Denver ...

Danny's heart was beating too fast. He took a swallow of whiskey. He'd make the calls in the morning. No one could do anything till then anyway. And he was in no shape to be on the phone, not for a while yet.

Everyone would come to Columbus for the funeral— God, the funeral. At least someone else would be in charge of that. He tried to imagine all those people, crying. Telling them he was Colin's guardian now. Showing them whatever magic papers Tom had in the study. Seeing the worry in a hundred different faces.

Maybe he could just stay home with the boy. You couldn't take a three-year-old to his parents' funeral, could you?

He ought to call his own parents, too. His mother would come and stay for as long as he asked, would give him advice. Walt would, too. He had a girl a little older than Colin. Maybe he could bring her out, give Colin a playmate for a while. Walt was a decent guy. He'd do whatever he could.

Everyone would help him. This was a little kid—no one would turn away from Colin.

Even Kim. Maybe.

In truth Danny had no idea what Kim was going to do with all of this. She wasn't prone to dealing rationally with anything, let alone a crisis. She was only twenty-four, for God's sake; she'd quit as many jobs as he had, in ten years' less time. Just a month ago he'd loaned her a thousand dollars to bail her out on a credit card. He tried to see her bouncing Colin on her hip, like Brynn did. Even in his imagination she looked horrified.

He checked his watch again. Forty-five minutes had gone by since they had hung up. His mind couldn't stop racing—he saw Kim calling a lover. Driving to Alaska as fast as her little Mazda would take her. Bleeding to death in the median of I-270.

He had to think of something else. It was time to quit fucking around and open the lockbox.

The study was off the same hallway as Colin's room. Danny paused at the entrance, listening; he could just barely make out Colin's little whistling breaths through the cracked door. Danny still had his shoes on; now he slipped them off and walked carefully to the study in his damp socks.

The study had always been Tom's sanctum. He had a kind of fetish for Corleone-type rooms, for mahogany furniture, for green-shaded lamps and fountain pens. *This is where I feel most like a lawyer,* Tom had always said. Now the study felt, to Danny, exactly like a funeral home: too still, too dark.

He turned on the desk lamp and then walked to the antique rolltop in the corner. Inside he found the metal lockbox, and the key taped inside the top drawer, just as Tom had shown him.

Inside the lockbox was a stack of sealed manila envelopes, each labeled in Tom's neat hand. *Auto Titles. True Brew. Mortgage. Birth Certs.* And then, at the bottom: *In the event of the deaths of Tom Schultz and Brynn Matthews.*

Danny sawed the envelope open with a heavy gold letter opener. A sheaf of papers and envelopes, weighty and official, slid onto his lap. On top of the stack was a smaller, sealed envelope. FOR DANIEL O'DAY ONLY was written in marker across the outside.

Danny looked at the ceiling until the stinging in his nose stopped.

He turned the envelope around in his hands twice, wanting more than anything else not to open it. In fact, the hell with opening it. He wanted to take the whole stack over to the fireplace and *burn* it. Let everything revert back to how it ought to be. Someone in Tom or Brynn's family—Walt!— would take control of Colin, of all the other envelopes, of the whole goddamned mess.

No. Tom would have duplicates filed somewhere. He was that kind of guy.

Danny rubbed his mouth. He was such a shit. He couldn't destroy the papers because he wouldn't get *away* with it? How about because he'd promised his best friends? Because he was concerned about their *child*?

You see? he asked Tom, in his head. *You see what a mistake this was?*

He reached for the letter opener, sniffling.

Inside the envelope was a sheet of stationery, with a faded print across the background: one of those ancient yellow maps that showed dragons curling out of the oceans. The paper was filled up with Tom's handwriting:

Danny,

So it's about four in the morning and I'm in a weird mood. Go figure, huh? I hope in twenty years I'll show you this note and we'll laugh about it. If you're reading it before then . . . well, Brynn and I are dead, and you know what happened better than I do. (Or maybe you're just snooping, in which case you deserve the same creeps I've got. You're now obliged to come tell me, you dumbass.)

But anyway, if we're dead, and Colin is still alive, then everything in this envelope will guide you through what has to happen next. Our wills have been notarized and witnessed by our attorney— all you have to do is take the papers back to him, and he'll get the wheels rolling. He's a friend; you should trust him. Most of our possessions will be routed to you until Colin is old enough to take them. Brynn and I each have a life insurance policy, too—Brynn's will go to Colin, and mine to you. The money's enough to pay off the mortgage, if you need to go—and if you do, for God's sake don't hesitate. If the worst has happened I don't want you to feel trapped.

We videotaped just about all of Colin's infancy. I tried writing a note to the boy tonight, but I got too worked up. In the end it might be better to sit him down with those videos, when he's ready. They're in a fireproof trunk in the basement.

Now for the rough stuff. You know what my parents think of me. This probably won't come as news, but they don't like you either. The godless unwashed, etc. I'm sure they're going to contest your guardianship. I suppose it's possible Walt might, too, if the folks play him right. I know this is going to be rough on you; I know, somewhere along the line, it'll seem easier to let them win, but please don't. In the event I can't be Colin's dad, then you will do just fine. You think too little of yourself. I don't, Brynn doesn't, and Colin doesn't.

So go take care of all this, and do it right away. You had better grieve for us, but you don't have time to do it now.

Tell Colin we loved him, and tell him every day.

Tom

TWENTY MINUTES LATER, when Kim's quiet knock startled him, Danny was sitting on the couch, the whiskey bottle between his thighs, Tom's letter turned facedown on the cushion next to him. He rose quickly enough that he nearly spilled the booze, and the room spun a bit. Good, he thought. Good for me. He opened the door.

Hi, baby, he said.

Hey, Kim said, and walked just inside, but not very far. I had to call Amanda for a ride, she said. I'm still pretty out of it. She hugged her elbows across her chest and glanced past Danny across the living room.

As glad as Danny was to see her, she looked like hell. Kim's round face was pale and bleary, her eyes red-rimmed behind her glasses, her short brown hair uncombed and limp. Most of the time she was brash, sexy and bow-lipped—he liked her energy, the way she looked in a black leather jacket and a skirt that hugged her plump hips. But now, in a sweatshirt and jeans, drained and serious, she seemed more like the babysitter's mother than the Kim he was used to.

Even so, that she hadn't yet embraced him made his throat constrict.

You're alone? she asked.

Yeah. I thought I told you—

I—I thought there would be ... cops, or something. Or family.

He explained to her about where the families were. Kim swayed slowly in the center of the living room, staring at everything but him.

She'd never been comfortable in Tom and Brynn's house—she'd even given them bitter superhero names: Supermom and Lawyer Boy. Their house was the Hall of Catalogs. That's not fair, he'd told always her. But in truth he'd never been comfortable in this house either. Colin, actually, had made it better—more chaotic, less like a museum. But Brynn had even gotten Colin into the act, telling him how fun it was to clean, to *Put it where it goes.* Colin, lately, would try to shut drawers or cupboards even before Danny was done with them, his round face frowning and aggrieved. *No, Uncle Danny, it doesn't go like that.* Brynn thought this was the funniest thing she'd ever heard. *Uncle Danny's messy, isn't he?* she said, while Colin pointed and shrieked, *Yeah! Messy!*

Danny told Kim, It's just us, for a while.

Jesus, she said. There ought to be, you know, agencies. Someone . . . She ran a hand through her hair, and never finished the thought.

Hey, he said, holding up the glass. You want some?

You're drinking?

Yeah. You—come on, don't look at me like that.

It's just that there's, you know, a kid in the other room. Maybe being drunk isn't such a good idea.

Danny looked at the bottle and then set it down on an end table. You know, he said, maybe I need some comfort here. From you.

Kim stared at him as though he had just materialized out of vapor. Then she blinked and nodded.

I'm sorry, baby, she said, and clung to him.

He kissed the part in her hair. She smelled like bar smoke, like distant beers. He liked it—that was the smell of a gig, of people laughing, and the feeling he got when the band first kicked it in and the whoop went up from the crowd. Of his own sore fingers picking up a cold bottle afterward. Being noisy and happy in the early morning. Stumbling into bed with Kim. He wondered when—if!—he'd ever feel that again.

Kim pulled away, long before he wanted her to. Where's Colin? she asked.

Sleeping.

He hasn't woken up at all?

No. They say he sleeps through the night these days, and . . . shit, I don't know what to tell him anyway. He's going to ask for his mother.

He wanted very badly to touch her again, but Kim had crossed her arms.

Can I see him?

Danny took her down the hallway off the living room; her boots clacked on the floorboards, and without Danny asking she steadied herself quickly against the wall and pulled them off. He pushed open Colin's door, then remained standing in the doorway, so that Kim would have to squeeze next to him to see inside. She did, her hip rubbing against his.

Colin was asleep still, lying on his stomach. He was a tall kid for his age, and he looked even taller, stretched out in the dark. On his kid-sized bed, if you squinted right, he looked almost the size of a teenager.

Before Danny could stop her Kim turned sideways and walked inside the room, just ahead of the hand Danny was about to put on the small of her back. The boards creaked, and he whispered, Hey, and then followed her.

She turned and put a finger to her lips. Then she knelt on the braided rug beside Colin's bed, her knees giving off two distinct pops, loud as firecrackers. Colin's hand twitched on the mattress. Kim didn't do anything for a few long seconds, her face turned away from Danny's. Then she reached out and pulled the sheet gently over Colin's rear. He squirmed for a minute, bicycling his legs, but then stilled. Kim rose up.

In the living room Danny whispered, What was that about?

She sat down on the couch. I was praying, maybe.

Kim, he knew, had grown up religious, but fell away from it in college. He had no idea she still prayed about anything.

She saw the look on his face. Special occasion, she said, her mouth twisting. Okay. I need a drink now.

He went into the kitchen for another shot glass and poured her one. She drank it quickly and sat with her eyes closed.

Can I sit with you? he asked.

She nodded, and scooted over, but Danny sat close

enough to her that when the cushions sank, their hips pushed together. He put a hand on her knee and she covered it with her own hand.

What about other friends? she asked.

Huh?

Other friends of theirs. They have to know people with kids.

Danny nodded, ashamed he hadn't thought of this. Yeah, he said. Brynn hangs out with some women in the neighborhood. They have, like, this Kid Club, where they host play dates—

There should be someone here who knows something about kids. Christ. I don't. I mean we can probably get him fed, but . . .

Maggie, Danny said. There's a woman named Maggie. I think she lives on this street, even. She's here a lot.

Maggie had a daughter—something cutesy and awful, was it Kaylee?—who wasn't much younger than Colin. Colin was sweet on her. Danny had been over for one of the afternoon play groups—Brynn had talked him into bringing his guitar and playing for the kids, croaking out folk songs: "This Land Is Your Land," shit like that. The kids had loved it, though, had sat looking at him after "Puff the Magic Dragon" as though Danny had just ridden down from the sky on the back of old Puff himself. After the performance Danny sat in the living room watching the kids, while Brynnie and the mothers admired her herb garden in the backyard. Colin watched television while leaning on Danny's knees. Then an older boy, maybe four, began pinching Kaylee, who started to shriek. Danny had shifted, said, *Hey.* But before he could stand up, Colin turned away from the television, then went and stood between Kaylee and the bully. *Stop it,* Colin said to the boy, his face suddenly twisted with rage. *You stop it now.* The bully went wide-eyed and squeaked. Every kid in the room stopped talking and stared at Colin. Colin took Kaylee by the hand, and led her over to the couch. She sat by Danny's feet and picked up a toy. Colin leaned back against Danny's legs again. Like nothing had happened.

He was brave, he was such a brave kid. Christ almighty. Not nearly brave enough.

Kim said, We should get Maggie over here. She probably knows a lot about Colin. What he likes. Kim stood. Do you remember where she lives?

It's too early, she won't be up.

Kim glared at him. Colin's an orphan! People died! I don't give a shit if they're having Christmas fucking dinner!

Hey. Hey! Keep your voice down. Okay?

Well, Jesus, we have to do something!

It's not like we're fucking clueless. I've babysat the kid. Okay? He likes yogurt and graham crackers and bananas. He's not allowed to drink anything with food coloring or caffeine in it. He can use the toilet. All right? We don't have to wake those poor people up.

He watched Kim wilt a little. His anger shocked him; ten minutes ago, if he'd thought of it himself, he'd have run crying to Maggie's. But Kim had assumed he had no handle whatsoever.

Kim whispered, I just—I don't know what to do.

Sit with me. Come on. Let me worry about Colin, if it bugs you, okay? I need you right now.

She was sobbing. It doesn't bug me, I just—

She came to him and sat down, and he couldn't make out anything she said. He put an arm around her shoulders.

Lie down with me, baby. Shh. Lie down. We've got a little time. Okay?

She sniffled into his shoulder, grabbing handfuls of his shirt, and nodded. He let gravity take them both down.

He stroked her right hand, and that was when he felt it: the ring he'd given her, three months ago. She was wearing it tonight—on more than one occasion in the last month she hadn't, and Danny had been driving himself crazy, trying to figure out what that meant. Trying to figure out if Kim was sending him signals, codes. He held her hand up to his mouth so that he could see it. He hadn't thought to look for the ring when she came in. But here it was. She had worn it to see him. Kim met his eyes, looked briefly at his thumb rubbing the ring. The corners of her mouth twitched in a way he couldn't read, and then she hid her face in his shoulder and cried and cried.

I'm okay, she kept saying. I'm okay.

SHE'D SAID THE same thing, months ago. When he gave her the ring. The whole thing had been a much bigger ordeal than Danny had expected. Not that the ring was expensive—it was only a Celtic heart in silver, old and tarnished in a way that made it seem a little more beautiful. He'd found it at a vintage store he and Kim liked to go to, and he was so pleased—finding it before she did—that he bought it without thinking of what to say when he gave it to her. What it meant. But you couldn't just give a ring to a woman. A ring always meant *something*.

So he'd asked Brynn her opinion, one afternoon when both of them were going over the schedule in the back room of the coffee shop.

Brynn turned the ring over in her hand. When she held it the ring seemed shabby, and Danny wished he'd asked Tom instead. But then Brynn smiled, and he felt a little better, and she handed the ring back to him delicately, which made him feel a lot better.

I don't want her to think it's *that* kind of ring, Danny told her. But I don't want to pretend like it doesn't mean *any*thing.

Have you talked about getting married before? Brynn asked.

No.

It's been almost a year, Brynn said, her voice sliding, insinuating. Even though he knew she didn't care for Kim that much. Kim and Brynn were both way too friendly around each other; Danny knew women, he guessed, well enough to understand what that meant. And Brynn had a way of asking questions—So what does Kim *do*? What kinds of plans does she have?—that seemed designed to produce shitty answers.

And anyway, he told her, I don't want to be married. I don't think Kim does either.

Oh, Danny, Brynn said. And that was how she was different from Tom: every now and then, she could make him feel bad for being someone she wasn't.

He bristled. So that means something's wrong with me?

No, of course not, Brynn said, but she looked at him with a kind of sorrow anyway. Danny—you know Tom and I love you. I just want someone to love you like he and I love each other.

You think I can't have that without a wife?

Brynn was already retreating a little, in her eyes, looking away from him and down at the schedule. No, she said. You're right.

Come on, he said. Say it.

Well, she said, I just think it means something—something important—to make a commitment to someone else. She looked·at him. I never used to want to be married—did you know that?

Huh-uh.

I didn't, she said. I was too independent. But I wanted *someone*—I didn't want to be alone. And then I met Tom, and I fell in love, and then everything was different. I couldn't seem to make enough promises to him. She smiled. Like all of a sudden I wanted a child. *With* Tom.

I can't help but notice, Danny said, that we're talking about kids. Again.

I think it's all connected, Brynn said. I wanted a baby because of Tom. Sometimes I think having Colin was just a way of saying to him: This part of me will always be around. You know? This is the future, and it matters. She glanced at Danny. Does that make sense?

Yeah.

Brynn looked at the ring in his hand. Does Kim make you feel like *that*?

Danny couldn't tell if this was one of Brynn's I-see-something-you-don't-see questions. But it didn't feel that way. Danny put the ring in his pocket. I love her, he said.

Brynn smiled. Like they'd been arguing, and she'd won.

She said, So maybe give her the ring and see what *she* wants it to be?

That was a better plan than any Danny had come up with,

no matter what Brynn tried to read into it. So later that night, when he was off work, he went to Kim's apartment. Kim was in a foul mood that night—at the time she worked as a receptionist for an accounting firm, and had just changed bosses, and the new guy was a prick. Danny made her spaghetti while she leaned against the refrigerator behind him, smoking and ranting.

Kim's mood couldn't get to him; he hummed to himself while chopping tomatoes and bell peppers for sauce. Standing there with her, listening to her complain with less and less heat, he found himself thinking that this—this whole scene, the dinner, the words that didn't mean anything, the smell of food, the knowledge that, later on, he'd be curled up naked with her in the mess of pillows on her living room floor, listening to records—all of it felt... extendable. Not like Brynn described it—not the whole business of marriage and children, none of that. But he didn't want it to end either. And when, testing himself, he thought about losing Kim, about her sitting in this kitchen, doing these same things alone, or with another man, the grief made him want to stop and embrace her.

After dinner, when they were drinking wine on the couch, he said, I got you a ring. He felt himself blushing. Not *that* kind... but I got you one.

She sat up, while he dug in his jeans pocket. A ring?

He held it out to her.

Oh my God, she said. Danny! Is this from the Attic?

Yeah, I found it yesterday.

God, I love it! How'd you know?

I don't know. It just seemed like something you'd want.

She stared at him, wide-eyed. So what kind of ring *is* it?

He grinned. Dunno. How about a let's-go-steady ring?

She laughed, in the way that meant she was nervous. Should I wear it on yarn around my neck?

If you want. Kimmy?

Yeah.

You okay?

I'm okay. Yeah. She kissed him. I'm okay.

They made love after that, Danny stripping Kim of everything except the ring. And when they lay in bed afterward, they talked for a long time about moving in together, when Kim's lease was up next August.

But nothing had ever come of it. August was coming on fast. And more and more, Kim had started feeling skittish to Danny, more likely to go out with her college friend Amanda than to his shows, more likely to fall asleep next to him watching TV than naked in bed.

Tom told Danny this was natural. I'm lucky to get laid twice a month, he said. Does she tell you she loves you?

Yeah, Danny said. Not as much, though.

I'd ask her. Just bring it up casually. Don't make a big deal out of it.

Do you ever talk about it with Brynn?

Oh, I bitch constantly. But man—we've got a kid. We've got an excuse. Tom looked at him and grinned. Being single's harder, always was.

But Danny had never brought it up with Kim. He'd been too afraid. Instead he'd been acting—he knew—pathetic, bringing Kim gifts and flowers when he knew she would be in too poor a mood to receive them, trying to seduce her when he knew he'd get rebuffed. He spent more and more time drinking and brooding about how quickly they'd fallen in together—the way Kim had come right over to him after a show, obviously starstruck; the way they'd spent the first week opening up to each other, rarely leaving Kim's bed. The way she used to look at him, like she was amazed, like he wasn't ten years older and fatter and lonelier.

He remembered with more and more shame how grateful he'd felt, when Kim told him she loved him. How he'd been too happy to sleep, staring into the dark and thinking that his troubles were over.

And all the while the ring appeared, disappeared from Kim's finger: like just another thing she wore, depending on her mood.

THEY LAY TOGETHER on the couch for almost an hour, Kim's back pressed against Danny's belly. He rubbed a little arc over the seam of her jeans, a few inches either way. He knew she wasn't sleeping—he could feel her breathing, her occasional sniffle. But they didn't speak.

Finally Kim took his hand and held it against her breasts, his fingers squeezed tight in a way that suggested he shouldn't caress her. But not unfriendly either.

Danny? she asked—her voice, after all the quiet, startled him. What's going to happen to us?

He closed his eyes—here it came. He said, I don't know. I don't want kids.

Me neither. But I promised.

She was quiet for a while, and he couldn't help himself. I don't want to lose you, Kimmy.

After a long pause, she said, Me neither.

Danny almost broke in half with relief.

But I will, she added, shifting. Everything's different now. I love you, but that's because of a way things were that . . .

I know. But it's not my fault.

Kim said, Do you want me to be his—his mother? I mean—

I don't know, Danny said. If you asked me yesterday, I would have said that things—that I was a little worried—

Yeah, she said quickly.

—But that I wanted us to work it out. And if that's true, then—

Then maybe we'd end up here sooner or later anyway? With a kid?

Maybe. I don't know. But it was possible, yesterday.

She turned to him, cheeks wet. Is it all right if I don't know yet?

Sure, he told her. I love you. Do you know that? I really love you.

What else could he say?

She turned and kissed him. Many times, she wouldn't say I love you back—but when she kissed him, like this, he understood that's what she meant. He returned the kiss, pressing himself into her big soft body.

His mouth opened wider; so did hers. For a few minutes they twined together, sinking into the couch cushions. Kim was always a voracious, wet kisser; it drove him nuts. No different now. Danny started to tingle. He rocked his hips a little, found his hands wanting to feel her, to slide down to her rear end. That little thrill of chaos again: Why not, why the fuck not? Who was around to care?

Kim plucked at his hand. Danny, she said, and sat up.

He groaned. He felt sixteen again, drunk on two beers, caught groping in the dark after a school dance.

Can't you just hold on to me? she said. For a little while?

Sure, he said. Kim lay quietly next to him while he looked up at the ceiling, while his blood slowly flowed back to where it was supposed to.

After several minutes the rise and fall of her shoulder slowed down; he felt her blow longer breaths across his cheek. Jesus. Asleep. *That* was any better than making love? She wanted to get away as much as he did, no matter how righteous she got about it.

She didn't want much of him. Certainly no part of the present.

He shifted and sat up, then lifted Kim's legs off his thighs. She murmured. Bathroom, he said.

When he'd stood he saw Tom's letter crumpled down between the cushions. He pulled it out and smoothed it against the arm of the couch. Hey, Tom, you died and I tried to get laid in your house.

You're a pal.

Danny's house now. His couch. His minivan in the driveway.

His son.

Could he get out of it? What if he went to the attorney with Walt and said, I don't want any part of this? What if he told Kim he would?

Danny walked through the kitchen and into the back bathroom. He peed and washed his hands. His face in the mirror was puffy, his eyes bloodshot, his nose raw.

On the way back he paused in front of Colin's door. He listened for the boy's breathing. What had Tom and Brynn done to the poor little guy? Here Danny was, trying to figure a way to weasel out of a trap—thinking about papers and at-torneys and getting lucky—when, the whole time, Colin was in more trouble than he could even understand.

He pushed open the door.

The stars on Colin's ceiling shone that pale glow-in-the-dark green. Danny walked a few steps inside. He couldn't make himself go to Colin yet, so instead he looked around at the shelves, the plastic tubs against the walls—everything put away neatly. It was a good room, a good place for a kid to be: happy, full of toys. Like Danny's own had been. He and Tom had spent days in his room, as kids—between the two of them they'd had a ton of *Star Wars* junk. Had he ever been happier than in those days? When his parents had vanished into the background, and it was just him and Tom, making shit up?

Danny stood over Colin, asleep on his back with his mouth hanging open.

The boy didn't look much like his father. In the face he was narrower, his nose longer—he'd look more like Brynn, the older he got. From the both of them he had height; the doctor thought he'd top six feet as an adult. Danny tried to see him that way: thin, with Brynn's thick auburn hair cut short, parted on the side. What color were his eyes? Danny couldn't remember. Not brown, not like Brynn's, not—

Not black, not filled up with blood.

They'd made Danny look at Polaroids. On the way to the morgue he'd been trying to imagine seeing the bodies them-selves, but the attendant told him they used pictures these days. He waited for a long time in a small windowless room. The policeman who'd called Danny asked him if he wanted coffee, and when the coffee came it was pretty good. A social worker sat with him for a while, and told him about people he could talk to, gave him pamphlets and a business card. In case he felt like it tomorrow, or anytime. *It's important that you gather up people who'll help you. Do this as a team.* The morgue attendant—a woman who seemed barely out of her teens, from a too-bouncy ponytail all the way down to a scattering of acne on her cheeks—told him that he should take his time. Tom and Brynn's faces hadn't been hurt too badly, she said, but in death—in car accidents—people looked different. In this case the force of the crash had caused his friends' eyes to hemorrhage. They would be darker than he remembered. He ought to prepare himself.

She was right. The people in the pictures did not look like Tom and Brynn. No. No, they did. Their faces were like gray latex masks of Tom and Brynn, lying slack and hollow without heads inside to keep them shaped. The one on the right had Tom's hair and beard. The other looked like Brynn, except her features were tilted, everything pulled down and to the right. He remembered seeing their bare collarbones, and thinking that outside the edges of the photos they were naked, and that seemed wrong to him, terribly wrong.

They had different expressions. Tom looked like he was telling a joke. His mouth was open and his lip was a little curled, showing his teeth. His black eyes were slitted, his head tilted back a bit. Brynn was sadder. She looked more dead; her skin more blue. Blood dotted her shoulder and her jaw, hinting at something awful down below. Her hair was frizzed around her head; she'd had it up in a bun when she left work at five. Her eyes were rolled up—white at the bottoms, black at the tops—her mouth open a little wider. Like, of the two of them, she was the one who had been facing forward, who had seen what was coming for them. Like she wanted to tell Tom, to warn him, but Tom wasn't listening.

He told the attendant, *I've seen enough.*

They'd been out to dinner. Probably running a little late. They always seemed to be hurrying home, so they could stand where Danny stood now: looking down on their sleeping child. So they could effortlessly do what Danny couldn't seem to find the courage to do: bend down and kiss Colin's forehead, pull his covers up, risk waking him. Love him.

Did he love Colin?

He loved Tom. He had come to love Brynn. But their son? Shouldn't he feel more than he did? If he was any type of good person at all, shouldn't his heart open up to this poor kid? Yesterday he would have said, yeah, he loved Colin. Of course. He's my godson.

But today?

What if the Devil popped into the room and offered a deal? You can have Tom and Brynn back. It's a simple thing. Give me the boy and I'll bring them back. Would he do it? What was Colin, anyway? He was three, barely formed. Everyone loved children so goddamned much—but what about the parents? What about them? Just because they had a kid, their lives were all of a sudden worth less? All their work, all their love and effort, was gone, and nothing was left but a kid who couldn't even begin to understand the loss—was that an even trade?

He thought about Tom's parents, or Walt, trying to take Colin. If one of them was here right now, offering to take on the burden, would Danny fight? Could he? His first urge would be to go hysterical with relief. To grab Kim's hand and run.

He thought about the way Colin would latch onto his hand—sometimes to take him places, to show him toys. But sometimes he'd just reach out and hold it, like that was the most natural thing in the world to do.

Who'd been happier to see him, lately? Colin, or Kim?

Danny sat heavily on the floor next to Colin's bed. He was the worst person alive. He *did* love the boy. He did. Maybe not like his parents did—but that wasn't Colin's fault. None of it was Colin's fault. Danny wished he could apologize to someone who would understand.

He tried to imagine it. Saying: *I love you, Colin.*

Lately he'd been teaching Colin about the guitar. His fingers were too small to do much, but Danny brought his Martin over and taught Colin how to hold it, showed him that different strings made different sounds. Danny held down chords and Colin strummed raggedly with a pick, after each success looking up at Danny in wonder. Colin got excited these days when he saw the guitar case. Sometimes Danny would strum and Colin would warble the ABC song—which, at his age, was mostly just nonsense, but still.

Sometimes Danny would put Colin on his shoulders and chug around the backyard like an engine, pumping his arms, and Colin would pull on his ponytail whenever he needed to sound the whistle. He'd shriek up there, almost convulsing with happiness.

But Danny was only thinking of good times. Of playing.

Colin still peed on the floor every once in a while. He had to be bathed. And the playing itself—that took hours and hours; you couldn't just turn on the TV and let the poor kid's mind rot. And then there was the small matter of his personality and his education, all the good feelings and thoughts and karma that Tom and Brynn put into his head simply by being around. The confidence.

And, of course, any minute now Colin would wake up and ask where his mother was. And after a night of fucking around, Danny still didn't have an answer to that one, did he?

But really, how hard a question was it? There was only one answer. Danny would say, *Mommy and Daddy are asleep, but they can't wake up*. Other people would say, *Mommy and Daddy are in heaven*, and he would tell Colin that it all meant the same thing. *Mommy and Daddy had to go away*. It would be awful. Colin would cry; they'd all cry. Nothing could prevent that.

What he needed to be thinking about instead were the questions looming farther down the road, when Colin was older, when whether Danny lied or told the truth mattered a hell of a lot more.

Danny saw himself years from now, sitting at a table in a small, dark kitchen. Colin sat across from him—a teenager maybe, or even a young man. Colin was tall, handsome—he had scruffy red hair, Brynn's narrow face. Tom's glasses, maybe. He wore a black T-shirt.

Danny couldn't say where they were—not in this house, anyway, but a place much poorer, dingier. Like an apartment. A place like Kim's, only Kim was nowhere around. How could she be? That was too much to hope for, too much to ask of her, of anybody.

The apartment looked like the sort of place where people might have a lot of arguments. And why not? He and Colin had both lost too much to be happy all the time.

But they weren't arguing, not now. They held cans of beer, and Colin was smoking—Sorry, Brynnie, he picked it up someplace. Worse things could happen.

What were they like? Colin asked him. He had Tom's voice: rich, believable.

Danny heard himself say, *They loved each other. They loved you. They even loved me.*

They were good people?

He saw himself reaching across the table, putting his hand on top of Colin's. The boy's face turned inward. Getting sad. Worried.

They were the best people I ever knew, Danny told him. *And you got half of each of them.*

He might have been dozing. Kim's hand on his shoulder made him jerk. He looked at the bed, where Colin lay, still sleeping. Kim settled down onto the rug beside him.

She whispered, What are you doing?

I didn't want him to wake up alone. As Danny said this, he realized it was true.

She nestled closer to him.

I woke up alone, she said.

She had to know what that sounded like.

Kim—

No, it's okay. She said this next to his ear. It was . . . a joke. I'm sorry. I don't know what to do.

Me neither, he said. You probably can't win with me for a while.

He couldn't see her eyes in the shadows, exactly, but he knew she was looking at him. She whispered, Can I sit here with you?

Danny squeezed her shoulder.

Yeah, he said. Sure.

She moved closer. He thought again, panicked, of all the things they had to do. One of them ought to go over to the coffee shop and put up a sign, right away. The morning shift was just about due to arrive.

But Kim lowered down and rested her cheek on Danny's leg, and pulled his forearm to her chest. She kissed his hand and tucked his curled fingers under her chin. He rubbed her fingers. He touched her ring.

He watched Colin, who lay still, quiet—unaware that the world was about to end, the moment he opened his eyes. Danny reached out and put his other hand on Colin's pillow, next to his hair, and listened to the room, quiet except for their breathing.

The shop could wait. All of it could, just a few more minutes. If that was all the time they had left, the three of them, then Danny couldn't bear to spend it any other way.

A Single Awe

And [I] understood, in the endless instant
before she answered, how Pharaoh's army, seeing
the ground break open, seeing the first fringed
horses fall into the gap, made their vows,
that each heart changes, faced with a single awe
and in that moment a promise is written out.

—Brenda Hillman,
"Mighty Forms"

WHILE DANA MACARTHUR'S HUSBAND BRYAN WAS BUSY unwrapping gifts with his tellers, she slipped away—finally— from the Sentinel Savings holiday party to smoke her only cigarette of the night.

Smoking was allowed inside the banquet hall—the upper reaches of the ceiling had been foggy for hours—but Dana was trying to keep her backsliding hidden. She'd quit last New Year's, more or less, as a promise to Bryan. *Honey,* he'd say, *I just don't want anything to happen to you.* And how could she disagree? But she missed her cigarettes, missed the private time they'd always given her. All night she'd watched the bankers get drunker and drunker, watched Bryan fuss happily over them, and felt, more and more, as though she was standing alone in the room. Why not go the distance?

She almost escaped the banquet hall unnoticed. But at the doorway to the lobby, turning the corner too fast, she nearly walked into the chest of a man she knew: Jimmy, a new teller at Bryan's bank, just out of college, tall and trim and smelling faintly of beer.

Excuse *me,* Jimmy said. He bowed a little, swept his hand forward in mock gallantry. Milady.

Dana sidestepped him with only a murmur of acknowledgment. She had met Jimmy just once before tonight, while stopping by the bank for a lunch date with Bryan a few weeks earlier. She'd noticed Jimmy right away—you couldn't help but notice him. He was handsome in a catalog-model way: sandy-blond, with a symmetrical face and slim hips, and a half smile she bet he'd practiced. He'd winked at her, when they first shook hands across the counter. She decided then not to pay him much mind. Most bankers, she'd found, were a lot less slick than they hoped.

But earlier tonight, while Bryan and the other branch managers handed out bonus checks, Dana had caught Jimmy staring at her from the other side of the room, his arm slung across the shoulders of a short, pretty blonde. He'd grinned at Dana, rocked on his feet; the woman stared wide-eyed at the party over the rim of her plastic cup. The quickness of his smile disturbed her; Dana had looked away. Bryan had reintroduced them not long after. (*You remember Jimmy? Of course.* His handshake, firm and dry. The woman's name was April. His wife or girlfriend, Dana couldn't remember.)

In a small, shadowed nook just outside the entrance to the

hall, Dana lit up, feeling small and furtive. Snow swirled past her, sparse and gritty. The parking lot shone with a glittering veneer of ice—another eggnog and she might have trouble negotiating it in her heels. There'd be some bruised asses later, when the party let out. Dana watched headlights crawl east on Henderson. The roads would be getting bad, too.

She thought about Jimmy's wink, his smile. She tried to make herself angry, but the feeling wouldn't take. Dana was twenty-seven—hardly old—but in the past couple of years, it was true, people like Jimmy and April had come to seem younger and younger—more like the high schoolers in Dana's algebra classes than the kind of people she and Bryan were. Which was like no one, except in the way they acted. Everyone in the banquet hall was either too young, drinking too much, or middle-aged, trying to seem young by drinking too much. Jimmy might be nothing more than a boy in a grown-up's body, but at least he didn't pretend to be someone he wasn't.

And anyway: whatever else in him might be flawed, Dana could certainly appreciate his grown-up body.

As she thought this the pneumatic door to her left wheezed, and Jimmy himself appeared, leaning his torso outside, craning his neck left and right. Dana froze—her nook was just out of his line of sight. But Jimmy walked outside anyway, shrugging on an overcoat. He turned a half circle, and then spotted her. He grinned, feigning surprise.

Dana, hey, he said. He pointed at her hand. You looked like someone sneaking. I'm dying. Can I bum one?

She should have told him she was finished—which was the truth. But instead she said, Who says I'm sneaking? and extended her pack.

Jimmy laughed and took a cigarette. Well, he said, Bryan's been telling us all how you quit. He's real proud of you.

Dana wasn't surprised to hear it, but the news didn't make her any happier.

Our secret, all right? she said.

Jimmy put the cigarette between his lips and patted his coat pockets. Hey, I'm not legal either. April'd have a damn kitten.

Dana held out her lighter, but Jimmy said, Got one. He probably had his own cigarettes, too. He lit up, took a drag, and sighed. Then he leaned companionably back against the brick.

You know, he said, I'm glad to see you here tonight.

He glanced at her sideways and blew out a plume of smoke, half smiling. What a piece of work.

Is that so? she asked.

He laughed. Yeah, it is. And not just because that's a killer dress.

Dana could scarcely believe she'd heard him. Jimmy had gone right for her vanity, newly bruised. She had found the dress a few days earlier, shopping on a whim—she'd discovered, with a little thrill, how good she looked in it. The dress was black, with long sheer sleeves, and an ankle-length skirt slit up to mid-thigh. Probably not appropriate for a Christmas party, but its lines and color favored her, showed her off. She'd been dieting, had flattened her stomach a little; in the dress all that work seemed worth it. To teach she only wore sensible clothes; maybe once or twice a year did she have a chance to look this good.

So why was she surprised that someone had noticed?

And . . . hadn't she wanted other men to notice? In the

days since she owned it, if she was being honest, she had imagined strangers seeing her in it. Admiring her. Even re- moving it from her. The good-looking man buying ties in the next department—she'd seen him in the mirror, caught in the act of looking away, as she held the dress up against her body. Or even—she had indeed thought this—a man like Jimmy. Maybe even Jimmy himself. A man who winked at the boss's wife when she visited the bank in her jeans and run- ning shoes. What would a man like that think of her in a dress like this?

Now she knew. She kept her eyes out on the parking lot.

Thank you, she said, keeping her voice neutral. Where's your girlfriend?

Jimmy grinned as though Dana had done something wonderful.

Inside, he said. Ladies' room. There was a line—I saw my window and took it.

Dana crushed out the butt of her cigarette. Instead of a Christmas party she should be standing outside of some fifth- year senior's house, listening to the blare of speakers propped in a window, trying to keep track of her center of gravity. Jimmy could ask, *What's your major?* She could tell him to fuck off. Or she could lean on his arm.

Your husband's quite a guy, Jimmy said to her.

Thank you, Dana said—inanely, as though she'd made Bryan the way he was.

He's crazy about you. Dana, Dana—that's all he talks about.

Jimmy gave her that sideways glance again. It was un- canny—was she wearing a sign with her troubles on it? Did men like Jimmy have a radar for insecurities? Probably.

She'd tried to surprise Bryan with the new dress tonight. *My my my,* he'd said, when she came out of the bathroom wearing it. A flicker in his eyes, a dimple in his cheek—and she'd felt grateful, taller, stronger. Like the old days, that was all it took. He was knotting his tie. She wanted him to drop it, to come over to her. To feel him pull her closer when he kissed her. But instead he said, *You look fabulous, hon,* and then went back to frowning at his crooked knot.

And she'd seen the evening rolling out ahead of them: after the long tedium of the party she and Bryan would have to stay late, to make sure the drunk tellers all got home safely. They wouldn't be alone again in their bedroom until at least three in the morning, and by then they would stink of sweat and stale smoke, and Bryan might very well be asleep, turned to the wall, before the dress was even off.

She should, she knew, go inside. End this line of thinking before it extended any further.

Instead she shook another cigarette from the pack. She started to dig for her lighter, but Jimmy held out his. Dana leaned forward toward his cupped hands. His arm pressed against hers through the sleeves of their coats. He was wearing cologne: just a hint escaped from the collar of his shirt.

Jimmy was saying, No, I mean it. I love working for Bryan, we all do. Heck of a nice guy.

He sure is.

Can I ask you something, though? His eyes were glittering with secrets.

Dana took in a breath, barely knowing what to hope for. Sure, she said.

So I've been hearing this rumor.

She knew, then, what he was going to ask, and felt a surge of disappointment so strong she almost began to cry.

She said, Go ahead.

Is it true that—I mean, I heard that— Jimmy laughed at himself. Is it true he saved someone's life once? That's why . . . ? Jimmy moved his fingers up and down over his right forearm, indicating Bryan's scars.

Dana wondered what sort of look was on her face.

Hey, Jimmy said, I'm sorry, I didn't mean to offend you. Really.

But she had no one but herself to blame for his asking. When Dana had been just—just a kid, five years ago, she had stood in a corner at a Sentinel dinner party and told the story of Bryan's burns—his heroism—for the first time. Back then she had been proud. She wanted the people who worked with him to know what Bryan had done, what he was. And it was possible that the reason Bryan Macarthur was now a branch manager had something to do with that story, circulating out there in whispers. Dana and Bryan had never discussed this possibility, but she knew they had both thought it. He'd been upset—sad—when he found out she'd told.

He'd said, *They look at me differently. I'm nothing special.*

She'd told him, *You are to me.* Then she kissed him, deeply.

Now she took a breath.

It's true, she told Jimmy. We were in college together, in Colorado. We went to the mountains on a ski trip. We were driving through a blizzard and found a wrecked car. Bryan pulled a woman out after the car caught fire.

Dana pushed back her coat and dress sleeve. She held up her wrist in front of Jimmy and turned it.

He and I dragged her up to the road, she said. I got burned a little, too.

Jimmy looked at the scar twisting from her forearm down to the base of her thumb.

Jesus, he said, leaning back. That's pretty fucking brave.

It happened quickly, Dana said.

That's a strange thing to say.

She shrugged. He was right. She couldn't explain why she'd said it . . . or why she'd shown him the scar, which she usually kept hidden. It was nothing—not compared to Bryan's. Her face flushed, and she hoped Jimmy wouldn't notice. She was lingering too long—what did she think was going to happen, anyway? What *could* happen? She had to end this, get back inside.

When she looked up from readjusting her sleeve, Jimmy was leaning forward, too close.

You've got some more secrets, I bet. I thought so when I first met you.

Dana pulled back, almost by instinct.

I'm sorry, she said. I have to get inside. Good night, Jimmy.

She took a step, her stomach jumping, but Jimmy said, Wait, and even though she told herself to keep going, she turned around anyway.

Jimmy took hold of her hand. He was taller even than Bryan, and she had to arch up to kiss him. His lips were cold, his breath tasting of cigarette smoke and the sting of a breath mint. He opened her mouth wide; she returned the pressure. His hand slipped down the back of her long coat and squeezed at her rear end, and for a moment she was pressed against him from her knees to her shoulders.

Then Dana put a hand inside Jimmy's open overcoat—his stomach, under the smooth silk of his shirt, was stony-hard—and pushed. Jimmy rocked back. He smiled and brushed a thumb wonderingly across his lips.

What was that? Dana asked, and though she meant to sound angry, her voice quavered.

You wanted me to, he said.

He was right. She wanted him to kiss her again. She wanted, in fact, to pull him into an empty car and do a lot more than kiss him. Since meeting Bryan she'd never kissed another man—her body felt light, her ankles wobbly.

But she said, I'm going inside. Don't ever do that again.

You might change your mind, Jimmy said. He dug in his pocket and handed her a business card. She took it the same way she'd kissed him—her body acting a second ahead of her will. Don't call me at home, he said. My cell's there on the card.

I'm not going to call you, she said, and dropped the card into the snow.

He smiled, like he knew something she didn't, and then shrugged. That's too bad, he said, and then put his hands in his coat pockets and walked past her. You're a very sexy woman, Dana.

Bryan could fire you for this.

She hated the shrillness of her voice.

Jimmy walked backward for a few steps. Well, I guess if I have a job Monday morning, I'll know you didn't tell him.

The pneumatic door wheezed open and Jimmy walked inside; the party—voices and laughter and warmth—spilled out. The door closed on the noise, on Jimmy, and she was alone again.

Dana leaned against the brick wall for a few minutes, in shock.

She didn't want to return to the party, but she had to. Bryan would worry if she was out of sight any longer; even now he might be looking for her. But she fumbled her cigarettes as she transferred them from her pocket to her purse, dropping them into the dark corner. She almost didn't pick them up—they'd gotten her into this trouble in the first place. But she knelt all the same. The cigarettes lay on an old crust of snow, next to Jimmy's business card. She crumpled the card and dropped it into her purse; she'd throw that away inside, in the bathroom.

The lobby was almost empty, except for a young couple Dana didn't know, who spoke loudly and fondly at each other. Dana walked past them, down a side hall and into the women's restroom. There was, of course, no line.

She splashed water into her mouth and chewed a handful of breath mints; she reapplied her lipstick. In the mirror, under the fluorescents, she looked too pale. Exactly like a woman who'd just done something she wasn't proud of.

Bryan spotted her the moment she reentered the hall; he broke away from a knot of laughing employees to jog over. He was wearing a Santa hat that flopped against his ear, bouncing with his movements. On Bryan—gangly and tall—it looked even more ridiculous than it was supposed to. His expression was, at once, eager and sheepish.

What is that? she asked.

I know, I know—the tellers got it for me. And a nice pen, too. He kissed the top of her head. You're cold, he said, drawing back.

I was getting some air.

His lips tightened. Uh-uh. You were smoking. I can smell it.

She tried to play it off like a joke: I don't know what you're talking about.

Honey, you were doing so well—

That was it—she wanted to slug him. Bryan, I don't want to hear it.

He looked at her, his face falling a bit. Come on, he said, his voice low. I'm only trying to help.

What would he do if she started a scene, here? The party was his baby, one of his great achievements at Sentinel: *There's too much separation around here. We need to be closer if we're going to get the right kind of work done.*

But why was her anger Bryan's fault, why was anything Bryan's fault? She was the one who'd just been groped by one of his employees.

Before she could reply, Bryan looked over her shoulder and brightened. Dana turned and saw, to her horror, Jimmy and April approaching, coats draped over their arms.

Hey, you two, Bryan said. Don't tell me you're leaving already?

She's got to work tomorrow morning, Jimmy said, smiling mildly into the air, squeezing April's shoulders. April's eyes were glittering with drink; she leaned into Jimmy's chest as though he'd permanently bent her. She wore, Dana saw, dangling reindeer earrings with little red stones for noses.

You know what I found out? Bryan said to Dana, beaming. These two are engaged.

Last week, April said. She held out her hand, and Dana, trying hard not to stare at Jimmy in outright amazement, pretended to examine the ring.

That's beautiful, Dana said.

Hey Jimmy, Bryan said. Let me talk at you for a minute. Not work?

Only for a minute.

Can you believe this guy? Jimmy said, to both women, and winked at Dana again. Then he and Bryan walked away a few steps, where Bryan began talking with his hands.

He's so funny, April said. Dana didn't know which one of the men she meant.

So, Dana said—because she had to say something. Have you set a date?

Jimmy, twenty feet away, swept his eyes across her. He'd done this on purpose. A word from her and she could expose him. She ought to.

April smiled at her question and scrunched up her face. Next June, she said.

Not long now, Dana said, her throat tight. She tried to feel pity—this poor girl was clueless. Jimmy had probably fucked around on her dozens of times. Or maybe April knew, was following some blind hope that she'd be able to change him, rein him in with a ring.

But either way, Dana couldn't bring herself to look for long at April's future, all the pain that was waiting for her out there. No. April was beautiful and lush, and when Dana looked at her she couldn't help but imagine her kissing Jimmy, naked with Jimmy in all her cheerleaderish glory, the two of them lit with amber light, like in a movie. If he had this, what could he possibly want with Dana?

He wanted her, she knew, because she was different: small and dark and slim. And, of course, forbidden.

Jimmy just loves your husband, April was saying. I got to

talk to him tonight. He's so nice. April leaned closer, and put her hand on Dana's wrist. Her breath smelled like wine. She said, We're both so lucky.

Dana stared at her.

Jimmy and Bryan came back over to them then, Bryan laughing heartily, and Jimmy smiling broadly at Dana.

You guys be careful going home, now, Bryan said.

Goodbye, April said, shaking Dana's hand. It was so nice to meet you.

Congratulations, Dana said. Then she shook Jimmy's hand coolly.

See you around, Jimmy said, grinning.

I'm sure you will, she said, hoping that in this light no one could see the color in her cheeks.

AFTER JIMMY AND APRIL left, Dana retreated to a corner, drinking another eggnog and trying not to be noticed. She watched Bryan work the room, traveling from one laughing knot of employees to the next. They all loved him. And they should—Bryan loved all of *them*. Dana tried not to think of Jimmy, of the feel of his stomach under her palm. But she could remember it with tremendous clarity, just by closing her eyes.

Half an hour later Bryan returned to her.

Hi there, he said. I'm sorry. Okay?

He bent to kiss her temple; she turned her head. She couldn't help herself.

I'm sorry, too, she said quickly. I—I'm not feeling well.

What is it? Bryan moved in close to her, putting a hand on her waist. Honey?

My stomach. I drank too much.

Bryan began looking around—trying to spot, she guessed, the bathroom, or a chair where she could sit. His Santa hat jingled.

She touched his elbow. Honey, I'm sorry—but can you run me home? I don't think I ought to drive, and I have to lie down.

His eyes widened. She had to admit a grim little satisfaction in screwing up his careful plans. Or else why would she have asked?

Yeah, Bryan said. Umm—let me talk to Dave and Mary—

Okay. I'll go sit in the car, all right? I'm sorry.

Now she meant it. Bryan looked frantic.

Outside the snow was falling heavily; the sculpted bushes growing against the brick of the reception hall were already prettily frosted. Dana moved carefully across the parking lot, steadying herself on the hoods of other cars, half expecting Jimmy to pop up from the shadows, smirking and beautiful. By the time she was inside the car, she had the shivers. She turned on the heater and sat with her hands in her armpits, watching her breath curl smokily against the passenger window, and through it, the snow piling up on the hood of the next car over.

But this was only Ohio snow—only a tease. Dana had grown up in Colorado, where the snow didn't fuck around. She missed the mountains in winter, the acres of hip-deep snow that would never be tracked up, dirtied with slush.

The snow had been a lot worse than this, the night of the accident. That was for sure. It piled up on top of a coating of ice, riding winds that swirled over the caps of mountains. That was another thing you almost never saw in the Midwest: the kind of snowstorm that frightened you, that spawned disasters.

She'd kissed another man. Jimmy had kissed her, and she'd kissed him back, and then she'd pushed him away.

Bryan opened the door and folded himself behind the wheel. How you doing? he asked.

Better. She waved her hand. Fresh air.

We'll get you home, Bryan said and stroked her knee. His voice was regretful. He was thinking, maybe, that he'd have to hold her hair out of the way while she puked into the toilet. His hand lingered a bit on her knee, his thumb moving in circles. She put her hand over his and pressed down. Maybe she could convince herself the kiss hadn't really happened. Bryan didn't deserve any of this: what she'd done, what was in her head.

It had been a kiss, nothing more. In the end Dana had brushed off Jimmy in the right way.

Maybe when they were home, she could make amends. She would tell Bryan she'd lied about being sick. Maybe she'd pull him down on the bed before he went back to the party. She wouldn't even take off the dress.

Dana leaned her head against the seat while Bryan put the car into gear.

No, the dress would come off. Bryan had a thing about her belly. If it happened—if—he would end up sitting in front of her on the bed. He'd kiss her navel, then stretch his long neck and lick at her nipples, and sigh: *I love you, Dana.* He'd say this three times during lovemaking. In the vicinity of her belly and breasts, and then when he entered her, and again when he was coming. As though, if he didn't, Dana would roll out of bed, aghast. Each time he'd say it, he'd meet Dana's eyes, checking.

I love you, too, she'd say, each time. Or sometimes she'd just kiss him, hard, putting her fingers in his hair.

Bryan would make love to her.

Jimmy would have fucked her. He'd have no trouble using the word.

Dana remembered: she hadn't thrown away Jimmy's card.

Without looking at her hands, she felt her purse, making sure the clasp was closed. She rubbed sweat off her palms and into the wool of her coat. The slick reflections of streetlights shone on the pavement. Bryan drove slowly, hunched over the wheel, hands at ten and two. The heater roared, and he muttered at the idiots who wouldn't slow down, who couldn't see it was for Crissakes *snowing*.

AT THE TIME of the accident, Dana had been dating Bryan for two months. They were both students at the University of Colorado. They'd met in a statistics class. The professor was Japanese and had trouble with names, and so kept a seating chart; Bryan was Macarthur, and Dana was McKinnon. They'd started talking before class, then during the walk out of the room. Soon they were trading notes. She spent a long time looking at Bryan's hands as he wrote—his handwriting was beautiful and looping, like a woman's. He had long, delicate fingers. When she finally held them, during a movie, she found they were delightfully soft. A few nights later she took him to bed.

The ski trip was a surprise; Bryan called her on a Friday morning and asked if she wanted to go away for the weekend. They drove up to Breckenridge with two of Bryan's friends from the business program, tanned fraternity boys with perfect white teeth, who talked openly and excitedly about the snow bunnies they hoped to lay before the weekend was over.

Dana thought she and Bryan were along only because Bryan drove a Cherokee that still smelled new.

But in their fake Swiss chalet, after sex by the fireplace, Bryan told her he loved her, and Dana saw the weekend differently, as Bryan must have planned it: as a romantic getaway. A chance for fireside declarations.

Dana wasn't sure then what exactly she felt for him. She liked him fine—but love? She was charmed by his niceness—everyone who knew him was. But when she thought about him, he added up only to an outline of a man. He wasn't handsome, though he was far from ugly. He was athletic, and liked to hike and run. He liked sitting under a blanket with her and watching television. He read a lot of science fiction. He was capable of talking for hours about banking or economic theory, and how he wanted to reform this or that. Sometimes he wrote letters to the school newspaper, about how, for instance, Democrats could never understand fiscal responsibility. When she talked about her homework, or her student teaching, he listened attentively—but he asked her questions in a way that always made her suspect he had rehearsed them. An entry in his Day Runner: *Things to ask Dana.*

Bryan's family had money, but he was generous. He treated her to the weekend in Breckenridge, and offered in a way that didn't make her feel embarrassed, poor. He was nice, attentive to her, unfailingly polite.

But the truth was, when they weren't in bed, Dana was often bored. That boredom made her feel horribly petty—but she couldn't rid herself of it, no matter how hard she tried. And on the ride up to Breckenridge, listening to his buddies pretend to laugh at his jokes, she understood she could never last with him.

She kept quiet as they settled into their room. But there, despite herself, she began having a good time. Bryan was cheerful and hyperactive, almost clownish. She liked the kitschy chalet with the big fireplace. She liked the enormous bed, and the snowy domes of the mountains just outside their balcony. And she liked what she felt most guilty about—the sex with Bryan, on the bed, on the pile carpet in front of the fireplace.

Dana didn't want to be the sort of woman who would stay with a man because he was good in bed—which Bryan, to her shock and surprise, was, and had been from the very start. His long, knobby body *fit* hers, somehow. In bed his earnestness, his willingness to please her, had definite advantages. And he was so overjoyed to be with her that, for the first time since she'd lost her virginity, she felt she was good at sex. She enjoyed telling Bryan to hold still, to lie back and let her take care of things. She liked the look he got on his face, stunned and worshipful.

And then, too—after sex with Bryan she felt *differently* about everything. She liked the smell of his skin. She'd laze in bed with him, her head in the crook of his shoulder, and feel what she could only call contentment. She understood what she had always made fun of her girlfriends for insisting: that a man could make her feel safe. Lying next to Bryan, naked and drained, she was able to think about her grades, about paying her bills, about her coming job search, and not feel overwhelmed.

Whenever she thought she had to be done with him, that she couldn't listen to him talk about the Fed for another minute, her mind would circle back to one of those tranquil, still moments, and she would wonder: Is *that* what love is?

And so, after he told her he loved her, Dana could only reply, I don't know, Bryan. I've never been in love before. I don't want to say it if I don't mean it.

Okay, he said, looking down. That's okay, Dana.

And there—she *hurt* for him. He turned away from her, naked and suddenly not so glad about it, and she wanted to hold him.

But not to tell him.

She said, Just give me time, okay?

He nodded and put his face against her shoulder.

When they were dressed he said, Let's go to dinner. The two of us alone.

Sure, she said, brightly. That'll be nice.

He drove her up and over Fremont Pass, to a little place in Leadville—he had, it turned out, made reservations for them earlier in the day. He'd never doubted she'd say she loved him, too. They had expensive steaks. Dana drank a lot of beer. Bryan, when he said anything, spoke with an edge of panic.

Halfway through dinner snow started coming down hard, and the proprietor—a small, sideburned man with a belt buckle shaped like a buffalo—came over to their table and said that if they wanted to get back to Breckenridge tonight, they'd better get a move on.

Outside snowflakes pricked at Dana's cheeks. The sun had set during dinner, and the wind cut and hissed out of almost total darkness; the storm clouds blocked even the glow of the moon. She looked at the highway, already whitened, and felt a twist in her stomach.

Farther up the pass the highway was thickly covered, but Bryan's Cherokee did all right, grumbling along in low gear. They saw only one other car, taking the switchbacks about a half a mile ahead and upslope, its taillights blinking on and off through the trees. Bryan's lips were tight. She felt awful for him—but that wasn't the same as loving him, was it? She wondered whether or not she should sleep with him when they got back to the chalet. What that would make her, if she did, or didn't.

At the crest of the pass the winds rocked the Jeep; the back wheels started to shimmy. The snow seemed to jump out of the dark at the windshield. And then, slowing to ease around a sharp hairpin, Bryan said, Shit. Oh shit.

What? she asked. He was going to say they were through; she knew it, tensed for it.

Bryan pulled the Cherokee over to the side of the road. The other car, he said. I've been following its tracks. Look.

In front of the Cherokee's headlights Dana could barely see the tracks the other car had left, approaching the hairpin. They led straight ahead—too straight. She understood: the car hadn't turned. Ahead on the bank was a broken section of guardrail, and above it, just visible, was a black window where the pine branches had been shaken naked of snow.

Then the wind picked up, and the whole road was lost in whiteout. Bryan might not have seen that curve either.

The Cherokee rolled to a stop, where it sat unevenly on a plow drift. Call 911, Bryan told her, handing her his car phone. Then he opened his door. Dana dialed as he stumbled through the snow. She told the operator where they were.

We're sending someone, the operator said. Is anyone hurt?

I don't know. My boyfriend is trying to get to the car.

Bryan looked over the edge of the road, then turned back to her, stricken.

When Dana hung up she climbed out of the Cherokee and tried to follow Bryan's tracks to the edge. The temperature had dropped at least ten degrees, and the snow hit her face like flung sand. Dana could just hear a noise over the wind, though: a scream—a woman's—harsh and scraping.

In high school Dana had worked as a lifeguard. She tried to recall her CPR training—but now she couldn't think of what to do, only of how nervous she'd been on the job. What would she do, if anyone really needed help? If someone down below in the water stopped moving? If someone started *screaming?* Dana had never seen anything truly awful in her life that was not on television. She paused in the snow. This was it: *this* was the emergency. Someone wouldn't scream like that unless she was in agony. This was going to be blood and bone.

Hurry! Bryan shouted, and dropped off the edge of the road.

The slope fell away steeply; Dana remembered from the drive in that the drop was hundreds of feet, down to a twisting riverbed. But in the snow and dark she could barely see anything—except for the headlights of the wrecked car, still shining, maybe fifty feet below. The trees were sparse near the road, and then thickened farther down. The snow on the slope was unbroken. The car must have gone airborne— ramped off the road and then gotten caught in the trees. Now it was turned over on its roof, jammed against three pines grown close together, like a wall.

Bryan blundered down twenty feet ahead, plowing a trail. Dana followed him. Off the road the wind was a little quieter. But the screams were louder: Dana thought she could see dashboard lights through one of the car's side windows. She could smell gasoline, exhaust—they stood out, here in the clean, cold air.

Bryan was sliding down the steepest part now on his hip, and then he was at the wreck. Dana followed, faster, heart thumping in her throat, snow finding its way beneath her clothing, next to her skin. The underside of the car—a sedan—was hissing. Clumps of snow fell onto it from the tree branches overhead and sizzled and smoked. This close, the smell of gas was heavy and moist, like something she could spit whole from her mouth.

The sedan's passenger window faced uphill, and was broken; this was where the screams were coming from. Bryan knelt down and looked inside. The wind caught his hair, tufting it. And then—just when he called out, Hello?—the car caught fire.

The flames bloomed out, black and blue and orange, from the rear of the car, like the petals of a flower opening up. Dana stood transfixed by them—by the shifting colors, the way the insides of her body seemed to move with the flames. For a moment the warmth felt good. But then the fire blazed, hurting her eyes, following lines across the car's underbelly, toward the people inside. And Bryan.

The woman screamed louder. Bryan shielded his eyes, sat back on his haunches and made a deep wordless sound, as though he'd been startled awake. The flames were only a few feet from his head. The tree trunks had lines of fire on them now, like glowing vines. Dana flinched back, moving crablike up the slope. The skin on her face tightened. She could barely think. She saw Bryan in outline next to the car, rocking for-

ward and back with his arm flung up, the fire making a noise
now, that familiar whoosh and mutter over the howling of the
wind, the trees all around gaining outline and shadow and
everything moving.

And Bryan bent forward. Dana wanted to scream, No,
but she couldn't. He dropped to his hands and knees and
crawled through the narrow broken window until only his legs
were visible.

She should have moved forward. She remembered wanting to—not to save the screaming woman but to save Bryan,
to grab his legs and pull him back out. He was going to die,
she knew. She was watching a man die. And understanding
this was awful—she had never been more frightened of anything in her life. The woods and the flames loomed. She could
not feel her body anymore—she was somewhere between
herself and Bryan, somewhere up in the air.

Bryan's knees twisted and dug into the snow. The fire was
inside the sedan—she could see its glow on the dashboard
past Bryan's shadow. The screams intensified; Bryan grunted,
then shouted, Pull it! Pull! You have to! The trees were catching, the branches crackling—underneath the snow, the wood
was still kindling dry from the past summer's drought. Sparks
fell down over the car in little firework showers.

And then Bryan wriggled out. He was smoking; his arms
were smoking. He ducked as the fire licked over his head, into
the front wheel well. Then he knelt again and reached into the
car and pulled out the woman. Slowly, slowly.

The woman was burning. She wore a ski jacket, and it was
on fire. Her arms beat at the window frame, at Bryan. Bryan
heaved and she came free, legs trailing uselessly. She was

shrieking like an animal. Bryan kept dragging her. His face twisted away from the burning woman, his cheekbones glowing a ghastly yellow.

Bryan's own jacket caught flame. He gave the woman one last heave, then wrapped her in his arms and rolled both of them into the deep snow.

Dana! he called, his voice torn, a screech.

And *that* moved her. Her limbs came unlocked. Bryan was alive.

Dana floundered across the slope to him, threw handfuls of snow on his back and arms. He was trying to take off his jacket, which was smoking, flaming. Dana grabbed hold of one of the sleeves and pulled. A new smell was coming out of the car—like meat cooking. Someone was still inside, was burning, was dying. The smell was coming off of Bryan, too, off of the woman. Parts of Bryan's jacket had melted and clung in strands to his arm and shoulder. His hair was smoking. Dana felt a horrible searing pain on her own forearm, where his jacket was twisted around her arm. She jammed it deep into the snow until she felt the cold seep into the pain.

The woman wasn't screaming anymore. Dana looked at her, even though she would have given anything not to. The woman had blond hair, now streaked with blood, burned away down to the skull on one side. Her face was a mess: rust-red where it wasn't blackened. She was awake, Dana saw, her mouth opening and closing, panting almost. The woman's eyes—the whites were shockingly bright against her swollen cheeks—kept rolling from side to side.

Come on, Bryan said.

He couldn't use his right arm. Dana's own arm hurt, but she put her hands under one of the woman's arms, and Bryan put his good hand under the other, and they pulled her up the slope, away from the burning car, the blazing stinking white fire of the burning tires, the smell of the man burning inside—her husband. They found this out later. Her husband. They were locals. He'd been drinking and going way too fast.

He'd died before the fire, Bryan told her that night, in the hospital. He spoke during a brief period of wakefulness, before they medicated him into oblivion. He lay very still, his arm bandaged up to the shoulder.

Bryan whispered, His neck was broken. I checked.

As though she was worried he might not have rescued enough people, as though she was angry at him for having failed. Dana was glad the man had been dead. If he'd been alive, Bryan would have gone back in for him, and both of them would be dead now. She knew that.

Is she all right? Bryan asked. His lips were swollen, cracked.

She's in intensive care. They don't know if she'll live.

But the woman had lived. Her back was broken, and she was horribly scarred, but she was still alive, living now with a sister in Colorado Springs. She and Bryan exchanged Christmas cards.

Bryan had nodded, then closed his eyes.

Looking back, Dana wasn't sure when it happened—when the moment that changed everything truly fell. Before the crash she had been ready to leave Bryan. But sitting next to his hospital bed, she felt she'd rather die than lose sight of him again. She felt . . . peaceful: the same sort of peace that had always settled around her after making love to him, as she curled against his long, thin body. But she couldn't say what had happened to make it so. Bryan had done a wonderful, courageous thing—had done it without thinking. And when he had gone into the car, Dana had lost herself—a part of her had come unmoored, and waited for Bryan to come out alive before drifting back to her.

Dana leaned forward. Her insides seemed to pull her down to him. She whispered to Bryan, I love you.

And saying it to him felt good, true.

Bryan smiled up at her, even though she knew it must hurt his mouth. His good hand brushed hers. Then the painkillers caught him, and he drifted away.

NOW, IN THE CAR, Dana dozed, too. She dreamed, as she often did, about the accident. Sometimes she had night-mares—she was the woman trapped in the car, screaming to Bryan, who paced outside in the snow, deciding. But some-times they didn't frighten her at all. Tonight she dreamed that she never got out of the Cherokee, that she watched the whole thing on a television, inside, knowing how it was going to turn out.

Honey, Bryan said, shaking her. We're home.

She was all the way into the house before remembering she'd kissed Jimmy.

Bryan walked with her into their bedroom, his hand on her waist, as though she might fall over. He pulled back the bedcovers and she lay down on the cool sheets, stretching her-self. She started to bend her knees, to reach down for a heel, but he stilled her with a hand. She closed her eyes: Bryan was going to undress her. Her blood surged. If he made love to her now she would forget Jimmy. She'd feel the familiar rub of her husband's stomach, his hip bones—how could she have forgotten that?

Bryan slipped off one of her heels, then the other. He

reached up under her dress to grab the waistband of her hose. She let him lift her hips. His fingers curled under the fabric, next to her skin. The fingers on his left hand were soft, the ones on his right a little rough and bumpy, from the scars. She liked the feel of her hose sliding down her thighs, and off.

Are you awake? he whispered, leaning over her.

Mm-hmm.

Turn on your side. I'll unzip you.

No, she said. She opened her eyes and curled her bare heel around the back of his thigh. His loosened tie fell into a jumble on her collarbone. She used it to pull him in closer, between her legs.

Bryan said, Huh—but he let himself be pulled. I thought you were sick, he said.

She kissed him, tightening her calves around his rear end.

Sick of the party, she murmured. That's all. She lifted her hips and dropped them and lifted them again.

Honey, he said.

They hadn't made love for a long time after the accident. The first time was in the summer. Bryan had taken a semester off, staying at his parents' house in Columbus. His family flew Dana out from school to see him on weekends. Once the bandages were off, Bryan had been nervous about letting her see his scars. But one night, while his parents were out, Dana undressed him, insisting.

It's awful, he told her, not meeting her eyes. *I won't blame you if—*

Nothing about you could ever be awful, she said.

His arm and his chest looked bad—worse than she'd imagined, the tissue there the color of baked ham—but she didn't let it show on her face. Instead she leaned down to kiss him on his ribs, found the scars dry and hard under her lips. The sensation wasn't bad—she was reminded of touching a friend's pet boa, finding the scales dry and smooth. *Can you feel that?* she asked. *No,* he whispered. *It's all right,* she told him. She had seen terrible things, and Bryan's arm was not one of them. His hips were fine and his thighs were fine. His lips were still soft and gentle, the touch of his good hand light. His hair had grown back out. His penis was fine, silky and untouched. Rocking, she watched his eyes, which were lovely and brown and kind.

He cried when they were done, holding her against the soft left side of his body. *I love you,* he said, hoarse. *I love you, too,* she said. *I will always love you.* That he loved her, that he had looked at the fire and chosen to suffer it, both seemed to come from the same place in him. He had seen, each time, what she hadn't been brave enough to see. She sighed next to him, traced his nipple with her fingers, touched his scars. She would not let herself be repulsed by him.

But ever since, he preferred to keep his shirt on all the same.

Now Dana loosened his tie, pushed it over his head.

Honey, he said, as she started to unbutton his shirt. Honey. Yes?

What are you doing?

I think you know.

You lied to me, he said, smiling.

A little. Come on.

I have to get back, he said. You know that.

Not yet.

Later, he said. I'll be back in two hours.

Bryan . . .

He rolled on his side, away from her. Just two hours. Sleep until I get back. He saw her face. Look, he said, people need to get *home*. I promised I'd drive some of them. You don't want them out on the roads, do you?

He could be condescending when she'd been drinking.

I won't be awake in two hours.

He sighed. I appreciate the gesture, I do, but . . . I can't just abandon my post. I'm a boss, I'm working tonight.

Jesus, Bryan. Dana sat up and let out breath.

He kissed her hair. It's my *job*.

She knew what she was doing to him. He couldn't stand her being upset. He'd be frantic until he could get back to her.

Go, she said.

No. Look, I can stay. Let me call—

Bryan, go, she said. The moment's passed, all right?

Two hours, he said. Not even that.

She thought he looked relieved.

When he was gone, she undressed and slid under the covers. She looked at her own arm on the bedspread: pale, spotted here and there with moles. Her one scar twisted up and around her wrist. They'd had to pull some of Bryan's melted jacket off her skin, like a piece of taffy stuck to its wrapper.

She was a terrible person. Why was she dissatisfied with anything? She wasn't as scarred as Bryan; Bryan wasn't as scarred as the woman he'd pulled from the car, who was hideous. And the woman was alive—her husband was not.

Poor, drunk April had been half right: Dana was lucky.

But she thought of Jimmy anyway, the card he'd slipped her. She remembered the way he had kissed her, the feel of his

hand on her rear. She thought—she couldn't help herself—
of his smooth, muscular stomach. Of bare, unscarred skin
under her hands. He'd be quick, inconsiderate. He would not
tell her he loved her. But he'd be good. Dana pictured April
with her back arched, Jimmy's blond head turning between
her thighs.

At three thirty Bryan came home. Dana pretended to be
asleep, listening to him undressing with great care in the dark,
sliding gently into bed next to her. His arm crept across her
waist. She felt a gentle kiss on her shoulder. He was still sorry.

Wake me up, she thought. *Touch me.*

But he didn't. He curled next to her, and soon he was
snoring, his arm limp and heavy across her hip.

In the hospital in Denver, Dana had insisted on sitting
next to Bryan, after the doctors cleaned and bandaged him.
She was told at first she wasn't allowed, but one of the para-
medics who brought them in had told the story: that this man
was a hero. Dana heard the nurses whispering to each other
about it. Dana, bandaged herself, wouldn't let go of Bryan's
good hand. His right arm was bandaged thickly to the shoulder.
His hair was burned on one side; his right cheek was blotchy
and blistered. He stank. A nurse put her hand on Dana's shoulder, and said, He'll be under soon. We're giving him painkillers.

Can I stay until he sleeps? Dana had asked.

Bryan watched her with glazed eyes, murmuring sense-
lessly—they'd given him plenty of drugs already.

After a long sigh the nurse said, All right. She bustled
around the dark room. Bryan closed his eyes, let out a long,
whistling breath.

Then Dana saw the nurse was looking at her, smiling hopefully.

Is it true? the nurse asked. What he did?

It's true, Dana said. She wasn't surprised when the nurse embraced her.

When the nurse had gone, Dana leaned over and kissed Bryan, pressing carefully, softly, against his swollen lips. Bryan murmured again. His breathing was so gentle she had to keep very still in order to feel it. She uncovered his good arm from beneath the sheet and traced it with her fingers. She whispered to him that she loved him. She told him about the wedding they would have, the names of the children they would have. She let herself go, into every dream she'd ever dared have.

When that car burst into flames, she and Bryan each had time for one decision, one thought. Bryan, in a second, had dived forward; he had saved the woman's life. That was the sort of person he was. Dana had thought about this at the hospital, her hand on Bryan's wrist, her mouth close to his ear—and had decided what *she* was, too. She hadn't cared if the woman in the car had lived or died. Her thoughts, the entire rest of her life, had reached out and attached to Bryan, followed him twice into the burning car, until her future depended on whether he came out again. And he had.

But what had Dana done *tonight*, with Jimmy? What had she chosen? She had kissed Jimmy, had pushed him away, had kept his card—and these actions seemed not to have come from any conscious thought at all.

She thought of Jimmy's number, crumpled in her purse. The flat muscles of his stomach under her palm. The way he'd looked at her.

More and more these days she was remembering: when the fire started, she'd had one *other* thought.

Her heart had gone to Bryan, yes . . . but just before that, for a long moment, she had thought of nothing, seen nothing, but the flames. They'd bloomed across the underside of the car: deep black, then a lovely shifting blue, then curling orange.

And she was the sort of woman who could be filled up by them, whose body could sway to them. Because they were so strange, so beautiful. Because, in that terrible wind and cold, she had been so grateful for their heat.

Abandon

I.

AN HOUR AFTER THEY BREAK INTO THE CABIN, BRAD SITS
with Mel on the edge of the porch, his arm across her shoulders, watching wind blow across the lake—is it Humming-
bird Lake? Gopher Lake? They saw the name on a sign coming
in, but now neither of them can remember, even Mel, who's
been here before. Whatever it's called, the lake isn't that big:
maybe a quarter-mile across, a little more than that in length,
its shores choked with cattails. Just a puddle compared to
Lake Superior, ten miles to the north. Kind of ugly, Brad
thinks. But private. Theirs.

Lake Inferior, Mel says, shading her eyes. Poor little baby
lake.

We'll keep it company, Brad says.

The cabin behind them is inferior, too. It's not so much a cabin, in fact, as it is a fishing shack, two rooms wide, without electricity or running water or even a fireplace—the last time she was here, Mel told him, there'd been a generator parked in the little shed out back, but it was gone now. The only furniture is a card table and two metal chairs, and a small cot folded around a thin, moldy mattress. It's not even close to the love nest Brad's spent the entire drive trying to imagine.

But a quiet hour on the porch with Mel, watching the sun glint off the lake water, smelling the piney breeze, has chased away most of his disappointment, brought back a little of the looping excitement that gave him the idea for this trip in the first place. He's still with Mel, after all, and they're alone.

Man, he says, it'd be cool to live in a place like this.

It's peaceful, Mel says, then scoots closer. But we'd definitely need better furniture. And heat.

Though the sky is sunny and clear, and the breeze warm, every once in a while they've felt an unexpected chill—a reminder that, despite the summery temperatures lately, this is October. Yesterday in Chicago he and Mel were walking around in shorts and sandals, and even though they knew the Upper Peninsula would be cooler, they only packed light jackets for the weekend. Mel told him on the drive up that she's not even sure she remembered to bring socks—she's got only her ratty old black Chuck Taylors, the ones with the holes in the sides that show her bare feet.

He moves his hand to her lower back, spreading out his fingers to see how much of her he can cover. Which is a lot. He lowers his mouth to her ear and says, I guess we'll just have to use body heat.

She doesn't answer him—she's been strangely quiet, in fact, ever since they got here.

He gives up. Want to tell me what's wrong?

Mel sighs. I'm okay, she says. It's just hard to relax, you know? I keep thinking we're going to get *caught*.

We're cool, he says. No one's been down this road in a month.

Which is an exaggeration, but not much of one. They drove the entire eight miles of gravel road from the highway to the cabin without seeing a single car. Brad did catch glimpses of a couple of other cabins on the way in, but all of them looked a lot like this one: tiny shacks or trailers, locked up for winter. Even so, Mel urged him to park the truck near the lakeshore, where the cabin will hide it from view of the road.

Let's go be alone, he'd told her, back in Chicago, and now here they are: about as alone as two people can get. There's nothing around them except miles and miles of forest. Brad saw it from rises along the gravel road: an endless sweep of shadowy green hills, broken by patches of brown and yellow and gold. A sea of dirty water blown into gentle swells, beautiful and a little disturbing, all at once.

Maybe I'm just nervous, Mel says. And that sucks—you know? I mean, this is just what I wanted. I have to be able to trust my fucking happiness.

And this is another reason Brad loves her—sometimes it's like Mel is listening in on his thoughts.

Trust it, he says. We're going to be fine.

I will, she says, and lights a cigarette, then squeezes his knee. I do.

And by the time Mel's done with her cigarette Brad knows she's better, because she's started to talk—she's telling him, hands fluttering, about something she heard in one of her psychology classes, about people who live in solitude. Eskimo tribes, cosmonauts, Japanese soldiers on Pacific islands. He drifts away from her words, but keeps listening to her voice, which is beautiful, low and husky and sly. That she'd tell him any of this makes him feel smart. And proud, that she's talking with *him,* that she's agreed to show him this place, and that here they'll both be happier than they've ever been.

ONCE THE SUN SETS—they watch it from the porch, glowing orange and red through the pine branches woven together above the cabin—the temperature drops quickly. Brad and Mel move inside the cabin, lighting their way with a flashlight Brad found in the glove box of the truck. It's not much warmer inside. Brad bends down and holds his palm flat above the floorboards; cold rises through the wide cracks like smoke. He doesn't even want to stand still in here; how are they supposed to sleep?

Mel looks warily down at the cot and mattress, her jacket pulled tight around her.

We can still go get a motel, she says.

Which Brad doesn't want to admit he's been thinking, too.

No, he says. We came all this way, we're going to figure something out.

They go hunting, opening the cabin's few doors. There's an old bucket in the back room that Mel tells him has always been the toilet. In the only closet they find a couple of ratty sweaters, smelling of mothballs, and so enormous—Andy's dad, Mel says, making a face; He's such a fucking fatass—that even Brad can wear one like a nightgown. There's a quilt folded up in there, too, stinking of mold. In one corner of the

main room is a basin with cabinet space underneath, full of
tackle boxes without tackle and half-empty boxes of dish
soap. A long roll of tinfoil. A shoe box with two candles in it,
and matches. Large, unconcerned spiders.

In the small shed out back Brad finds a propane camping
grill, barely knee-high, and a squat little tank of fuel, the size
of a football, which feels full when he lifts it. He brings them
both inside.

See? he tells Mel, as she shines the flashlight at him. I'm a
genius.

In the center of the cabin's front room they make a tent.
They unfold the thin mattress onto the floor, between the legs
of the card table. At the head and foot of the mattress they
arrange the two chairs. Brad drapes the moldy quilt across all
of it; it's just large enough to reach the floor. They place the
grill on a sheet of the tinfoil underneath one of the chairs.
Then they crawl under the table. Brad starts the grill burning
with his lighter, and immediately heat spills out into their tiny
space.

They brought a blanket of their own, which Mel digs out
of her packs and spreads over their legs. Okay, she says, curling next to him. This is pretty cool.

And you wanted us to go to a *motel*, he says.

No! Mel slides her arms around his neck. No, this is better.

They hold pieces of lunch meat over the fire and eat them
between slices of bread. Brad opens a can of pop.

To home, he says, lifting it.

To home, she says, and leans against him.

They sleep in spurts. They agree not to leave the stove running. Just watch, Mel says, that thing'll spring a leak, and they'll
find a couple of skeletons when spring comes. But Mel sleeps

too deeply, so Brad ends up captaining the grill all night. He doesn't mind. He likes the whoosh of the fire starting, and the way Mel looks, sleeping in its glow. Even so, he always pauses before he spins the propane knob back down to zero—because the darkness that rushes in then is absolute. Their bodies blink out of sight, like neither of them ever existed.

But he loves what happens just afterward—how they feel their way toward each other; how Mel, even when she's asleep, burrows closer.

Even after two months with her he's still surprised by the joy he feels—the gratitude—in knowing that Mel needs him, and needs him close.

II.

When Brad first met her, he knew right away Mel was different.

He'd gone up to her at a club on the near north side. Mel was dancing like a madwoman—alone, it looked like, but having the time of her life. Brad wasn't; he'd struck out with two other girls. His eyes had passed over Mel before, but now he drank a beer and watched her, the way she kept going, never losing her energy. Not giving a shit. What the hell? he thought. He maneuvered next to her, and when she saw him dancing she grinned in a way that seemed to use all of her body—like they were old friends, and she'd been waiting for him to show up—and turned her body toward him, dancing like her joints were made of rubber, shaking her head so that he could only see glimpses of her eyes through her straight black hair.

She wasn't drop-dead beautiful, not like a lot of the girls in the place, but once Brad was up close he couldn't stop looking at her. She had a narrow face, but wide eyes, a wide mouth, and no makeup he could see. Everything she wore was black: a shirt with long sleeves, black velvet pants, high-top sneakers—but even though all of her skin was hidden, Brad could tell there wasn't much of her, underneath the clothes.

She laughed at him, almost the entire time they danced. Brad couldn't tell if she was happy he was around, or was just making fun of his dancing, but either way she didn't seem to want him to fuck off, so he kept close, laughed right back at her.

Later she grabbed his arm and led him to the bar. She stood on tiptoe and shouted over the music, Will you get me a beer? I'm underage!

He'd have guessed she would sound tiny, squeaky even, but her voice was deep and husky, like she'd smoked for twenty years. He imagined what she'd sound like, talking to him someplace quiet. Or moaning.

Tell me your name, he said, and I will.

She made a face. It's Mel.

Like Melanie? Melissa?

Worse, she said. Melody. But if you ever want to speak to me again, promise never to call me that. It's *Mel*.

He held his hand out. Mel, he said, I'm Brad.

She took his hand, made a pleading face. Brad, will you please please please buy me a beer?

He did, and then he bought her a couple more after that. And two hours later, well after midnight, when Brad's roommate, Lou, came by and glowered and jerked his chin at the door, and Brad told Mel, Hey, my ride's taking off, she grabbed his hand and said, No, stay, and so Brad shrugged, and Lou vanished without asking twice.

An hour later the club was closing down, and Mel said, You hungry? I'll buy you dinner. Least I can do.

She was shining with sweat. Her dancing had left her hair looking like a bird's nest. Brad himself stunk of sweat and smoke. His ears rung. And he couldn't stop smiling. He remembered that: right away, Mel had made him feel good.

Let's go, he said. I'm nowhere *near* tired.

Great, she said, I know a place. And she grabbed his hand and pulled him out the door, almost at a run.

MEL LED HIM to an all-night diner. There they sat in a back booth and ate hash browns and drank mug after mug of coffee. Mel kept asking him questions; right when Brad was sure he couldn't say another word, she'd ask, And *then* what?—and all the time her eyes would be bright, alert, widening and narrowing as though what he had to say was really and truly interesting, as though his life was some kind of adventure.

So he told her about growing up in Indiana, about his father being a prick, about his folks splitting up, about how he'd been alone with his mother for a long time, from when he was ten until he was seventeen, and how they always got along all right, even if he was a troublemaker—

You? Mel said, laughing.

(And sometimes—every day, actually—since then, he's wondered why she said that; he is, and always has been, a troublemaker, a fuckup. For as long as he can remember he's been doing the wrong thing, sometimes by accident, but a lot of the time just because he can't bring himself to give a shit. He has tattoos on his arms, he has long hair and a scraggly goatee and squinty eyes; if he showed up on a movie screen, everyone would think, *bad guy*, and wait for the hero to take him out.

But not Mel, not this one laughing girl asking *You?*)

Me, he said, heat in his cheeks.

And he told her: about his mother meeting his stepfather, Jim, at some church singles group, and how, once Jim moved in, he and Brad hated each other immediately; Jim was one of those guys who staked a claim, and this time the claim was Brad's mother. How Brad had spent the previous six years warning his mother about the men who'd come around, only to realize she'd gone and married the worst one. And then how, boom, one Sunday morning it all fell apart; Jim found some weed in one of Brad's jackets, and laid into him, and Brad couldn't help it; they'd all been living in the little house together for six months, and Brad's mother was walking around saying *Jesus loves you*, like some fucking zombie, and here was this shirtless hairy asshole standing next to the coffeemaker, jabbing a finger at Brad and telling him his mother didn't need all this bullcrud—

Mel laughed. He said that?

Brad did his stepfather's voice: *Boy, your mother's ten kinds of saint, and here you are tracking bullcrud all over her clean floors!*

You hit him, Mel said, and shook out a cigarette for him. Please?

Brad nodded and lit up. Yeah, he said. I couldn't let him use that kind of language.

Well, actually—he told her this—he kind of lost his shit, taking everything out on old Jim, screaming and threatening to kill him, and that ended with Jim grabbing the phone away from Brad's hysterical mother and, pulling a bloody bath towel away from his mouth, shouting: *I don't need a goldurned ambulanth! Thend the polith!*

And so Brad was arrested, and Jim pressed charges—*For your own good,* his mother told him, before adding, *I couldn't talk him out of it*—and Brad ended up with a three-month suspended sentence and a lot of time with a counselor. His mother told him it'd be better if he moved out, so he got a place with a buddy in Hammond. His mother begged him to apply to college, but—

No offense, he told Mel, but I really didn't see myself as a fucking scholar, you know?

She'd told him, earlier, that she was a junior at DePaul, was studying to be a teacher.

None taken, Mel said. People are different. When I was a kid I thought college was the coolest thing on earth, but I meet all kinds of great people who never go, and all kinds of shitheads who do.

She smiled at him, and he believed her.

So then what?

So *then* his mother was lonely without him, and started calling him every night to cry about his future, to beg him to come to church. And in the meantime Brad and his buddy got work as overnight floor cleaners; during the day they mixed music and drove around looking for old records at garage sales. And then one day his buddy came home and announced that he was tired of sitting on his ass, and that he had a little money saved up, and that if Brad had that much, too, then he knew a guy who'd sell him a brick of weed, and that the two of them could do pretty well for themselves. And Brad, who was so tired of cleaning fucking floors he could barely force himself out of bed—a night running the cleaner left his hands so shaky that he could barely work the sliders on his four-track—thought that was a pretty good idea.

For a while they did all right. Neither he nor his buddy got rich, that was for sure, but they covered their rent and their own smokes, and Brad managed to pick up a better board. But then—

You get caught? Mel asked.

Sort of. Mom had been sending me checks—she felt guilty about kicking me out, right? Turns out Jim didn't know about them. And *then* it turns out that one of the guys we were selling to was the son of someone Mom was in church with, and he got caught by *his* folks . . .

Ouch, Mel said.

Yeah.

And so the next night his mother showed up at his apartment, alone. He knew she'd found out, right when he opened the door: she was pale and thin-lipped and kept her hands folded in front of her.

He couldn't quite tell Mel what his mother said to him. He could feel Mel's eyes, wide and dark, wanting to believe anything he told her—and, more than that, to *feel* what he told her, whatever that might be—and holding out on her seemed wrong. Sneaky. But he wasn't even sure how to put it in words.

It was a bad scene, he said.

Did she call the cops? Mel asked.

She threatened to.

Which was a lie, more or less, though his mother had told him she'd considered it. What she said was, *Bradley, I've tried and tried to make you a son I could be proud of. But now I see you're like your father, and I'm done with men like him.*

Brad shouted at her, but he could see the way her face shut down, and that's how he knew she was telling him the truth: this was the same look she'd gotten when Brad used to beg her to leave his father, the man who'd beat her for ten years, who'd put her in the hospital twice with broken arms.

His mother, still blank, said, *Goodbye.* He waited for her to start to cry, to crack. He told himself to apologize, to cry and beg her. But his mother turned around and left.

He told *this* part to Mel: He decided that night to leave town for good. That next morning he split for Chicago, where he crashed with a guy he knew from high school. He got work at a club, sort of as a house roadie, and then one night at a party a girl he knew introduced him to a friend who sold pot, and sometimes meth, and he and Brad started trading stories about weird deals they'd seen, and at the end of the night the guy took Brad aside and said he might know a way to get Brad some work, and Brad said sure, and started selling weed the next week—

For real? Mel asked. She leaned forward, looking theatrically sly. You got any on you?

He looked at his hands and said, Oh, Mel, I wish I did.

And, cheeks burning, he told Mel that he was, at the moment, on probation. And that was because Brad had—because he'd gone *up,* for possession, and his PO was required to drug-test Brad once a month, and since pot stayed in the fucking system for so long—

You did *time*?

Yeah. Six months. I've been out three.

He waited for that empty look to come into her face; she was a nice girl, this Mel, but they'd reached the part of the evening when she'd figured out she was in the wrong place, when she'd decide she had to run back to her dorm or wherever— that Brad didn't just look like a bad guy but maybe *was* a bad guy.

But she said, They sent you up for *pot*?

Yeah. God, it was the worst. I sold to an undercover cop. Brad tapped his fingers on the table. It was all for shit. They only arrested me to get the guys up above me. The cops offered me a deal—you know, names for probation? But the guys I worked for would have fucked me up if I said anything. So jail it was.

Jesus. Was it bad?

He didn't know what to tell her about that either.

He thought of his cell mate, Delroy, stupid or brain damaged or both, who was in for trying to feel up his ten-year-old cousin. Delroy who sobbed, sometimes, when he was in one of those moods where he thought God was going to kill him; Delroy who would jerk off in the bottom bunk every night, with noisy grunts, sometimes right before sobbing. Delroy who, early on, had beat the living shit out of him, after Brad had yelled at him to keep it down. *You ain't my boss,* Delroy had said, at the end of it, grabbing Brad by the hair and giving his skull a knock against the cell wall. *You want me to fuck you?*

And Delroy was better than the rest of them. Brad could at least predict him.

He told Mel, Yeah, it was pretty bad.

Mel watched him, calm and even, and he could see: she was telling him she wasn't going anywhere.

God, she said. That sucks. I *like* pot. I *hate* that it's illegal. I get these anxious spells? She shook her head again. I could use some now.

Me, too, he said. The moment I'm off probation I'm going to smoke the biggest bowl known to man.

She smiled. I won't get you into trouble. I promise.

Mel held up her coffee mug, and Brad held up his, and they clinked them together. Coffee sloshed out of Brad's, all over the basket that held the salt shaker and the sugar packets. Story of my life, he said.

He looked at the clock and saw he'd been talking for two hours. Hey, he told her, now it's your turn. Tell me about *you*.

Soon, she said. Right now I want to go home.

She touched the back of his hand with a fingernail.

I want you to come with me. You okay with that?

He turned over his hand; she ran the same fingernail across the ball of his thumb, then pressed her palm flat against his.

Her irises were the color of strong, dark coffee.

He said, I'm okay with that.

III.

Late in the afternoon of their second day at the cabin, Brad relents—Mel's been bugging him all day to get his ass in gear—and the two of them head out to the nearest gas station for supplies, which they're starting to need.

But they haven't even made it halfway, the truck rattling and skating around the turns in the gravel road, when the engine begins to sputter.

What's wrong? Mel asks. She takes her feet in their torn sneakers down from the dash.

Don't know, Brad says. The CHECK ENGINE light comes on, glowing orange, and the truck stalls. Brad curses and steers toward the side of the road, only a few yards away from the drive to another small cabin: two ruts that vanish down into a hole in the trees.

On the drive up from Chicago they found that the truck's gas gauge can only be read as approximate. Now that they're stopped, the needle, which has been bouncing up and down around a quarter-tank, settles all the way down below E.

And Brad knows he's fucked up—he remembers it like a bill he forgot to pay.

Fuck me, he says. Out of gas.

Mel peers at the gauge. But we *got* gas.

When? he asks, scrambling.

Yesterday! At the gas station back on the highway.

They *didn't* fill up—but Brad can't say so to Mel, not yet. He climbs out of the truck and, on his hands and knees in the gravel, peers underneath at the tank, hoping he's wrong, hoping for a leak. He pops the hood and pretends to look at the engine.

They'd stopped at the same station they're headed to now, at the intersection of the gravel road and the highway. And while Mel was inside getting groceries—when Brad was supposed to be filling up the tank—he'd noticed that, through a break in the pines at the back of the station's lot, he could see Lake Superior. That endless blue glittering water, framed by the green pines, in the sunshine—he couldn't do anything but stare, smoking a cigarette, waiting for Mel to find him. And she had. She'd put her arm around him and said, *That's so beautiful*. She'd said, *I'm glad we did this,* and kissed him, and he'd kissed her back, and he'd been so busy thinking about how he was going to get laid when they reached the cabin that he forgot all about the gas.

Mel chews the side of her thumb and looks over the

engine, which is old and rusted and covered in sludge. Is it supposed to look like that? she asks.

Yeah, Mel, he says. It's really fucking old.

I was just asking.

He covers his eyes. I know, he says, and then turns to her. I forgot the fucking gas, all right?

She stares at him. How could you *forget*?

I just did. We were making out. I'm sorry.

Brad looks right and left, down the empty road, at the darkening valleys between the hills. The sky's bright blue, like it ought to be warm out—but it isn't. All day long it's gotten colder, windier. The trees around them are bending and shushing. Brad fumbles a cigarette out of his pocket, warms up his lungs. He sneaks a look at Mel.

She doesn't look mad at him. He's never seen her face look like it does now. She glances wide-eyed into the woods, up at the sky, and then again at him, her hands jammed into her jeans pockets.

What are we going to do? she asks.

Mel's *afraid,* that's what she is. He's being stupid again. Mel's the smart one; she's already thinking about the math: It's five thirty in the afternoon. They're maybe three miles away from the cabin, five miles—at least—from the gas station. The sun will be setting soon. They're both wearing T-shirts. No way they'll be able to walk for gas and back before sunset.

We need to get to the cabin, he says. If we go now we can just get there before dark.

But what about the food? she asks. The propane?

We've got a little lunch meat left. Right? And a six-pack. We've probably still got half a tank of propane. We'll be all right.

She's looking up at the sky. Probably? It's going to be cold tonight.

Mel, he says. We have enough. Come on.

He holds out his arm, and she stares at the sky for another few seconds before sliding underneath.

Okay, she says.

Brad turns to look at the truck, sitting out here in the middle of nowhere. Cars *did* come by—they'd seen their first one a little while ago: a yellow Jeep, heading the other way. What are the odds somebody will see the truck before they get it moving tomorrow? A local would be immediately suspicious. Brad's not sure how Lou got plates onto the truck, but he *is* sure he didn't do it legally. One person calling in those numbers might produce a policeman checking the cabins . . .

Wait, he says.

He walks down to the new cabin, tucked away in its pocket of trees. Its windows are empty and dark, and both cabin and drive are pretty well hidden away from the road.

Help me out, he says.

Mel sits behind the wheel, the truck in neutral, while Brad heaves himself at the inside of the driver's side door, again and again, until at last the old beast is rolling forward. Mel noses the truck, creaking, into the drive. The slope is just gentle enough to keep it moving, down into hiding, until the brake lights glow red in the shadows.

Before they leave Brad walks around to the back of the cabin. He tries the doors, but of course they're locked. He looks around, listens; the only sound is wind, woods.

Brad? Mel asks.

Maybe they've got some gas hidden around here, he says. Or extra clothes.

I don't know if that's a good idea—

Damnit, he says, you got a better one?

She turns away from him, and he's immediately sorry. This isn't *her* fault, this was never her fault; he's being a prick for no reason. This is shit his high-school counselor could have told him. He'll apologize on the walk back. He'll rub her shoulders tonight until she falls asleep.

He pries a rock out of the ground, then breaks a window near the back door, and reaches through to turn the dead bolt.

They find no gasoline, and no propane either, but he'd expected that much: this place is just as much of an empty shell as their own cabin—there *is* an electric space heater inside, and electrical outlets, but the power's off. In a kitchen cabinet Mel discovers six cans of tuna—Some fisherman *this* guy was, she says, and he's glad to hear her make the joke—and an unopened box of crackers.

A wool watch cap hangs on a hook by the front door, and a pair of gardening gloves, crusted with dirt. Brad takes them both. Before they leave the cabin he tugs the cap over the tops of Mel's ears.

She looks up at him, eyes big and dark. He'd give just about anything to take the worry out of them.

He puts his hands on her shoulders and makes himself smile, until Mel's smiling, too.

See? he says. Better already.

IV.

Mel's house was three L stops away from the diner, a big two-story house north of DePaul that looked like it ought to be condemned. Her five housemates lived upstairs, in the bed-rooms. Mel had a corner room in the basement, with her own door in the alley.

Her room was a disaster. Mounds of clothes on the bare concrete floor. A trash basket spilling over with empty cans of Diet Coke and beer. An unmade single bed. A little desk piled high with books and papers and a computer whose screen showed a picture of a raccoon. A low bureau with half its drawers pulled open.

Even in early summer the air had a basement's clammy chill.

Brr, Mel said. Come here.

Mel kissed like she smiled—with all her energy, with her entire body. She pressed her thighs against him, gripped the sides of his head with her long fingers. Sometimes she bit at his lips. After a few minutes she pulled him down onto the bed.

He tugged at her shirt. I want to look at you, he said.

Mel kissed his chin. You'll see things, she said.

He chalked that up to crazy Mel-talk—*what* would he see? Visions, coming from the ankh on her necklace? He stripped off her tight long-sleeved shirt, tingling at the sight of Mel's white belly, the glimmer of a red stone in her navel ring. The big nipples on her tiny breasts. He lifted Mel by the hips and kissed her between her breasts and then laid her back down, waiting all the while for her to catch fire, too, to pull at *his* clothes. But her face was placid—stoned, even—her eyes half-lidded, her lips holding a little smile. Her arms thrown limp above her head, wrists crossed.

He nuzzled her neck, her shoulders. He picked up one of her arms and kissed its length to her wrist—where he saw the long, thick scar, crossing the inside of her forearm. And another, smaller one underneath, like a shadow of the first.

Hey, he said.

Mel smiled in that sleepy way. Told you.

He picked up her other arm; this one had similar marks, except here the scar was shorter, more jagged. Mel traced it with a fingertip. I did this one second, she said. I was nearly unconscious.

Jesus, Mel. He looked at the scar again. When?

Just before I came to Chicago. Two years ago.

Why?

She smirked a little, and he knew that was a question a lot like *Was jail bad?*

I was unhappy, she said. But I guess you could figure that one out.

She held her wrists in front of her face, looking at the scars like they were bracelets she was thinking about buying.

Will you tell me about it? Brad asked. I mean, if you don't want to—

She leaned over and kissed him. Sweetly. Then she climbed off her bed and crossed the room to the bureau.

I'm sorry, she said, holding up a joint. I have to get high for this.

Go ahead.

Mel lit up and sat cross-legged on the foot of the bed, an ashtray beside her. She took a deep hit, closing her eyes. She turned her head away from him to blow out the smoke. Brad pushed away the urge to reach over for the joint. Instead he watched Mel's naked white chest expand and contract, watched the shadows between her ribs deepen. Her eyes took on a soft gleam.

She told him about her old boyfriend Andy, Andrew—and Brad could tell right away, just from the way Mel said his name, that she still loved him, would always love him; she almost didn't have to tell Brad the rest of the story. Andrew might as well have been in the next room, pacing, waiting for Mel's guard to drop so he could burst in.

They'd gone to neighboring high schools in Kalamazoo. Mel met him at a dance when she was a junior, and Andy was a senior; he was a friend of a friend. He was a terrible dancer, but he was—she said—so pretty that he got away with whatever the hell it was he was doing. He'd shown up with this horrible flouncy blonde, and the moment Mel looked at the two of them—the blonde thrusting out her boobs and Andrew looking down at them and grinning—she was suddenly and completely furious—

Why? he asked.

Oh, I was a good little church mouse then, she said.

You?

Yeah. I wore penny loafers. I played the clarinet.

You never would have talked to me, right?

She blew out sweet smoke. Oh, she said, I would have *prayed* for you.

But anyway: Mel went out onto the floor with a group of her girlfriends, and she ended up dancing right next to Andrew, and she got to, you know, putting herself into it—

Like how you dance now? Brad asked.

Mel blushed. Shut up!

—because Mel was trying to show him you could dance without rubbing your crotch on someone. And Andrew noticed, and the blond girl noticed, and Andrew was doing his thing right in front of Mel, and she did *her* thing—and then a slow song came on, and Andrew took her hand and pulled her in close. And she still hated him, but he was pretty, and as they slow-danced he talked with a low voice into her ear, telling her what a great dancer she was, and she found herself laughing at his jokes, or maybe at how much of a dumb ass he was. How smooth he *wasn't*. And then she realized he had a hard-on under his jeans, pressing against her stomach—and to her horror, she got turned on, too, and at the end of the night he asked if he could call her, and she knew she should have said no, but—

You just couldn't help yourself, Brad said.

Yeah, Mel said, and took a hit. He knew I'd say yes. Andrew saw right through me. Get this: on our first date he told me I was beautiful because I looked so sad all the time. What sort of thing is that to say to someone? But he got me. I ate it up.

Were you?

What?

Were you sad all the time?

Yeah, she said. Pretty much all my life. But anyway—

Andrew called her, and that weekend picked her up in a nice car and drove her out for a burger. They talked about tennis, which they were both good at, and later he drove her home. He kissed her in the car, all innocent and sweet. Her head spun; even after he dropped her off, when she was alone, she could barely catch her breath.

But first he asked if they could do it again sometime, which they did, and then again.

And then one night, when Andy's parents were gone, he talked her into a couple of glasses of wine, and after that they made out, and he unbuttoned her pants and touched her, and she told him she didn't want to, and Andrew said, *Okay* . . . but then went ahead and undressed her and held her arms down and said, *Shh,* and fucked her anyway—

Brad said, I want to kill him.

Mel let out a cloud of smoke. Me, too. But I stayed with him.

Why?

She shook her head, and said, Because a day later he called me up, and he was crying, and telling me how sorry he was. He told me he needed me. To make him a good man.

She sighed and looked at Brad. And he told me he loved me. I can't even tell you what that meant . . . you don't know how lonely I was.

Even now, when she was stoned, buzzed and tired and still smiling—just a little—he could hear her voice want to crumble under that word. He took her hand. Mel's eyes flickered to him. She laced her fingers in with his, and he knew he'd done the right thing.

And she told him that being with Andy was a lot like being hypnotized. Andy got to talking, and she just . . . believed him. She'd never kissed a boy before Andy, and now he was crying and holding her and telling her he wanted to make *love* to her—the right way this time—that he never wanted her to feel lonely again, and all the time he was touching her, so that her body wanted to make different decisions than her head . . . What could she say?

They ended up spending three years together. For a while everything was fine—like that one horrible night had never happened, like Andy really *was* good. Like she'd helped him become good. But then that fall he went off to school at

Northern Michigan, which was way up in BFE. And he wasn't there three months before he called her and told her he wasn't coming home that weekend, that he couldn't do this any more—

Let me guess, Brad said. He wanted to fuck around.

Mel nodded and looked at the ceiling. Yeah. Some friends told me they kept seeing him with different girls. I should have just hated his guts. But I was such a sap.

And she told Brad how the next three months ruined her. How she felt like she had before Andy—only everything was magnified now: she sat in church next to her parents, who loved Andy, who had no idea what their daughter had been through, and she understood she'd given up *everything* for him, and before that she'd given up *everything* for Jesus, and what was left? What was *she*? She tried praying, and she tried sleeping with the nice-enough guy from her class who took her to prom ... and each time she felt nothing. But when she thought about Andy, who had screwed her over—who had raped her—she missed him so much she wanted to pull off her skin. So one night—

One night, she said, I took a bunch of pills.

Mel had finished her joint now, and lay back next to Brad on the bed, her cheek tucked into the groove between his arm and his chest.

What happened?

I puked it all up—I didn't take nearly enough. My parents never even knew.

Jesus, Mel.

Yeah, she said. And then—

Then that Christmas, Andy showed up at her house, asking to see her. He was thinner, and looked like an entirely different person: he'd gotten that college-kid look, the Seattle-grunge thing all the boys were into. He'd grown a goatee. At first she didn't want to talk to him, but Andy started telling her just what she wanted to hear: That she was the only woman he'd ever loved. That since they'd broken up he had felt more alone than he could have dreamed—

She said, It was like listening to myself.

She broke down, holding him, kissing him, letting him take her right to bed. And later that night, out in his car, he offered Mel her first joint. She didn't want to, but Andy told her how calm it made him, how happy. His eyes lit up, the same way they did when he talked about their future together. *Do this with me,* he told her. *Let's be together like this.* So she tried it, and they smoked all night, and by morning she'd agreed to go to NMU, to be with him.

She was there for only a year. The Upper Peninsula was beautiful—she loved to walk on the lakeshore in summertime—but the winters were brutal and cold, and most of the time all she and Andy did was sit around with his horrible friends and get high. It turned out Andy was into harder stuff than pot—some of his rich skier friends had gotten him into coke. She took it without hesitating much; Andy wanted her to. And she kind of liked it—coke made her feel too buzzed to be unhappy. When the weather was warm they'd all sometimes drive farther up the coast, out into the woods, to a little cabin Andy's father owned. There they'd spend the weekend getting high and pretending to catch fish. Sometimes she'd even go by herself, to get away from Andy—he couldn't stand being high out in the woods with nothing to do. She'd dread going back to Andy's apartment, because when he was on coke he'd always want to fuck, and sometimes he'd get rough, and it reminded her, each and every time, of the first time, made her think that maybe he liked it that way . . .

But whenever she felt the most awful, he'd always look at her and lower his voice and say, *Hey, pretty girl,* and she'd think: But he loves me—

She said: I'd think, he's the *only* one who loves me.

And then, one night, at the end of her first year, she went to a party with him, and saw him talking with a woman she didn't know. A pretty blonde, the kind who always turned his head. Andy and the woman were standing in a quiet hallway at the back of a house, and while Mel watched the woman ran her hand from Andy's elbow down to his wrist, and he didn't pull away; he smiled and put his hand on the woman's waist, and Mel knew—

It was the worst, Mel said, whispering. Like my eyes had opened. All along I'd been alone. I started alone, and I only got more alone.

She turned her face to Brad. Have you ever felt like that? Like you were *nothing*? Like if you died no one would care?

Yeah, he said. In jail.

Her fingers twined and untwined with his.

The next weekend, she told him, she cut her wrists. She went home to Kalamazoo, because she knew if she tried it in the dorm someone would find her before it was over. She told her parents she was too sick to go to church, and when they were gone she filled up the tub and got in and swallowed a bunch of pills, and when she felt numb enough she cut her wrists with one of her father's razors.

It was really peaceful, she told him. It didn't even hurt much. It was like—it was like being as sleepy as you've ever been, and then closing your eyes and finally getting to go to sleep. Like giving up.

Brad could feel her breath on his shoulder.

She said, Turns out Mom was worried about me. Being sick and all. She came home early. I don't even remember what happened. One minute I'm in the tub, and the next I'm waking up and there's doctors, and my arms feel like they weigh a hundred pounds each, and I don't know whether to be happy or sad—

They put her in a center, because they tested her and found evidence of everything she'd been doing at NMU, and she cleaned up, and talked to counselors, and insisted to all of them she was fine, that she didn't ever want to do drugs again, or want to die. And, now that the coke was out of her system—now that Andy was out of it—she did feel better. Mostly. After a month they sent her back to her parents. She withdrew from school. They wanted her to go somewhere closer to home, but that, she knew, really *would* kill her. She felt free, finally. She wanted to go to USC—but after weeks of arguing her parents talked her into DePaul, where one of her uncles taught, where they'd wanted her to go in the first place.

So, she said, here I am. All better.

Brad said, So . . .

Well, yeah, I'm smoking *pot.* I get these, you know, panics? But nothing heavy.

No, I mean—do you ever feel like that? Like . . .

Like killing myself?

Yeah.

She got up and crossed the room again, and rooted in the same drawer that had produced her joint, and then came back with a brown prescription bottle full of pills. She dropped down onto her stomach next to Brad and set the bottle on his chest.

What's this?

My Celexa, she said. I'm supposed to take it for my anxiety, but I hate it. I've been saving it up. I ever have to do it again, I'll *really* do it.

You think you'll have to?

After a long time, she said, Probably not. I *think* about it all the time, but—hey, don't worry. I don't mean it like that.

So throw that out.

Mel picked up the bottle and held it in front of her eyes. She said, No. I kind of like having it, you know? It's like I'm testing myself. If I ever feel bad I take it out and look at it. And then I ask myself, how bad does it hurt? And so far it hasn't been that bad.

They make me nervous, he said.

She lowered her voice, spoke with a Russian accent, Not to worry. I am strong like bull.

Mel, you're nuts.

She said, I didn't tell you all of this so you could, you know, nurse me to health. Or pity me.

No. He ran his finger along her collarbone. I'm just trying to figure you out. You seem so . . . okay.

She grinned and rolled herself on top of him, then kissed him.

Who says I'm not?

V.

In the middle of their second night at the cabin, Brad wakes to utter darkness, but also to sound: a light tapping, followed by a howl.

He's confused at first. He just heard these same sounds in a dream—he and Mel were in her bed, and upstairs the house was full of wolves, who kept howling, their claws tapping on the ceiling above their heads—

He blinks into the dark, remembers: Mel is with him, and they're in Michigan, at the little cabin. In their makeshift tent. And it's cold. Cold like he's never felt—so cold that his cheeks are like sheets of stone, that his fingers don't want to curl. And the roaring sound is wind—horrendous wind, making the walls of the cabin creak, the windows rattle in their frames.

Brad pulls away from Mel—she mutters and slaps at the mattress where he's been—and crawls out of the tent. He reaches for the flashlight and then, on stiff legs, follows its beam over to the door.

When he opens it the wind bursts through, so cold and quick that Brad feels like he's being cut by knives. And—he can barely believe that's what he's seeing—there's *snow,* too, stinging his cheeks, swirling through the flashlight's beam. He trains the light on the porch—and sees the snow there is already several inches deep, drifting even higher up against the outside walls.

He crosses the room and shakes Mel awake.

What?

It's snowing.

What?

She climbs past him to look for herself. While she's gone

Brad lights the grill, and holds his stiff hands over the flames until they prickle. He's so cold he can barely think.

Mel scrambles back into the tent.

Did you look at the thermometer? she asks—she means the big round one, nailed to one of the porch rails. Her voice is thick, almost deadened.

No.

Fifteen degrees.

Jesus *Christ.*

What do we do?

It's a good question, but he can't think of what to say. The grill spills out heat like bathwater; he takes Mel's trembling hands and holds them close to it. The flashlight is still on, next to Brad on the mattress, and in its light Mel's face shines as white and cold as the snow. Her breath is coming in quick, steaming gasps.

Okay, he says finally. I guess we just have to stick it out till morning. We'll see what we're up against when the sun's out. Mel?

How can you say that? she asks.

She's looking at her lap now, shoulders heaving. Her hands are clutching into fists.

Her voice falls apart around the words, We're dead.

No! he says. Mel, come here.

She slides closer, her mouth twisted, her breath sour. She's never cried like this in front of him; she'll get teary over little things every now and then, but he's never seen her *sob.* It's awful. She might be right—his own body is numb with cold and fear—but he can't bear to watch her like this.

Come on, he says. Hey. Come on. We're not going to die.

She wails, How?

We'll think of something, he says. All I know is, we can't panic. Okay?

He holds her to him, strokes her hair, her cheeks, until— at last—she takes a long breath: shaky, but deep.

Then, in a small voice, she says what he's been thinking: But what happens when we run out of gas?

I don't know. I'm thinking. You think, too.

Brad—I've seen the snows up here. People die all the time—

Listen, he says. It's not going to snow forever. We'll wait it out. We haven't used much gas. Okay? So put on all your extra clothes and stay next to me. In the morning it'll be warm.

You don't *know* that—

No, he says, but that's what I'm going with.

She nods, but he can see the fear is still working at her. He remembers everything he's done to bring them here—urging her to come, forgetting to fill the gas tank—

Mel, he says. I'm sorry. This is my fault.

She shakes her head. No. No it isn't.

It is. And I'm going to figure something out. I promise.

She stares at him for a long time, her lips clamped shut. The wind rises, howling, and he holds his fingers against her cheek. She closes her eyes and nods.

Say it with me, he says. We'll be all right.

She puts her arm around her neck and whispers, We'll be all right.

BEFORE LONG Mel is drowsing, curled across him—and Brad's glad for this; when she's awake he's too worried about her, and his thinking isn't any good. He hovers over the grill and considers what options he can. There aren't many.

He told Mel they had enough gas, but that only was a guess—the grill doesn't have a fuel gauge. He keeps the flame on only long enough to warm the air around them. Every time he lights it Mel murmurs, and he holds her hands or her feet close to the heat. But then, when he spins the dial off, the cold rises through the mattress with awful speed, like water filling up a sinking boat.

His thinking is going nowhere. He's exhausted, but he's too afraid to sleep—would he be able to wake back up, if the room gets too cold? He holds Mel and listens to the wind. Some gusts shake the walls so much he closes his eyes and waits for the cabin to fly apart, for him and Mel to get sucked into the sky.

Some time later—neither of them brought watches; he has no idea how much time has passed, but it feels like a hundred years—he shuts down the grill and realizes he can see light, glowing through the quilt. He can see the outline of his own hand. The sun is coming up.

He disentangles himself from Mel and shuffles across the cabin floor to the doorway. When he looks outside he wishes right away that he hadn't.

The wind is still screaming, the snow still swirling down. So much has fallen that Brad can barely register it all—the drift against the cabin is a foot and a half deep, at least. He can't even see the lake—it's just a gray smudge, a lot smaller than he remembers it, appearing and disappearing in the gusts.

The thermometer on the post reads eight degrees. The numbers down this low have blue icicles painted on them.

When he ducks back inside the tent, Mel is awake, her eyes staring out from under the blanket. He wishes he could make his face seem hopeful, but he can't. And she can hear the storm as well as he can.

We'd better eat, he says.

For breakfast they have tuna on bread, and share a can of pop—they've been keeping the cans next to the grill, but even so what's in them is half slush, half syrup, almost too cold to swallow.

After they eat, they huddle, shivering, in the center of the mattress. And Mel tells him, I'm a little worried about my feet.

He takes them onto his lap. She's been wearing an extra pair of his socks, but they haven't helped; her feet feel like pieces of ice. He rubs them and rubs them, until Mel says they tingle, then he wraps them in one of his extra T-shirts.

She's not looking at him. He knows she's waiting for him to produce some sort of plan.

It'll stop soon, he says. We just have to be patient.

She doesn't answer him.

For a long time, they drowse. Sometimes the snow tails off, and when this happens—when the gray light glows just a little brighter—Brad shuffles to the front door, covers his face with his arm, and looks out at the deep white blanket, at the thermometer, which hovers near ten degrees without changing.

Sometimes he can tell Mel's awake—he can feel her staring—and he wants to ask her what she's thinking. But he never does. What's the use? She's probably going over the same bad plans he's been discarding since last night.

The gas station is eight miles away, more or less. The

gravel road keeps on going, deeper into the woods, and it's possible—just—that someone lives not that far away. Like maybe the owner of that yellow Jeep. But it's just as possible that the only thing down the gravel road is more woods. Or other empty cabins.

How many did they pass, on the drive in? Three? Two? He can't remember. And anyway, they can't count on any place out here being wired for electricity, or a phone. But heat— that's another thing. One of those other cabins *has* to have a fireplace, or a woodburning stove.

But this doesn't change the fact that any other place is at least three miles off. Probably farther. Which means walking. And they only have jackets. Mel's shoes have fucking *holes* in them.

And then—he's been trying not to think about this, but he has to—assuming they *are* able to get to the gas station, or a place with a phone, what will they say? By the time they reached anyone they'd have to be pretty fucked up—which means police, doctors, a hospital. Questions. And how would they answer them? *We were just out for a drive?*

He's got six months hanging over his head for violating probation, but add on breaking and entering, possession of a stolen vehicle—he'd be going back in for a long time, maybe even long enough to get bumped up from Cook County Jail to one of the penitentiaries.

Mel, he says.

What?

Talk to me, he says. It's too quiet.

I'm trying not to think anything, she murmurs.

He can understand that well enough. But her voice has a

quality to it he doesn't like—and he realizes: it's too even. She sounds too calm.

Tell me something, he says.

Like what?

Tell me where we're going to live.

She shifts, so that he can see her eyes. The apartment? she asks.

No. Like your dream house. Tell me about it.

I don't know, she says.

But then she talks. She tells him about North Carolina, a beach house she went to once, when she was in high school. After a while her hands start moving, above the quilt, shaping what she describes. The two of them will have a house like that one. A big house on stilts, out on the shore.

What's it like there? he asks.

Mel's voice is ragged, but she tells him about the sunrises. How it's so warm at night they'll be able to sleep outside on deck chairs, watching sunrises and sunsets. They'll have dogs that run with them through the surf. The water will be blue and the air will smell like salt. Their hair will turn blond from all the sun.

She stops, a shiver in her voice. Her eyes are blinking. Brad sits and lights the grill—they need the heat, but he also wants the sight of her face in the firelight.

He sinks back down next to her. Keep talking he says, and strokes her hair.

THE SUN DIMS. For the first time in hours the snow subsides, but the wind still sweeps and howls, and the needle on the thermometer drops—at sunset it points at six. When Brad shines the flashlight out at the lake he sees only white tree trunks, and wisps of snow, swirling and tattering above the ground like steam.

He lights the grill and lies back down—but no sooner has he huddled with Mel than, with a tiny, sucking pop, the fire goes out.

Oh God, Mel says, softly.

Don't panic, he tells her, almost by reflex, even though the sudden dark seizes his breath, too.

He turns on the flashlight, then fumbles in the odd shadows, trying to relight the fire. But it won't catch. He tilts the grill up and down, sideways, flicking Mel's lighter. He unscrews the propane tank, shakes it. It's too light.

Okay, he says. Okay.

Mel is watching him, long shadows across her face, the blanket clutched around her shoulders.

He hasn't been able to come up with much of a plan, but he tells Mel anyway. Listen, he says. We have to try and start a fire.

Where?

In the grill.

What about smoke?

I don't know. We can breathe through the blanket or something. Would that work?

She whispers, Maybe.

We need wood, he says.

They look around them. The entire cabin is made of wood, but for all its holes and cracks, it's sturdy. Brad starts to pound on the one interior wall, to see if he can pry loose a board. But he's got no tools. With just his hands it's going to take a while. Maybe too long.

Brad! Mel says. The closet—the shelves.

She's right. The three shelves are made of wood planks,

resting free on their braces. He stacks them in his arms. They're too thick to break apart; Brad tries kicking one a few times with his boot heel, but all he does is send a shooting pain up into his kneecap.

Whole, then. He leans the end of one shelf into the grill, into a nest of crumpled pages Mel has torn out of the paperback mystery she brought to read on the drive. The paper lights quickly, crackling. Mel watches the fire, her mouth hanging open. Her hair is like part of the room's shadow, clinging to her face.

Like everything else in the cabin, the wood is full of damp. Brad keeps tearing pages and stuffing them under the board. Finally the board starts to smolder; smoke spills out of the grill and into the tent. They quickly disassemble it. The smoke pours out and up, swirling through the room's drafty air before collecting against the ceiling. Brad's eyes and throat sting, but he pulls his sweater over his mouth and keeps lighting paper. At this rate he's going to use half Mel's book.

Finally the board catches; flames crawl along its sides. And the smoke boils up even faster. The cabin fills with orange light, odd shadows. The heat against Brad's face, his hands, nearly makes him weep with relief. He crouches low, close to the mattress, face-to-face with Mel. Her eyes are streaming, leaving sooty tracks along her cheeks. They cough and cough. Brad's chest tightens.

After another few minutes he starts to feel dizzy.

We've got to put this out, he tells Mel—his vision is so blurred that she's only a smudge in front of him, her cheekbones pulsing orange. We'll suffocate.

Mel shakes her head, puts a hand on his arm. Wait, she says.

She stares at him for a long time. Then she hugs him, puts her mouth next to his ear.

She says, I don't know, maybe—maybe this would be best.

He can barely believe he's heard her right. His eyes burn, his throat narrows. His breath is coming faster and faster.

She says, It would be quicker.

I can't fucking believe you.

Brad staggers to his feet and grabs the board by its un-burned end. He runs with it to the door, then outside into the cold and the dark, into the deep powdery snow on the porch. He jams the fiery end of the board down into the snow, and watches it sputter, watches the surface of the snow shift and hiss in the wind.

He stumbles back inside—his feet in their boots feel like pieces of concrete—waving smoke away from his face. The flashlight is still on, and in its small circle of light Brad sees Mel lying on her side on the mattress, sobbing, her fists curled beneath her chin. Brad crosses the floor to her on his knees, down where the air is still clear. He picks up the flashlight and aims it at the ceiling, seeing a thick layer of smoke, here and there forming whirlpools where holes in the roof or walls let in the wind.

Get under the blanket, he tells her, his teeth chattering.

She moans.

He can't help himself: he kicks the mattress until Mel looks up at him. He coughs and rubs his eyes and tries to keep the flashlight pointed at her.

I said cover yourself. I have to get the smoke out.

Mel throws the wool blanket over her head. Brad opens

the door again, and then flaps the quilt to wave the smoke toward the doorway. It begins to dissipate, a little; he keeps waving until his hands grow too numb. Then he builds the tent
again, over Mel. He climbs inside and points the flashlight
at her.

I'm sorry, she says, and turns her face away.

What the fuck was that about?

If we're going to die, she says, I don't want you mad at me.

Mel, we're not—

He wants to tell her *We're not going to die.* Wants to shake
her and tell her not to give up, that they'll never survive if she
can't even make herself try. But then it sinks in: the fire was his
last idea. They're out of heat. Mel's right; they probably don't
have long.

Brad? I just thought—

I know, he says. He holds out his hand. I'm—I'm just not
ready.

Saying this tightens his raw throat. Mel grips his fingers—
hers are so cold it's all he can do not to jerk his hand away.

I just don't want to give up, he says.

She sits and puts her arms around him.

There's nothing more to do, she says.

Brad thinks—at the same time—that she's right, and
that he hates the way she can sound so reasonable. Like this is
an argument she's won. But all the same he puts his face into
her hair. And though all of their skin is cold, he can feel, after
a while, a little bit of heat between them, a tiny pocket somewhere near their bellies. How long could it last?

Just hold on, she says.

It's my fault, he says.

No. She whispers this, runs her hands over his hair. No. You couldn't know.

He's sobbing now, like he can't ever remember crying—not when his mother told him she was done with him, not after the times he took a beating in jail. He can't stop whatever it is that's coming out of his throat, a sound so big and jagged that it hurts him to let it out. He keeps saying, No, over and over again.

It's not fair, is what he thinks.

Mel's crying, too—but softer, gentler. It's okay, she tells him. At least we're together.

He's just begun to calm down when the flashlight's beam starts flickering, dulling.

Mel has been crooning to him, whispering his name into his ear, and when he says, The light's going out, she actually laughs.

Figures, she says, and the beam gutters and dies.

He wonders if he's seen her for the last time. In the dark he tries to call up a picture of her face, and wonders if he'll be able to work his lighter with his frozen hands, at least long enough to take a look.

He thinks about how once when he was in high school he burned a blister onto his thumb, lighting candles with his mother's lighter after a power outage, and how angry he'd been at himself, when she told him he could use one candle to light another—

Holy shit, he says to Mel.

He clambers to his numb feet and crosses the room, feeling his way to the basin with his hands, his breath coming in quick gasps. Because he remembers, sees them almost like they're giving off light: underneath the basin, in a mold-covered shoe box, are two candles, and a book of matches.

VI.

Brad had known plenty of women before Mel. Ever since he'd wanted them to, he'd had no trouble getting girls to notice him—especially during the years he'd had extra weed falling out of his pockets. They came, they went, and that had always been fine. He tried, as much as he could, to be mellow, to avoid all the same stupid dramas he saw his friends falling into, over and over. He'd never dated anyone longer than a couple of months—he never understood the guys who *knew,* who all of a sudden went crazy for a girl, who one minute were ordinary guys and the next minute were acting like neutered dogs.

But after a few weeks with Mel, Brad couldn't decide who he was more like: some junior-high kid with a crush, drawing hearts on his notebook; or a junkie.

Ordinarily Brad hated using the phone—he'd go weeks without picking one up. Now he sneaked calls to Mel from the storeroom phone at the deli where he worked. It's me, he'd murmur, watching for his boss. Oops, gotta run. Mel would call him late on the nights they didn't spend together. Talk to me while I fall asleep, she'd say. And he would.

Mel was taking summer classes and working, in a university records office. On his free days Brad would catch the train to DePaul and hang out in the union, until Mel's class or her shift was over. He'd sit there in the middle of all those well-dressed students feeling like a fucking imposter, like everyone in the room knew he had no business there—and still that waiting was all right, because it meant more time with Mel. When she walked into the union and saw him—when her face lit up—it was worth it.

Finally Mel told him they couldn't touch until her homework was done; her grades were slipping. So they made a game of it. They'd sit at a coffee shop, at separate tables. Brad would read or listen to his little CD player while she did her homework, and if he caught her looking at him he'd shake a finger. When she was finally done she'd slip into the booth next to him and kiss him. Half the time they'd run to her place. The other half they'd sit late into the night and talk and talk.

She'd tell him about wanting to be a teacher someday, about how much she loved being around little kids. Back in Michigan she had what sounded like two dozen baby cousins and nieces and nephews. She missed babysitting them, reading to them. I think I'd be a good teacher, Mel said. Don't you?

Absolutely, he told her. She'd changed *him,* just in a matter of weeks; if she could open up his eyes, he figured she could open anyone's.

She was a genius, after all, at getting him to talk; if he so much as grunted she'd be all over it, asking him what he meant, and what did he think of this, or that, and here's what *she* thought of this, or that . . . keeping up with her, sometimes, felt kind of like being on speed.

One day, early on, Mel got him talking about the music he wanted to make, about how maybe someday he'd like to start a club, or produce records. He'd be happy as a DJ. Think about it, he'd say. *We* met at a club. That would be nice, you know? Running a place where everyone could dance and get happy and hook up.

Then he told her—and he was surprised by how quickly, nervously, the words came out—how he'd been thinking of getting out of Chicago. How when he was off probation he'd maybe go to Miami, where the club scene was so good.

Mel listened and smiled without parting her lips, but for once she didn't ask him any other questions.

THEN ONE NIGHT, two months in, Mel called him, saying, Brad, Brad, come over right now. He'd run to the L, thinking she was having some kind of emergency. But when he finally knocked on her door, she answered wearing only a bathrobe, holding a bottle of wine. They're all gone, she said, looking up at the ceiling. We're alone!

And so they ate dinner at the kitchen table upstairs, and drank right from the bottle, and rolled around on the living-room floor, and afterward they lounged naked and watched Letterman on the ancient black-and-white TV down in Mel's room.

It was then that she asked him, So do you ever think about what you're going to *do*?

What do you mean?

About Lou. About a place.

Lou had been rumbling, lately, about Brad moving out. Brad swallowed, wishing he didn't have to think about something so petty—not now.

I don't know, he said. Lou's all talk—it's not like he's going to do anything.

So can I ask you something?

Yeah.

I've been thinking, she said, and took his hand and held it up in front of her face, kneading his palm until his fingers were splayed. It's nice, being alone like this. Right?

You said it.

Yeah. So . . . maybe we should get a place.

Now he knew why she'd been so eager to get him drunk.

Don't say no, she said.

Mel, I've never lived with anybody. I mean, a girl.

I can see it on your face, she said. You don't want to.

That made him angry. She wasn't right. But . . . she wasn't wrong either. The thought had never entered his mind.

Brad lay very still, aware, as he hadn't been a minute ago, of Mel's warm flank pressed against him. If any other woman he'd ever been with had asked him, he would have said no. No way. He had to have his privacy, his own mess. That was bedrock, that was principle. Especially now . . . the moment probation was over he was going to be nothing but a little comic-strip cloud of dust. He'd be in Miami. And Mel still had a year of school, at least.

But then he realized: he hadn't been thinking, seriously thinking, about Miami for weeks. He'd been saying the words, but not seeing the pictures. Since going to bed with Mel he'd been thinking mostly of *Mel,* and not about beaches and clubs and the crowds of drunk college kids who arrived every spring, like geese.

So what the fuck was he afraid of?

She said, A little place. Just us.

We've only known each other a few weeks, he said.

Two months, actually. Her voice was edging already into sadness—he hated to hear it quiver, hated to think that was his fault.

Mel . . .

It's just—you make me *happy*. Nobody's ever made me feel happy. Not like this. You've made my whole life different.

And what she was saying now—that was it, *that* was what scared the shit out of him: her happiness. He could almost feel her hope, a little pulsing white spot between them on the bed. Waiting to glow brighter or die. And she wanted to put it right into his hands, to say: Hang on to this for me.

He wanted to tell her: Mel, I'm so going to fuck this up.

She sat up and sighed. I was kind of hoping for a response? You know, like, *I've been happy, too, Mel?*

Of course I've been happy. This is just—

A surprise?

Yeah, he said.

This isn't how I saw this going.

I know, I know—

Brad, she said, I love you.

He closed his eyes. She'd never said that to him before. But he'd imagined her saying it—late at night, sometimes, when he was too keyed up to sleep. And now, hearing it . . . if Mel so much as touched his shoulder right now he'd break down, he'd hold her all night and bawl into her hair.

He said, I just need to think.

Mel's voice was neutral. All right.

Can I still stay?

You asshole. Yes, I want you to stay.

They lay quiet for a long time. Mel turned away from him. Brad watched the tip of her ear.

Finally she said, We can think about it, and talk about it, and I'll even leave you alone for a while, if you want. But if you're going to stay in my bed, I kind of have to put you on the clock.

Mel—

You know I'm right. I'm done chasing the wrong people.

Then she turned, quickly, and kissed him on the forehead. Good night, she said.

But later that morning, while Mel slept, her back still turned to him, Brad saw it:

A little apartment, somewhere up in Lincoln Park, a few floors above the street. The balcony door was propped open— it was summertime. Down on the street he could see students walking back and forth, bags slung across their shoulders. Mel was at work, and he sat in front of a fan and listened to records on his headphones, or noodled with a keyboard. Their bed was in the corner, right under a window. He knew its frame rattled—but he also knew they never had to worry about being quiet, not here. They kept an ashtray in the window and would sit and smoke in the dark and watch the streets. They'd sleep with a breeze blowing over them, the sounds of traffic. And when it was time to get Mel up, he'd nuzzle the soft spot on her neck that vibrated when she moaned, or laughed.

He closed his eyes and wished—for maybe the first time since he was a kid—for everything to be different when the sun rose, for the room around them to be revealed as it should be.

Mel was better than anything that had ever happened to him. So why was he treating all of this like some big fucking tragedy?

It was, he told himself, time to grow the fuck up.

Mel, he said. *Mel.*

She turned to him. When her eyes opened she smiled, and he could tell: she already knew what he would say. Like all night she'd been waiting for him to catch up, to see what she'd already seen.

He said, Okay, and then described it to her anyway.

VII.

The third night never seems to end.

Brad lights one of the candles, jamming it between slats on the grill's rack. He and Mel pull the quilt down from the top of the table and drape it over their heads, and sit with the candle between them. Brad rubs and rubs Mel's feet, but she says she can't feel them anymore.

That's all she says to him, and all he can think to ask her about.

He keeps the candle burning until the space between them fills with heat. Then he pinches it out and huddles with Mel, rubbing every part of her he can, until he can't stand the cold, and lights it again. The candle burns slowly, but still it's getting shorter and shorter.

They're down, he knows, to only one more option. He's been trying to think of a way to tell Mel, a way that won't panic her, but he can't. He has no choice.

Mel.

When she says, What? it's the first word he's heard from her in hours.

Listen, he says. When the sun comes up I'm going to go for help.

He can hear her intake of breath. Her feet twist, a little, in his hands.

No, she says.

We don't have a choice.

You *can't*.

I have to. I should have gone yesterday. But I know—we aren't going to make it another day.

I'll go, too, she says.

He wants to cry. Mel, he says, you wouldn't make it.

They look at her feet, bundled in his lap.

You could carry me, she says. Piggyback.

He's thought about this. He says, I wish I could. But it's too far. I'm not strong enough. And you'll be warmer here with the candles.

Brad, she whispers. Please. Don't leave me alone.

It'll only be a few hours. A day at most.

That's too *long*. She pulls close to him. *Please*. I'd rather die with you here.

He can't tell her that this is exactly what he's afraid of.

Listen to me, she says. Her cold hands move, panicked, around his chest and neck. Let's say you make it. We'll be *arrested*. You'll go back to jail.

Of course she's thought of it, too.

As has he. But he's also been thinking, this last hour, of the apartment in Chicago—their place, the one they'll live in someday. The warm summer afternoons. And he's been thinking that if Mel is there—waiting for him, in a place like that—he can do the time.

He imagines the first day he's out, the two of them eating hot Chinese food, making love like they've never made it.

Yeah, he says. I know. But I can do it.

She starts to wail, pushing her face against his chest.

Mel, he says, stroking her hair. I got us into this. It was my idea. If I don't try to fix it—

He's about to say: *I'll never be able to live with myself.* But he doesn't.

She won't answer him.

You know it's the only way, he says. I'll go in the morning.

LATER BRAD brings one of the chairs under the blanket and sets up the lit candle underneath it. He's gone too long without sleep; the candle flame leaves yellow streaks across his vision. He nods off with Mel still clinging to him.

Later, he realizes she's crying again. The wind is still howling outside. Mel's cold hands are on his chin. His own feet are numb.

Brad, Mel whispers. I don't think we're going to make it until morning.

Sure we will, he says.

She puts her mouth against his ear. I want you to promise me something, she says.

What?

If I don't make it? And you do? Just leave. Leave me here.

Mel—

I mean it, she says. I don't want you to go to jail. Not over this. And I don't want you to feel bad. This wasn't your fault. Okay?

Her eyes are black holes, right in front of him.

Promise, she says. If you want to make me feel better, promise.

I promise, he says.

She kisses him. Her body is shaking, and cold, cold everywhere.

I love you, she says. Make me warm.

It's hard to do, but they manage. The blanket around them

fills up with heat. Brad's mouth is dry and cracked, but between them he imagines—it's so real he can almost see it—a glow, like from an electric stove's warm red coil.

Mel says, Tell me you love me.

And he does, over and over.

In the end he tries to pull out, but she says, No, it's okay. He feels, at once, dread, and joy, and a fluttering in his stomach—not just as he comes, but something else—like the feeling he's had, swimming, when he's stepped out over his head: the fear of sinking, and then the peace that comes after, when he's made himself relax, and float.

Mel rubs her hands across his lower back, and sighs. You're so warm.

Afterward she takes the candle and goes to visit the bucket. He can't keep his eyes open. She's gone for long time, and he's just about ready to shout for her when he hears her thumping quickly back. She's shivering wildly, and when she's under the quilt he rubs her, his own body cold and heavy.

Hold me tight, she says.

Later he thinks she's having a dream. Her hands are waving in the air above the blanket, and she gasps.

Shh, he says, grabbing a hand.

She mutters something that might be his name, and shudders, and curls to him.

Shh, he says. It's okay.

THE NEXT TIME he wakes, the cabin is still. The wind groans, but not as strongly as before. Brad looks for a long time at the quilt a few inches above his face, at the candlelight pulsing across the fabric, trying to remember where he is. He lifts the quilt—the cabin is still dark; it's still the same night. But there's an awful stink in the air, something other than the quilt's stinging mold.

He wonders when Mel will come back from the bathroom, because he's freezing, and then he knows she never left, that she is in his arms, and that she's gone cold.

His hand scrabbles for the candle and holds it next to her. Mel's turned away from him. He says her name, grabs her shoulder, shakes her. He turns her to face him. Her face is gray, her eyes only white slits. Bile streams out of her mouth.

HE LOSES TIME, for a while.

At first he talks to her, like maybe she's hanging on in there, somehow.

He tells her he loves her. He tells her he wants to die.

He asks, What the fuck did you *do*?

He asks this when he's trying to wipe her face clean, when he lifts her onto his lap and he finds the empty prescription bottle that's rolled underneath her. When he knows it wasn't just the cold that took her.

He tells her she's crazy, that he hates her. That he can't believe he ever loved such a crazy stupid selfish bitch.

He tells her he knows what she wants him to do, and he's not going to do it. He tells her he's going to fucking die anyway.

Not long after that the candle burns down to a tiny spark, and from there into nothing.

I won't light the other one, he tells her. But after a while the dark is too much, the cold is too much, and he does.

He huddles around the little flame, puts his hands over it until they fill with pain.

At one point he's sure that Mel's snuggled closer to him, and that her skin is warm. He rubs her feet and kisses her and tells her he's sorry, that he wants to marry her and live in a house on stilts next to the ocean.

LATER HE shudders awake. The candle's burnt down by a third. He can just see the part in Mel's hair, the white curve of her forehead. He touches her hair, pulls his hand back.

He can *see* her. There's more than candlelight around him.

Slowly, stiffly, he wraps the blanket around his shoulders and lifts up the quilt. The room's so bright it hurts his eyes— outside the windows, when he squints, he can see blue skies. And the air is different—it's warmer, he's sure of it. He's not so good on his feet, but all the same he walks and opens the door, to look at the thermometer. And there it is: twenty-five degrees. The sun glints off the flat field of snow that was once the lake.

He watches a sunbeam move slowly across the floor-boards. He drags the mattress over to it, sits in the heat next to Mel. When he feels the warming on his neck, he moans.

I told you, he says to her. You gave the fuck up!

He should go, he knows that. But the sun is so warm he can't think, can barely even make himself move.

LATER—just a couple of hours, he thinks, but he can't be sure—Brad hears a sound, one he can barely believe: a motor, a big one. He crosses the room to the back windows and peers out.

Out on the road a red pickup with a plow attachment rumbles by, throwing up a plume. He wonders if he's hallucinating it.

You see, he says to Mel. You *see* that?

You fucking coward, he says. He's not sure who he says this to.

Brad puts on every bit of clothing he can. He digs in Mel's purse and adds her cash to his own: he counts out seventy-eight dollars. He takes her cigarettes.

He opens the last can of tuna with his pocketknife and eats it with his fingers, even though the chunks are held together by a web of frost, and swallowing it stings his throat.

Just before leaving he turns to look at Mel from the doorway. And he can't bear the sight of her pale face—it's like she's awake, like he's leaving someone alive.

So he wraps her in the quilt. It's harder than he'd imagined. She's gone stiff, and she's heavy—he thinks, with a shameful surge of relief, that he really *couldn't* have carried her out. When he's done he sets her as gently as he can down on the mattress, and then sits with his hand on her, until the cold from her body begins to pulse up through the scratchy wool. Like she's pushing him away.

He thinks about leaving her ID, next to her on the mattress—but he can't make himself do that.

Fuck her, fuck all her stupid plans. He's going to get gas, and then he's coming back for her.

He tucks his chin into his sweater and walks outside.

VIII.

Brad and Mel spent all the next day celebrating: walking around downtown Chicago, talking about the place they'd get, the life they'd have.

They went to the shore in the afternoon. For early October the weather was obscenely beautiful: warm, almost summery, with a terrific breeze blowing in off the lake. Everyone in Chicago was out there with them, it seemed, and to Brad they all looked like he felt: stunned by good luck. For a long time they walked on the beach, and after that they sat on a bench outside the planetarium—a place Mel loved—looking at the whitecaps rolling ahead of the wind.

Mel kept talking about the Upper Peninsula of Michigan, her white face tilted toward the sunshine. She told him again about the fishing cabin she used to go visit—about how, when she was there alone, in weather like this, it was maybe the prettiest place she'd ever seen.

I wish I'd never been there with Shithead, she said, as they walked off the pier.

You and me both, he said.

I wish I'd gone with *you,* she told him. You know? Like I wish I could just empty out my memories. Replace him with you. I'd have been so *happy.*

She slid her arm around his middle.

We'd have fun up there, she said. Just the two of us. We're never *alone* here.

Brad watched the people making way for them—the sidewalks were so busy the two of them barely had room to walk like this, and if anyone paid any attention to them, in their happiness, it was only to be annoyed, to mutter *Watch it.*

And that was when—that was how—the idea came to him. It *swooped* in, like no idea ever had, except maybe the one that had come to him the night before, when he woke Mel up and told her he wanted to live with her.

He grabbed her arm and said, So let's go be alone.

What? she said. Go where?

That cabin.

She gave him a look. Yeah, okay. Except it's like a couple hundred miles from here. At least.

I mean it, Brad said, walking backward in front of her.

She laughed at him. It's not like the L goes there. But hey, if we start walking *now*—

Mel, he said. I really want to see it. I want to be alone with you.

She screwed up her face at him, half amused, half understanding. You're starting to worry me, buddy. You okay?

Just like that, the courage was there for him.

Mel, he said. I'm so in love with you I can barely fucking *think*.

He wished he could take a picture of the look on her face. You *love* me?

Yeah, he said. I love you, Mel.

She ran at him and squeezed him until he was sure she was hurting her arms.

He said, I love you and I want to live with you, and I want to *do* something—I don't know—something kind of nuts. Something *with* you. So why not? Let's go see your cabin.

Okay, she said. He thought she might be sniffling. That's great, really, but you know, we need a *car*. Which neither one of us has.

We'll take Lou's truck.

You really want to go back to jail, don't you?

No, he said. Look—I happen to know that truck's not exactly legal. Lou's not going to report the damn thing gone. And fuck him anyway.

Mel looked at him, appraising.

We've got the weekend, he said. We can both call in sick

on Monday. My PO just called—he won't try again till, like, next Thursday . . .

He knew he had her. He knew her—she *wanted* this. And she wanted him to ask her to do it, had *been* wanting it. Watching her face now—her smile spreading, her thoughts moving beneath and behind it—was like watching her tear open a present.

She said, This is so fucking crazy.

But you want to do it anyway.

She grinned and reached for him. You know I do, she said.

IX.

Brad trudges along the road toward the truck, his eyes mostly on his boots. The plow has left the road covered by a thin crust of snow, so white in the sunshine that his eyes water; not only is it slick, but his feet are numb enough that he'll stumble if he's not careful. And everything around him is so bright he can barely look at it: the hills are a dazzling white, the sky a blue as pure as paint. The sun gleams overhead; after a while Brad even starts to sweat under his clothes. From the trees come sudden thumps and hisses: snow falling in wads and sheets from the branches of the pines. He's thirstier than he can ever remember being. As he walks he scoops handfuls of snow into his mouth, swirling them down into tiny swallows of water.

And he keeps thinking: Mel died. I'm alone.

Before long he passes the truck, and even though he's looking for it, he's relieved that it's hard to spot: just a truck-shaped clump of snow down in the pines, next to the other cabin. Certainly the plow driver didn't notice it: a waist-high wall of snow blocks the drive.

Digging the truck out will be a lot of work. Better to think of that later.

For now Brad slogs on toward the gas station, trying to think of what he'll say there.

He should, he knows, go up to the cashier and admit everything. End all this. He should say: My girlfriend's dead back in one of the cabins. He should tell them his name, Mel's name. Let the official gears start turning.

But he told her he'd leave her. She made him promise.

Brad cries now, as he walks; no one is around to care, but still he covers his eyes, pinches his nose. Promised *what*? Mel tricked him. He didn't know what she was planning. When he promised her he thought they could both make it. And he'd been right. He'd been *right*. All Mel had to do was fucking believe him. To trust him.

So why had she brought her fucking pills with her?

He'd trusted *her*. He'd been alone in her room before—at any time he could have flushed those pills down the toilet. He'd thought about it, but he never had. He knew Mel had been testing him, when she showed them off. Seeing what he'd do, what he'd say. Whether she ever admitted it to herself or not, that's exactly what she'd done, and he'd passed. She trusted him, and so he trusted her, not to be stupid, to try and be happy—

And she brought them *here*.

He forces himself to take big breaths. To think. He *knows* Mel. He knows her better than anybody. She would say herself that nothing she ever did was simple. The pills probably went with her everywhere. Some people carried guns or rabbits' feet, or wore crucifixes, just in case of trouble. Mel carried her pills.

And—in her own sick way—she'd been right. The worst kind of trouble *had* come. Maybe she'd known that for people like her, like Brad, something would have to go wrong, sooner or later. Maybe, deep inside, she hadn't been surprised by any of their fuckups. He remembered the way she looked when the smoke was filling the cabin—how calmly she said, *It would be quicker.* Mel knew what sort of shape they were in a long time before he did.

Brad's walking faster and faster, slipping every now and then in the compacted snow.

But she'd been *wrong.* The sun had come out.

But she couldn't have known that, could she? All she had to go on was what Brad told her—which was that in the morning he was going for help. She had to make a guess— just like he did—about how well that idea would turn out. They both sat in that same cold room, thinking over the odds, and they both came to the only decisions they could.

And hadn't they made the same decision? If the sun hadn't come up—if Brad was making this same trip right into the teeth of the storm, through knee-deep unplowed snow, in that wind and cold—what would his chances be? He'd wanted to go only because he *might* save Mel. Even if that meant dying. Because he couldn't bear to sit still anymore and do nothing.

How was Mel's choice any different? She did what she could stand, and she did it because she loved him.

Brad sits in a snowbank and puts his face in his hands.

But how can he do what she wants him to? How can he leave her?

He tries to see the guy behind the counter at the gas station. Or a policeman. He tries to see himself opening his mouth, letting lies pour out.

The best story he could tell anyone wouldn't be words at all, but a picture. One he doesn't have. It would show him and Mel, lying close together, his arm around her, his chin on top of her skull, both of them quiet and still and connected, with all the things they did in their lives tucked in between them. And they wouldn't be in a cabin; they'd be eighty years old, under a thick quilt in a big house on a sunny beach, and nobody would find them but the children they didn't have, and nobody would truly be sorry about them dying like they did, because anyone who knew them would know they were *supposed* to go this way; that they loved each other so much that if one of them died first, the other couldn't stand to live a single second more.

He should never have lit the other candle last night. He should have opened up the door and taken off his clothes. He should have held on to Mel and just let it happen. But he didn't. He couldn't.

He's such a fucking coward.

It's now—shuddering, melted snow soaking into his clothes, snot running down his chin—that Brad hears a vehicle coming. He stands and wipes his eyes and sees a splotch of red far down the road: the plow. It's heading back up the other side of the road, grumbling and scratching, snow piled in front of it like a breaking wave.

He should wait until it's the last second and then jump out in front of it. Mel's dead and alone in the cabin and here he is, alive. He's a stupid fuckup who's going to die sooner or later—what did Mel think she was saving him for, anyway?

What's he going to do? What could he ever fucking do without her?

He wades off the side of the road into the deep snow, into the trees. The plow rolls closer, loud and alive and healthy. Brad leans against a pine. He should get it over with, right now.

The plow roars by, and Brad crouches low, his face against the wet bark, and shuts his eyes, until the noise of the plow's engine fades almost to nothing.

By the time he reaches the gas station he's gone cold inside. He's been squinting against the snow so long that, inside the shop, all he can see are waves of color, the silhouettes of shelves and racks and the man behind the counter. He smells cooking meat, and his stomach squeezes so hard he almost cries out.

He goes to the restroom and waits until his vision comes back, then looks at himself: he's red-eyed, drawn, his skin gray where it's not filthy. He drinks handful after handful of water from the sink, then scrubs his face, wets and ties back his hair.

In the shop he buys a hot dog, a pair of sunglasses, thin gloves, and prepays for a gallon of gas, in a small plastic can. The man behind the counter is thick, wearing a hunting cap, and never takes his eyes off Brad. Can he see Brad's hands shaking? A radio behind the counter is playing twangy country music, and Brad wants to stare at it; music is the strangest thing he can imagine, right now.

Out of gas? the man asks, still staring.

Yeah, Brad says.

Where at?

Back on 35, Brad tells him. I let it go too long.

Where you in from?

The man's eyes have narrowed; it's not a friendly question. But Brad's practiced this part.

He says, I was up at NMU all weekend with friends. Got stuck in with the snow. I was in a hurry to get home, so I didn't even look at the gas gauge. Brad tries a laugh, and it sounds so crazy he winces.

The man counts out his change, working his lips. That was one hell of a blow, he says. Ain't seen anything like that before. Hey—you need a ride back to your car?

Nah, Brad says, swallowing fear. Don't trouble yourself.

The man looks relieved, nods to himself.

Thanks, Brad says.

You take care now, the man says, and before Brad is halfway out the door he turns up his radio to a blare.

THREE HOURS LATER Brad parks the truck outside his and Mel's cabin.

He's sore, trembling—he's had to dig out the truck, scooping snow with his arms, tromping down wheel ruts with his boots. He saw no one until he had the truck out onto the road; then the same yellow Jeep he and Mel had seen two days before rattled by, and the driver tooted his horn. Brad watched it in the rearview mirror until it rounded a curve and was gone.

He could have driven off, back to Chicago, once the truck was running. Left Mel, like she wanted. He told himself to— he sat in the cab, on the newly cleared road, and tried to urge himself on, to take the left turn and go. He didn't have the balls to do himself in—so what else was there to argue?

But he turned right. He drove back to the cabin, amazed at the feeling of driving, of how simple and easy a thing it was. How quickly he was able to make it back to her.

Mel got her goodbye. He wants his, too.

The road is still empty in both directions, but he's parked in the open. He'll have to hurry. Brad opens the door of the truck and wades down the snowy drive—the sun has sunk the morning's thick powder down into wet cement—and up to the cabin door. The thermometer says it's forty degrees.

He takes a breath, preparing himself. He thinks, with a crazy swimming hope, that maybe Mel will be awake. Stranger things have happened. Maybe she'll be sitting on the mattress, waiting to see him, or mad as hell, he doesn't care which—

But everything is as he left it. The room is tight and close and stinks of smoke. The sunshine streaming in has made long wobbly rectangles on the floor, but after sitting in the truck with the heater blasting, the place feels like a refrigerator.

Mel is where he left her; a lump in the quilt, so still and small you might not notice a human shape, if you weren't looking.

Brad walks over to her, the boards creaking under his boots. He touches the quilt, his hand still shaking. It's cool. He presses his hand down until he feels her underneath, hard as stone.

He sits and puts both hands on the blanket, trying to figure out what he's touching. He thinks he's got her arm. He strokes it, up and down.

He should at least leave her ID with her. It'll be summer, probably, before anyone comes for her, and there—there won't be much left of her then. He swallows with a dry click at the back of his throat.

Brad forces himself to move, to stretch across the mattress for the purse in Mel's backpack. He digs out her DePaul ID—she's stone-faced in the picture, like she's angry—and drops it next to her on the mattress. He takes her driver's license; in this picture she's smiling. He slips it into his own wallet.

She doesn't have any paper with her, or else he'd leave a note—maybe on the door, where whoever comes in ...

He stops, sits still, watching the door. Because he *knows* who.

The cabin belongs to Andy's family. And it'll be one of them who finds her, when it's warmer. One of them—maybe Andy, but probably Andy's father—will see Mel's ID. And what will he think?

The obvious: That Mel came here because she loved Andy. Or because she was trying to hurt Andy. Because she gave a shit about Andy.

Brad thinks about this story spreading: about Andy getting a call, about Mel's family getting a call, and Mel's friends. After those phone calls Mel would change, just like that, would become a whole new person. She wouldn't be the girl who told Andrew off, who got her life together. Instead she'd be that sad, sick girl who never got over her first love, the poor little thing who couldn't live without her prince fucking Andrew.

Brad can't let it happen. Not like that.

So he kneels and scoops up Mel—she's twice as heavy as he remembers her—and staggers with her to the door. And even though he falls several times, even though by the time he does it both he and the quilt are covered with snow, he carries her across the drive to the truck, and into the passenger seat. She'll only fit curled to the side, with her head leaning against the door—it's the best he can do, for now. He buckles her in so she'll stay put.

He runs back inside, one last time, for her things. He's frantic now, his breath coming in pants, scouring the cabin for anything that will reveal who was here.

He leaves the bucket in the bathroom full of their waste.

Let Andy hear about *that*.

HE DRIVES SOUTH. The truck sloughs the last of its snow when he's finally on the highway and can drive at speed. The main roads are clear, but down side roads, in driveways, Brad can see people digging out their buried cars, clearing downed tree limbs, blowing snow off sidewalks. He stops at another gas station, fills up the truck, keeps driving. More and more cars appear around him.

He tries the radio for a while. The news talks about how this storm is the worst the UP has had in twenty years. People have died. An old man, of a heart attack, shoveling his walk. A teenaged boy, who drove off the road into a tree. Two people whose boat is missing on Lake Superior. A vagrant frozen in a park in Sault Sainte Marie.

He turns the radio off. Every now and again he glances sideways, at Mel wrapped up beside him. He turns the radio back on. He feels no better, either way.

When he crosses the border into Wisconsin, the sun is low and swollen off to the west, and he watches it, feeling numb and stupid—for a long time he can't figure out what day it is. He counts back the hours, and is shocked to find that not even a full twenty-four hours have passed since Mel died.

And all the while, as he drives, he tries to figure out how to do it. How to leave her.

At first he thinks he should find a hospital. A busy one in Milwaukee, maybe, where he might be able to sneak in and out of the parking lot. But he knows people who tried to drop off OD'd friends on hospital sidewalks before, and almost always they got spotted, their license numbers written down. If he's going to do this, he needs to think of something better than a stupid junkie trick.

He thinks about taking her back to her house, tucking her into bed, leaving her there. But she has too many roommates; someone would see him. Even if they didn't, they know she's been gone, and that Brad has a key.

There's only one way he can think to do it that's even halfway safe. He starts checking the road signs for a rest stop.

Mel's roommates will be a problem no matter what he does. They know him, they'll ask questions. He'll have to tell them—who is he kidding? He'll have to tell everyone—her friends, the people at the deli, probably even the cops—the same story, over and over: *Mel ran away, and I don't know why. She told me it was over Friday night. I've been going crazy trying to find her.*

Or maybe he should tell them *he* broke things off. Give her a reason to vanish. Maybe he'll need to remind everyone that Mel's always been capable of this kind of thing.

He thinks about trying to speak to another girl sometime. One of those silly, glittery girls in the clubs. Dancing with her. Listening to the story of her life. Going to bed with her.

Hearing her whisper to him, *Have you ever been in love?*

Once, he'll say.

What happened?

She left me, he'll say, and the next day he'll leave that girl, and the one after. He'll change his phone number and quit his job and move to another city. He'll live alone for the rest of his life.

FIFTEEN MINUTES LATER Brad pulls into a rest stop—exactly the kind he needs: isolated, out in the country. The sun is down below the horizon, but still glowing. He turns off the truck and unbuckles Mel's seat belt. Then he climbs out into the lot. He's almost alone, except for a couple of semis parked a hundred yards away, too far to see anything. The night is warm and wet; the smells of turning leaves and melting snow and Lake Michigan are all mixed in the air. In a few days it'll be like the storm never happened.

Brad spots a hooded pay phone next to the restrooms, and heads for it, digging in his pockets for change. His heart thumps and thumps, like footsteps up a long staircase.

He's holding the receiver in his hand, ready to dial, when a station wagon pulls off the highway, and parks in the space right next to the truck. Brad hangs up and walks quickly through the thick snow to a picnic table, out of the light. He watches a family—mom and dad and three young kids—spill out of the wagon. None of them seem to see him; none of them notice that a truck with a dead body inside is only inches away.

He waits out their trip to the bathrooms and to the vending machines, listens to their distant, happy chatter. They're like aliens. The father herds everyone back inside the wagon, and Brad wonders how the man—so obviously not a fuckup—got to be where he is.

An urge comes over him: he should go up to the man,

shake his hand, tell him what happened. But he can't do it, can't move. And then the station wagon drives away.

Brad wipes his nose on the sleeve of his jacket. The rest area's still empty. On the interstate only a few headlights are moving slowly past. He's as alone as he's going to get.

He walks back to the pay phone. While he dials he tries to make out Mel's outline through the passenger window.

A woman's voice says, Emergency Response, and Brad tells her what he's been practicing:

Someone's died of an overdose.

Then he walks away from the phone, toward the truck, leaving the receiver off the hook so they can trace the call.

He opens Mel's door. She starts to fall out; he lunges for her, hooks an arm underneath the blanket where he thinks her shoulder might be. She feels as hard as a piece of wood in there. He ought to just keep easing her down—put her on the sidewalk like he planned, and then drive like hell. But his grip isn't right—he's sure he's going to drop her. He bends his knees and heaves her back into the truck, harder than he'd like.

When she's back on the seat he sees that a strand of her hair has come loose, at the top of the blanket. Short and black, dirty and limp.

He stares at it for a few seconds, the weight of her body pressed against his chest. Then he runs his finger across the strand. Her hair feels like he remembers—unbearably smooth.

He closes Mel's door, softly, so as not to hit her.

Brad's mouth is cottony. He walks quickly around the truck and climbs behind the wheel. For a few seconds he puts his hand on the keys in the ignition. Maybe another hour with her will be enough.

But it won't be. It just won't. There's nothing left to do, not anymore. The call has been made; the receiver is still dangling, off the hook. Right now police are on the way.

He touches her hair again. He has to put her on the sidewalk, drive away.

Or not.

This new idea doesn't come crazily—not like the one that sent him and Mel off to Michigan in the first place. It doesn't make him shake, like knowing he loved her did. It doesn't feel painful, like punishment. Not like telling everyone lies will. Not like having to say he stopped loving her.

You promised, he hears her say.

Mel, he tells her, it's different now.

This, he can do.

He puts his arm around Mel and draws her close to him. He touches the loose strand of hair with his lips. He's braced himself for a smell, this close to her, but there's nothing now, except the odors of the cabin—mold, smoke—clinging to the quilt. He moves his hand across the cloth, feeling, through it, Mel's ear, the line of her neck, the curve of her skull.

While he waits, he closes his eyes and remembers his first sight of her, the way she was dancing: like a crazy woman, her little body whipping out and around at the joints, her fists clenched and her teeth bared, her hair flying wild as she swung her head, like she was saying *no no no* to everyone but him.

He remembers the surprises: The scars across her wrists. The deepness of her voice. The way she'd curl up when she laughed. The way that, happy or sad, she'd cling to him. How proud that always made him feel. How, the night she asked him to live with her, she seemed to know all along he'd say yes.

Brad remembers that entire night, from start to finish: how afraid he was, at first—but also how easy he'd found it, in the end, to give in. How Mel had been angry at him, but only until he reached for her, held her tight and told her the truth: that he'd tried and tried, but he just couldn't imagine a future where she wasn't with him.

All Through the House

Now

HERE IS AN EMPTY MEADOW, CIRCLED BY BARE AUTUMN
woods.

The trees of the woods—oak, maple, locust—grow
through a mat of tangled scrub, rusty leaves, piles of brittle
deadfall. Overhead is a rich blue sky, a few high, translucent
clouds, moving quickly—but the trees are dense enough to
shelter everything below, and the meadow, too. And here,
leading into the trees from the meadow's edge, is a dirt track,
twin ruts with a grassy center, winding through the woods and
away.

The meadow floor is overrun by tall yellow grass, thorny
vines, the occasional sapling—save for at the meadow's center. Here is a wide rectangular depression. The broken remains of a concrete foundation shore up its sides. The bottom

is crumbled concrete and cinder, barely visible beneath a thin netting of weeds. A blackened wooden beam angles down from the rim, its underside soft and fibrous. Two oaks lean over the foundation, charred on the sides that face it.

Sometimes deer browse in the meadow. Raccoons and rabbits are always present; they have made their own curving trails across the meadow floor. A fox lives in the nearby trees, rusty and quick. His den, twisting between tree roots, is pressed flat and smooth by his belly.

Sometimes automobiles crawl slowly along the track and park at the edge of the meadow. The people inside sometimes get out, and walk into the grass. They take photographs, or draw pictures, or read from books. Sometimes they climb down into the old foundation. A few camp overnight, huddling close to fires.

Whenever these people come, a policeman, fat and gray-haired, arrives soon after. Sometimes the people speak with him—and sometimes they shout—but always they depart, loading their cars while the policeman watches. When they are gone he follows them down the track in his slow, rumbling cruiser. When this happens in the nighttime, the spinning of his red-and-blue lights makes the trees seem to jump and dance.

Sometimes the policeman comes when there is no one to chase away.

He stops the cruiser and climbs out. He walks slowly into the meadow. He sits on the broken concrete at the rim of the crater, looking into it, looking at the sky, closing his eyes.

When he makes noise, the woods grow quiet. All the animals crouch low, flicking their ears at the man's barks and howls.

He does not stay long.

After his cruiser has rolled away down the track, the woods and the meadow remain, for a time, silent. But before long what lives there sniffs the air, and, in fits and starts, emerges. Noses press to the ground, and into the burrows of mice. Things eat, and are eaten.

Here memories are held in muscles and bellies, not in minds. The policeman, and the house, and all the people who have come and gone here, are not forgotten.

They are, simply, never remembered.

1987

Sheriff Larry Thompkins tucked his chin against the cold and, his back to his idling cruiser, unlocked the cattle gate that blocked access to the Sullivan woods. The gate swung inward, squealing, and the cruiser's headlights shone a little ways down the track, before it veered off into the trees. Larry straightened, then glanced right and left, down the paved county road behind him. He saw no other cars, not even on the distant interstate. The sky was clouded over—snow was a possibility—and the fields behind him were almost invisible in the moonless dark.

Larry sank back behind the wheel, grateful for the warmth, for the static spitting from his radio. He nosed the cruiser through the gate and onto the track, then switched to his parking lights. The trunks of trees ahead dimmed, turned orange. The nearest soul, old Ned Baker, lived a half mile off, but Ned was an insomniac, and often sat in front of his bedroom window watching the Sullivan woods. If Larry used his headlights, Ned would see. Ever since Patricia Pike's book had come out—three months ago now—Ned had watched over the gated entrance to the woods as if it was a military duty.

Larry had been chasing off trespassers from the Sullivan place ever since the murders, twelve years ago in December. He hated coming here, but he couldn't very well refuse to do his job—no one else was going to see to it. Almost always the trespassers were kids from the high school, out at the murder house getting drunk or high—and though Larry was always firm with them, and made trouble for the bad ones, he knew most kids did stupid things; he couldn't blame them that much. Larry had fallen off the roof of a barn, drunk, when he was sixteen—he'd broken his arm in two places, all because he was trying to impress a girl who, in the end, never went out with him.

But activity in the woods had picked up since the Pike woman's book appeared. Larry had been out here three times in the last week alone. There were kids, still, more of them than ever—but also people from out of town, some of whom he suspected were mentally ill. Just last weekend Larry had chased off a couple in their twenties, lying on a blanket with horrible screaming music playing on their boom box. They'd told him—calmly, as though he might understand—that they practiced magic and wanted to conceive a child there. The house, they said, was a place of energy. When they were gone Larry looked up at its empty windows, its stupid dead house-face, and couldn't imagine anything further from the truth.

The cruiser bounced and shimmied as Larry negotiated the turns through the woods. All his extra visits had deepened the ruts in the track—he'd been cutting through mud and ice all autumn. Now and then the tires spun, and he tried not to think about having to call for a tow, the stories he'd have to make up to explain himself. But each time, the cruiser roared and lurched free.

He'd come here with Patricia Pike. He hadn't wanted to, but the mayor told him Pike did a good job with this kind of book, and that—while the mayor was concerned, just as Larry was, about exploiting what had happened—he didn't want the town to get any more of a bad name on account of being uncooperative. So Larry had gone to the library, to read one of Pike's other books. He picked one called *The Beauties and the Beast*, with the close-up of a cat's eye on the front cover. The book was about a serial killer in Idaho in the six-ties, who murdered five women and fed them to his pet cougar. In one chapter Pike wrote that the police had hidden details of the crime from her. Larry could understand why—the killings were brutal; he was sure the police had a hard enough time explaining the details to the families of the vic-tims, let alone to ghouls all across the country looking for a thrill.

We're going to get exploited, Larry had told the mayor, waving that book at him.

Look, the mayor said, *I know this is difficult for you. But would you rather she wrote it without your help? You knew Wayne better than anybody. Who knows? Maybe we'll finally get to the bottom of things.*

What if there's no bottom to get to? Larry asked, but the mayor had looked at him strangely and never answered, just told him to put up with it, that it would be over before he knew it.

Larry wrestled the cruiser around the last bend, and then stopped. His parking lights shone dully across what was left of the old driveway turnaround, and onto the Sullivan house.

The house squatted, dim and orange. It had never been much to look at, even when new; it was small, unremarkable, square—barely more than a prefab. The garage, jutting off the back, was far too big, and knocked the whole structure out of proportion—made it look deformed. The windows were too little, too few.

Since the murders the house had only gotten worse. Most of the paint had chipped off the siding, and the tiny pig-eyed windows were boarded over—kids had broken out all the glass years ago. The grass and bushes of the meadow had grown up around it, closing it in, made it look like the house was sinking into the earth.

Wayne had designed the house himself, not long after he and Jenny got married; he'd had no idea what he was doing, but—he'd told Larry, showing him the plans—he wanted the house to be unique. *Like me and Jenny,* he'd said, beaming.

Jenny had hated the house. She'd told Larry so, at her and Wayne's housewarming dinner.

It's bad enough I have to live out here in the middle of nowhere, she'd said under her breath, while Wayne chattered to Larry's wife, Emily, in the living room. *But at least he could have built us a house you can look at.*

Larry had told her, *He did it because he loves you. He tried.*

Don't remind me, Jenny had said, swallowing wine. *Why did I ever agree to this?*

The house?

The house, the marriage. God, Larry, you name it.

When she'd said it she hadn't sounded bitter. She looked at Larry as though he might have an answer, but he didn't—he'd never been able to see Jenny and Wayne together, from the moment they started dating in college, all the way up to the wedding; *I do,* Wayne had said, his cheeks wet, and Jenny's face had gone all soft, and Larry had felt a pang for both of them. At the housewarming party he told her, *It'll get better,* and felt right away that he'd lied, and Jenny made a face that showed she knew he had, before both of them turned to watch Wayne demonstrate the dimmer switch in the living room for Emily.

The front door, Larry saw now, was swinging open— some folks he'd chased out two weeks ago had jimmied it, and the lock hadn't worked right afterward. The open door and the black gap behind it made the house look even meaner than it was—like a baby crying. Patricia Pike had said that, when she first saw the place. Larry wondered if she'd put it into her book.

She had sent him a copy, back in July just before its release. The book was called *All Through the House*—the cover showed a Christmas tree with little skulls as ornaments. Pike had signed it for him: *To Larry, even though I know you prefer fiction. Cheers, Patricia.* He flipped to the index and saw his name with a lot of numbers by it, and then he looked at the glossy plates at the book's center. One was a map of Prescott County, showing the county road, and an X in the Sullivan woods, where the house stood. The next page showed a floor plan of the house, with bodies drawn in outline, and dotted lines following Wayne's path from room to room. One plate showed a Sears portrait of the entire family smiling together, plus graduation photos of Wayne and Jenny. Pike had included a picture of Larry, too—taken on the day of the murders—that showed him pointing off to the edge of the picture while EMTs brought one of the boys out the front door, wrapped in a blanket. Larry looked like he was running—his arms were blurry—which was odd. They'd brought no one out of the house alive. He'd have had no need to rush.

The last chapter was titled "Why?" Larry had read that part all the way through. Every rumor and half-baked theory Patricia Pike had heard while in town, she'd included, worded to make it sound like she'd done thinking no one else ever had.

Wayne was in debt. Wayne was jealous because maybe Jenny was sleeping around. Wayne had been seeing a doctor about migraines. Wayne was a man who had never matured past childhood. Wayne lived in a fantasy world inhabited by the perfect family he could never have. *Once again the reluctance of the Sheriff's department and the townspeople to discuss their nightmares freely hinders us from understanding a man like Wayne Sullivan, from preventing others from killing as he has killed, from beginning the healing closure this community so badly needs.*

Larry had tossed his copy in a drawer, and hoped everyone else would do the same.

But then the book was a success—all Patricia Pike's books were. And not long after that the lunatics had started to come out to the house. And then, today, Larry had gotten a call from the mayor.

You're not going to like this, the mayor had told him.

Larry hadn't. A cable channel wanted to film a documentary based on the book. They were sending a camera crew at the end of the month, near Christmastime—for authenticity's sake. They wanted to film in the house, and of course they wanted to talk to everybody all over again, Larry first and foremost.

Larry took a bottle of whiskey from underneath the front seat of the cruiser, and, watching the Sullivan house through the windshield, he unscrewed the cap and drank a swallow. His eyes watered, but he got it down and drank another. The booze spread in his throat and belly, made him want to sit very still behind the wheel, to keep drinking. A lot of nights he would. But instead he opened the door and climbed out of the cruiser.

The meadow and the house were mostly blocked from the wind, but the air had a bite to it all the same. He hunched his shoulders, then opened the trunk and took out one of the gas cans he'd filled back at the station, and a few rolls of newspaper. He walked to the open doorway of the house, his head ducked, careful with his feet in the shadows and the tall grass.

He smelled the house's insides even before he stepped onto the porch—a smell like the underside of a wet log. He clicked on his flashlight and shone it into the doorway, across the splotched and crumbling walls. He stepped inside. Something living scuttled out of the way: a raccoon, or a possum. Maybe even a fox; Wayne had once told him the woods was full of them, but in all the times Larry had been out here he'd never seen any.

He glanced over the walls. Some new graffiti had appeared: KILL 'EM ALL was spray-painted on the wall where, once, the Christmas tree had leaned. The older messages were still in place. One read: HEY WAYNE, DO MY HOUSE NEXT. Beside a ragged, spackled-over depression in the same wall, someone had painted an arrow and the word BRAINS. Smaller messages were written in marker—the sorts of things high-school kids write: initials, graduation years, witless sex puns, pictures of genitalia.

And—sitting right there in the corner—was a copy of *All Through the House,* its pages swollen with moisture.

Larry rubbed his temple. The book was as good a place to start as any.

He kicked the book to the center of the living-room floor, and then splashed it with gas. Nearby was a crevice where the carpet had torn and separated. He rolled the newspapers up and wedged them underneath the carpet, then doused them, too. Then he drizzled gasoline in a line from both the book and the papers to the front door. From the edge of the stoop he tossed arcs of gas onto the door and the jamb until the can was empty.

He stood on the porch, smelling the gas, and gasping—he was horribly out of shape. His head was throbbing. He squeezed the lighter in his hand until the pain subsided.

Larry was not much for religion, but he tried a prayer anyway: *Lord, keep them. I know you have been. And please let this work.* But the prayer sounded pitiful in his head, so he stopped it.

He lit a clump of newspaper, and, once it had bloomed, touched it to the base of the door.

The fire took the door right away, and flickered in a curling line across the carpet to the book and the papers. He could see them burning through the doorway, before thick gray smoke obscured his view. After a few minutes the flames began to gutter. He wasn't much of an arsonist—it was wet in there. He retrieved the other gas can from the trunk and shoved a rolled-up cone of newspaper into the nozzle. He made sure he had a clear throw, and then lit the paper and heaved the can inside the house. It exploded right away, with a thump, and orange light bloomed up one of the inside walls. Outside, the flames from the door flared, steadied, then began to climb onto the siding.

Larry went back to the cruiser and pulled the bottle of whiskey from beneath his seat. He thought about Jenny; he thought about camping in the meadow as a boy with Wayne. He had seen this house being built; he'd seen it lived in and died in. Larry had guessed he might feel a certain joy, watching it destroyed, but instead his throat caught. Somewhere down the line, this had gotten to be his house. He'd thought that for a while now: the township owned the Sullivan house, but really, Wayne had passed it on to *him*.

An image of himself drifted into his head—it had come a few times tonight. He saw himself walking into the burning house, climbing the stairs. In his head he did this without pain, even while fire found his clothing, the bullets in his gun. He would sit upstairs in Jenny's sewing room and close his eyes, and it wouldn't take long.

He sniffled and pinched his nose. That was a bunch of horseshit. He'd seen people who'd been burned to death. He'd die, all right, but he'd go screaming and flailing. At the thought of it his arms and legs grew heavy; his skin prickled.

Larry put the cruiser in reverse and backed it slowly away from the house, out of the drive and onto the track. He watched for ten minutes as the fire grew, and tried not to think about anything, to see only the flames. Then he got the call from Lynn at dispatch.

Sheriff?

Copy, he said.

Ned called in. He says it looks like there's a fire out at the Sullivan place.

A fire?

That's what he said. He sees a fire in the woods.

My my my, Larry said. I'm on old 52 just past Mackey. I'll get there quick as I can and take a look.

He waited another ten minutes. Flames leaked around the boards on the windows. The downstairs ceiling caught. Long shadows shifted through the trees; the woods came alive, swaying and dancing. Something alive and aflame shot out the front door—a rabbit? It zigged and zagged across the turn-around, and then headed toward him. For a moment Larry thought it had fled under his car, and he put his hand on the door handle—but whatever it was cut away for the woods to his right. He saw it come to rest in a patch of scrub; smoke rose from the bush in wisps.

Dispatch? Larry said.

Copy.

I'm at the Sullivan house. It's on fire, all right. Better get the trucks out here.

Twenty minutes later two fire trucks arrived, advancing carefully down the track. The men got out and stood beside Larry, looking over the house, now brightly ablaze from top to bottom. They rolled the trucks past Larry's cruiser and sprayed the grass around the house and the trees nearby. Then all of them watched the house burn and crumble into its foundation, and no one said much of anything.

Larry left them to the rubble just before dawn. He drove home and tried to wash the smell of smoke out of his hair, and then lay down next to Emily, who didn't stir. He lay awake for a while, trying to convince himself he'd actually done it, and then trying to convince himself he hadn't.

When he finally slept, he saw the house on fire, except that in his dream there were people still in it: Jenny Sullivan in the upstairs window, holding her youngest boy to her and shouting Larry's name, screaming it, while Larry sat in his car, tugging at the handle, unable even to shout back to her, to tell her it was locked.

1985

Patricia Pike had known from the start that Sheriff Thompkins was reluctant to work with her. Now, driving in his cruiser with him down empty back roads to the Sullivan house, she wondered if what she'd thought was reticence was instead real anger. Thompkins had been civil enough when she spoke with him on the phone a month earlier, but since meeting him this morning in his small, cluttered office—she'd seen janitors with better quarters—he'd been scowling, sullen, rarely bothering to look her in the eye.

She was used to this treatment from policemen. A lot of them had read her books, two of which had uncovered information the police hadn't found themselves. Her second book, *On a Darkling Plain,* had overturned a conviction. Policemen hated being shown up, even the best of them—and she suspected from the look of Thompkins's office that he didn't operate on the cutting edge of law enforcement.

Thompkins was tall and hunched, perhaps muscular once, but now going to fat, with a gray cop's mustache and a single thick fold under his chin. He was only forty—two years younger than she was—but he looked much older. He kept a wedding photo on his desk; in it he had the broad-shouldered, thick-necked look of an offensive lineman. Unsurprising, this; a lot of country cops she spoke to had played football. His wife, next to him, was a little ghost of a woman, dark-eyed, smiling what Patricia suspected was one of her last big smiles.

Patricia had asked Thompkins a few questions in his office, chatty ones designed to put him at ease. She'd also flirted, a little; she was good-looking, and sometimes that worked. But even then Thompkins answered flatly, in the sort of language police fell back on in their reports. *It was at this point in time that I, uh, approached the scene.* He looked often at his watch, but she wasn't fooled. Kinslow, Indiana, had only six hundred residents, and Thompkins wasn't about to convince her he was a busy man.

Now Thompkins drove along the interminable gravel roads to the Sullivan woods with one hand on the wheel and the other brushing the corners of his mustache. Finally she couldn't stand it.

Do I make you uncomfortable, Sheriff?

He widened his eyes and he shifted his shoulders, then coughed. He said, Well, I'll be honest. I guess I'd rather not do this.

I can't imagine you would, she said. Best to give him the sympathy he so obviously wanted.

He told her, If the mayor wasn't such a fan of yours, I wouldn't be out here.

She smiled at him, just a little. She said, I've talked to Wayne's parents; I know you were close to Wayne and Jenny. It can't be easy to do this.

No, ma'am. That it is not.

Thompkins turned the cruiser onto a smaller paved road—on either side of them was nothing but fields, empty and stubbled with old broken cornstalks, and blocky stands of woods, so monochromatic they could be pencil drawings.

Patricia asked, You all went to high school together, didn't you?

Abington, class of '64. Jenny was a year behind me and Wayne.

Did you become friends in high school?

That's when I got to know Jenny. Wayne and I knew each other since we were little. Our mothers taught together at the elementary school.

Thompkins glanced at Patricia. He said, You know all this already. You drawing out the witness?

She smiled, genuinely grateful. So he had a brain in there after all. It seems I have to, she said.

He sighed—a big man's sigh, long and weary—and said, I have nothing against you personally, Ms. Pike. But I don't like the kind of books you write, and I don't like coming out here.

I do appreciate your help. I know it's hard.

Why this case? he asked her. Why us?

She tried to think of the right words, something that wouldn't offend him.

Well, I suppose I was just *drawn* to it. My agent sends me clippings about cases, things she thinks I might want to write about. The murders were so . . . brutal, and they happened on Christmas Eve. And since it happened in the country, it never made the news much; people don't know about it—not in the big cities, anyway. There's also kind of a—a fairy-tale quality to it, the house out in the middle of the forest—you know?

Uh-huh, Thompkins said.

And then there's the mystery of *why*. There's a certain type of case I specialize in—crimes with a component of unsolved mystery. I'm intrigued that Wayne didn't leave a note. You're the only person he gave any information to, and even then—

He didn't say much.

No. I know, I've read the transcript already. But that's my answer, I suppose: there's a lot to write about.

Thompkins stroked his mustache and turned at a stop sign.

They were now to the right of an enormous tract of woods, much larger than the other stands nearby. Patricia had seen it growing on the horizon, almost like a rain cloud, and now, close up, she saw it was at least a mile square. The sheriff slowed and turned off the road, stopping in front of a low metal gate that blocked a rutted dirt track; it dipped away from the road and into the bare trees. A NO TRESPASSING sign hung from the gate's center. It had been fired upon a number of times; some of the bullet holes had yet to rust. Thompkins said, Excuse me, and got out. He bent over a giant padlock and then swung the gate inward. He got back behind the wheel, drove the cruiser through without shutting his door, then clambered out again and locked the gate behind them.

Keeps the kids out, he told her, shifting the cruiser into gear. Means the only way in is on foot. A lot of them won't walk it, at least when it's cold like this.

This is a big woods.

Probably the biggest between Indy and Lafayette. 'Course no one's ever measured, but that's—that's what Wayne always told me.

Patricia caught his drop in volume, glanced over to see his mouth droop.

The track curved right, then left. The world they were in now was almost a sepia-toned old film: bare winter branches, patches of old snow on the ground, pools of black muck. Patricia had grown up in Chicago, but had relatives on a farm downstate; she knew what a tangle those woods would be.

What a curious place for a house. She opened her notebook and wrote in shorthand.

This land belongs to Wayne's family? she asked.

It used to. Township owns it now. Wayne had put the land up as collateral for the house, and then when he died his folks didn't pay on the loan. I don't blame them for that. The bank sold it to the town a few years back, on the cheap. The town might sell it someday, but no one really wants farmland anymore. None of the farmers around here can afford to develop it. An ag company would have to buy it. In the meantime I keep an eye on the place.

Thompkins slowed, and the car jounced into and out of a deep rut. He said, Me, I'd like to see the whole thing plowed under. But I don't make those choices.

She wrote his words down.

They rounded a last bend in the track, and there, in front of them, was a meadow, and in the center of it the Sullivan house. Patricia had seen pictures of it, but here in person it was much smaller than she'd imagined. She pulled her camera out of her bag.

It's ugly, she said.

That's the truth, Thompkins said, and put the car into park.

The house was a two-story of some indeterminate style—not quite a Cape Cod, but probably closer to that than anything. The roof was pitched, but seemed . . . too small, too flat for the rest of the house. The face suggested by its windows and front door—flanked by faux half-columns—was that of a mongoloid: all chin and mouth, and no forehead. Or like a baby crying. It had been painted an olive color, and now the paint was flaking. The track continued around behind the house, where a two-car garage jutted off at right angles, too big in proportion to the house.

Wayne drew up the plans, Thompkins said. He wanted to do it himself.

What did Jenny think of it? Do you know?

She joked about it. Not so Wayne could hear.

Would he have been angry?

No. Sad. He'd wanted a house out here since we were kids. He loved these woods.

Thompkins undid his seat belt. Then he said, I guess he knew the house was a mess, but he . . . it's hard to say. We all pretended it was fine.

Why?

Some folks, you just want to protect their feelings. He wanted us all to be as excited as he was. It wouldn't have occurred to us to be . . . blunt with him. You know that type of person? Kind of like a puppy?

Yes.

Well, Thompkins said, that was Wayne. You want to go in?

The interior of the house was dark—the windows had been boarded over with sheets of plywood. Thompkins had brought two electric lanterns; he set one just inside the door and held the other in his hand. He walked inside and then motioned for Patricia to follow.

The inside of the house stank—an old, abandoned smell of mildew and rot. The carpeting—what was left of it, anyway—seemed to be on the verge of becoming mud, or a kind of algae, and held the stink. Patricia had been in morgues and, for one of her books, had accompanied a homicide detective in Detroit to murder sites. She knew what death—dead human beings—smelled like. That smell might have been in the

Sullivan house, underneath everything else, but she couldn't be sure. It *ought* to have been.

Patricia could see no furniture. Ragged holes gaped in the ceilings where light fixtures might have been. Behind the sheriff was a staircase, rising up into darkness, and to the right of it an entrance into what seemed to be the kitchen.

Shit, Thompkins said.

What?

He held the lantern close to the wall, in the room to the right of the foyer. There was a spot on the wall there, a ragged, spackled patch. Someone had spray-painted an arrow pointing at it, and the word BRAINS.

Thompkins turned a circle, with the lantern held out. He was looking down, and she followed his gaze. She saw cigarette butts, beer cans.

Kids come in here from Abington, Thompkins said. I run them off every now and then. Sometimes it's adults, even. Have to come out and see for themselves, I guess. The kids say it's haunted.

That happens in a lot of places, Patricia said.

Huh, Thompkins said.

She took photos of the rooms, the flashbulb's light dazzling in the dark.

I guess you want the tour, Thompkins said.

I do. She put a hand on his arm, and his eyes widened. She said, as cheerfully as she could, Do you mind if I tape our conversation?

Do you have to? Thompkins asked, looking up from her hand.

It will help me quote you better.

Well. I suppose.

Patricia put a tape into her hand-held recorder, then nod-ded at him.

Thompkins lifted the lantern up. The light gleamed off his dark eyes. His mouth hung open, just a little, and when he breathed out a thin line of steam appeared in front of the lantern. He looked different. Not sad, not anymore. Maybe, Patricia thought, she saw in him what she was feeling—which was a thrill, what a teenager feels in front of a campfire, know-ing a scary story is coming. She reminded herself that actual people had died here, that she was in a place of tremendous sadness, but all the same she couldn't help herself. Her books sold well because she wrote them well, with fervency, and she wrote that way because she loved to be in forbidden places like this; she loved learning the secrets no one wanted to say. Just as, she suspected, Sheriff Thompkins wanted deep in his heart to tell them to her. Secrets were too big for people to hold—that was what she found in her research, time after time. Secrets had their own agendas.

Patricia looked at Thompkins, turning a smile into a quick nod.

All right then, the sheriff said. This way.

Here's the kitchen.

Wayne shot Jenny first, in here. But that shot didn't kill her. You can't tell because of the boards, but the kitchen window looks over the driveway, in front of the garage. Wayne shot her through the window. Jenny was looking out at Wayne, we know that, because the bullet went in through the front of her right shoulder and out the back, and we know he was outside because the glass was broken, and because his footprints were still in the snow when we got here—there was no wind that night. Wayne's car was in front of the garage. What he did was, he got out of the driver's side door and went around to the trunk and opened it—best guess is the gun was in there; he'd purchased it that night, at a shop in Muncie. Then he went around to the passenger door and stood there for a while; the snow was all tramped down. We think he was loading the gun. Or maybe he was talking himself into doing it. I don't know.

We figure he braced on the top of the car and shot her from where he stood. The security light over the garage was burned out when we got here, so from inside, with the kitchen lights on, Jenny wouldn't have been able to see what he was doing—not very clearly, if at all. I don't know why she was turned around looking out the window at him. Maybe he honked the horn. I also don't know if he aimed to kill her or wound her, but my feeling is he went for a wounding shot. It's about twenty feet from where he stood to where she stood, so it wasn't that hard a shot for him to make, and he made most of his others that night. Now down here—

[The sheriff's pointing to a spot on the linoleum, slightly stained, see photos.]

Excuse me?

[Don't mind me, Sheriff. Just keep talking.]

Oh. All right then.

Well, Jenny—once she was shot, she fell and struggled. There was a lot of blood; we think she probably, uh, bled out for seven or eight minutes while Wayne . . . while Wayne killed the others. She tried to pull herself to the living room; there were . . . smears on the floor consistent with her doing that.

[We're back in the living room; we're facing the front door.]

After he'd shot Jenny, he walked around the east side of the house to the front door here. He could have come in the garage into the kitchen, but he didn't. I'm not sure what happened from there exactly. But here's what I think.

The grandmother—Mrs. Murray—and Danny, the four-year-old, were in the living room, in here, next to the tree. She was reading to him; he liked to be read to, and a book of nursery rhymes was open facedown on the couch. The grandmother was infirm—she had diabetes and couldn't walk so well. She was sitting on the couch still when we found her. He shot her once through the head, probably from the doorway.

[We're looking at the graffiti wall, see photos.]

But by this time Jenny would have been . . . she would have been screaming, so we know Wayne didn't catch the rest of them unawares. Jenny might have called out that Daddy was home before Wayne shot her; hell, this place is in the middle of nowhere, and it was nighttime, so they all knew a car had pulled up. What I'm saying is, I'm guessing there was a lot of confusion at this juncture, a lot of shouting. There's a bullet hole at waist height on the wall opposite the front door. My best guess is that Danny ran to the door and was in front of it when Wayne opened it. He could have been looking into the kitchen, at his . . . at his mother, or at the door. I think Wayne took a shot at him from the doorway and missed. Danny ran into the living room, and since Mrs. Murray hadn't tried to struggle to her feet, Wayne shot her next. He took one shot and hit her. Then he shot Danny. Danny was behind the Christmas tree; he probably ran there to hide. Wayne took three shots into the tree, and one of them, or I guess Danny's struggles, knocked it sideways off its base. But he got Danny, shot his own boy in the head just over his left ear.

[We're looking through a door off the dining room; inside is a small room maybe ten by nine, see photos.]

This was a playroom. Mr. Murray and Alex, the two-year-old, were in it. Mr. Murray reacted pretty quick to the shots, for a guy his age—but he was a vet, and he hunted, so he probably would have been moving at the sound of the first gunshot. He opened that window—

[A boarded window on the rear of the house, see photos.]

—which, ah, used to look out behind the garage, and he dropped Alex through it into the snowdrift beneath. Then he got himself through. Though not without some trouble. The autopsy showed he had a broken wrist, which we figure he broke getting out. But it's still a remarkable thing. I hope you write that. Mr. Murray tried his best to save Alex.

[I'll certainly note it. Wayne's parents also mentioned him.]

Well, good. Good.

Sam and Alex got about fifty yards away, toward the woods. Wayne probably went to the doorway of the playroom and saw the window open. He ran back outside, around the west corner of the house, and shot Sam in the back right about where the garden was. There wasn't a lot of light, but the house lights were all on, and if I remember right the bodies were just about at the limit of what you could see from that corner. So Sam almost made it out of range. But I don't know if he could have got very far once he was in the trees. He was strong for a guy his age, but it was snowy, and neither he or the boy had coats, and it was about ten degrees out that night. Plus Wayne meant to kill everybody, and I think he would have tracked them.

Sam died instantly. Wayne got him in the heart. He fell and the boy didn't go any farther. Wayne walked about fifty feet out and fired a few shots, and one of them got Alex through the neck. Wayne never went any closer. Either he knew he'd killed them both, or he figured the cold would finish the job for him if he hadn't. Maybe he couldn't look. I don't know.

[We're in the living room again, at the foot of the stairs.]

He went back inside and shut the door behind him. I think he was confronted by the dog, Kodiak, on the stairs, there on the landing. He shot the dog, probably from where you're standing. Then—

[We're looking into the kitchen again.]

—Wayne went to the kitchen and shot—he shot Jenny a second time. The killing shot. We found her facedown. Wayne stood over her and fired from a distance of less than an inch. The bullet went in the back of her head just above the neck. He held her down with his boot on her shoulder. We know because she was wearing a white sweater and he left a bloodstain on it that held the imprint of his boot sole.

He called my house at 9:16. You've seen the transcript.

[How did he sound? On the phone?]

Oh, Jesus. I'd say upset, but not hysterical. Like he was out of breath, I guess.

[Will you tell me again what he said?]

Hell. Do you really need me to repeat it?

[If you can.]

Well . . . he said, Larry, it's Wayne. I said, Hey Wayne, Merry Christmas, or something like that. And then he said, No time, Larry, this is a business call. And I said, What's wrong? And he said, Larry, I killed Jenny and the kids and my in-laws, and as soon as I hang up, I'm going to kill myself. And I said something like, Are you joking? And then he hung up. That's it. I got in the cruiser and drove up here as fast as I could.

[You were first on the scene?]

Yeah. Yeah, I was. I called it in on the way, it took me a while to—to remember. I saw blood through the front windows, and I called for backup as soon as I did. I went inside. I looked around . . . and saw . . . everyone but Sam and Alex. It took me . . .

[Sheriff?]

No, it's all right. I wasn't . . . I wasn't in great shape, which I guess you can imagine, but after a couple of minutes I found the window open in the playroom. I was out with—with Sam and Alex when the deputies arrived.

[But you found Wayne first?]

Right, yes. I looked for him right off. For all I knew he was still alive.

[Where was he?]

Down in here.

[We're looking into a door opening off the kitchen; it looks like—the basement?]

Yeah. Wayne killed himself in his workroom. That was his favorite place, where he went for privacy. We used to drink down there, play darts. He sat in a corner and shot himself with a small handgun, which he purchased along with the rifle. It was the only shot he fired from it. He'd shut the basement door behind him.

. . . You want to see down there?

———

THEY SAT for a while in the cruiser, afterward. Thompkins had brought a thermos of coffee, which touched Patricia; the coffee was terrible, but at least it was warm. She held the cup in her hands in front of the dashboard vents. Thompkins chewed his thumbnail and looked at the house.

Why did he do it? she asked him.

Hmm?

Why did Wayne do it?

I don't know.

You don't have any theories?

No.

He said it quickly, an obvious lie. Patricia watched his face and said, I called around after talking with his parents. Wayne was way behind on his loan payments. If he hadn't worked at the bank already, this place would have been repossessed.

Maybe, Thompkins said, and sipped his coffee. But half the farms you see out here are in the hole, and no one's slaughtered their entire family over it.

Patricia watched him while he said this. Thompkins kept his big face neutral, but he didn't look at her. His ears were pink with cold.

Wayne's mother, she said, told me she thought that Jenny might have had affairs.

Yeah. I heard that, too.

Any truth to it?

Adultery's not against the law. So I don't concern myself with it.

But surely you've heard something.

Well, Ms. Pike, I have the same answer as before. People have been sleeping around on each other out here for a lot longer than I've had this job, and no one ever killed their family over it.

Thompkins put on his seat belt.

Besides, he said, if you were a man who'd slept with Jenny Sullivan, would *you* say anything about it? You wouldn't, not now. So no, I don't know for sure. And frankly, I wouldn't tell you if I did.

Why?

Because I knew Jenny, and she was a good woman. She was my prom date, for Christ's sake. I stood up at her and Wayne's wedding. Jenny was always straight, and she was smart. If she had an affair, that was her business. But it's not mine now, and it's not yours.

It would be motive, Patricia said softly.

I took the bodies out of that house, Thompkins said, putting the cruiser into reverse. I took my friends out. I felt their necks to see if they were alive. I saw what Wayne did. There's no reason good enough. No one could have wronged him enough to make him do what he did. I don't care what it was.

He turned the cruiser around; the trees rushed by, and Patricia gripped her coffee with both hands to keep it from spilling. She'd heard speeches like this before. Someone's brains get opened up, and there's always some backcountry cop who puts his hand to his heart and pretends the poor soul still has any privacy.

There's always a reason, she said.

Thompkins smirked without humor; the cruiser bounced up and down.

Then I'm sure you'll come up with something, he said.

December 25, 1975

In the evening, just past sundown, Larry went out to the Sullivan house again. He and the staties had finished with the scene earlier in the day—there hadn't been much to investigate, really; Wayne had confessed in his phone call, yet Larry had told his deputies to take pictures anyway, to collect what evidence they could. And then all day reporters had come out for pictures, and some of the townspeople had stopped by to gawk, or to ask if anything needed doing, so Larry decided to keep the house under guard. Truth be told, he and the men needed something to do; watching the house was better than fielding questions in town.

When Larry pulled up in front of the house, his deputy, Troy Bowen, was sitting behind the wheel of his cruiser by the garage, reading a paperback. Larry flashed his lights, and Bowen got out and ambled over to Larry's car, hands in his armpits.

Hey Larry, he said. What's up?

Slow night, Larry said—which was true enough. He said, Go get dinner. I'll cover until Albie gets here.

That's not till midnight, Bowen said, but his face was open and grateful.

I might as well be out here. It's all I'm thinking about anyway.

Yeah, that's what I thought. But I don't mind saying it gives me the willies. You're welcome to it.

When Bowen's cruiser was gone, Larry stood for a moment on the front stoop, hands in his pockets. Crime-scene tape was strung over the doorway, in a big haphazard X; Bowen had done it after the bodies were removed, sniffling and red-eyed. It had been his first murder scene. The electricity was still on; the little fake lantern hanging over the door was shining. Larry took a couple of breaths and then fumbled out a copy of the house key. He unlocked the door, ducked under the caution tape, and went inside.

He turned on the living-room light and there everything was, as he'd left it this afternoon. His heart thumped. What else had he expected? That it would all be gone? That it hadn't really happened? It had. Here were the outlines. The bloodstains on the living-room carpet, and on the landing. The light from the living room just shone into the kitchen; he could see the dark swirls on the linoleum, too. Already a smell was in the air. The furnace was still on, and the blood and the smaller pieces of remains were starting to turn. The place would go bad if Wayne's folks didn't have the house cleaned up soon. Larry didn't want to have that talk with them, but he'd call them tomorrow—he knew a service in Indianapolis that took care of things like this. All the same he turned off the thermostat.

He asked himself why he cared. Surely no one would ever live in this place again. What did it matter?

But it did, somehow.

He walked into the family room. The tree was canted sideways, knocked partway out of its base. He went to the wall behind it, stepping over stains, careful not to disturb anything. The lights on the tree were still plugged into the wall outlet. He squatted, straddling a collapsing pile of presents, then leaned forward and pulled the cord. The tree might go up, especially with its trunk out of water.

Larry looked up at the wall and put his hand over his mouth; he'd been trying to avoid looking right at anything, but he'd done it now. Just a few inches in front of him, on the wall, was the spot where Danny had been shot. The bullet had gone right through his head. He'd given Danny a couple of rides in the cruiser, and now here the boy was: matted blood, strands of hair—

He breathed through his fingers and looked down at the presents. He'd seen blood before, he'd seen all kinds of deaths, mostly on the sides of highways, but twice because of bullets to the head. He told himself to pretend it was no different. He tried to focus, made himself pick out words on the presents' tags.

No help there. Wayne had bought gifts for them all. *To Danny, From Daddy. To Mommy, From Daddy.* All written in Wayne's blocky letters. Jesus H.

Larry knew he should go, just go out and sit in his cruiser until midnight, but he couldn't help himself. He picked up one of Jenny's presents, a small one that had slid almost completely under the couch, and sat down in the dining room with the box on his lap. He shouldn't do this, it was wrong, but really—who was left to know that a present was missing? Larry wasn't family, but he was close enough—he had some rights here. Who, besides him, would ever unwrap them? The presents belonged to Wayne's parents now. Would they want to see what their son had bought for the family he'd butchered? Not if they had any sense at all.

Larry went into the kitchen, looking down only to step where the rusty smears weren't. Under the sink he found garbage bags; he took one and shook it open.

He sat back down in the dining room. The gift was only a few inches square, wrapped in gold foil paper. Larry slid a finger under a taped seam, then carefully tore the paper away. Inside was a small, light cardboard box, also taped. He could see Wayne's fingerprint caught in the tape glue. He slit the tape with his thumbnail, then held the lid lightly between his palms and shook out the container onto his lap.

Wayne had bought Jenny lingerie. A silk camisole and matching panty, in red, folded small.

Jenny liked red. Her skin took to it, somehow; she was always a little pink. The bust of the camisole was transparent, lacy. She would look impossible in it. That was Jenny, though. She could slip on a T-shirt and look like your best pal. Or she could put on a little lipstick and do her hair and wear a dress, and she'd look like she ought to be up on a movie screen someplace. Larry ran his fingers over the silk. He wondered if Wayne had touched the lingerie this way, too, and what he might have been thinking when he did. Did he know, when he bought it? When had he found out?

Don't be coy with me, Wayne had said, on the phone. He'd called Larry at his house; Emily would have picked up if her hands weren't soapy with dishwater. Larry watched her scrub at the roast pan while he listened. *I know,* Wayne said. *I followed you to the motel. I just shot her, Larry. I shot her in the head.*

Larry dumped the lingerie and the wrappings into the garbage bag.

He took the bag upstairs with him, turning off the living-room light behind him and turning on the one in the stairwell. He had to cling tight to the banister to get past the spot where Wayne had shot the dog—a big husky named Kodiak, rheumy-eyed and arthritic. Kodiak didn't care much for the children, who tried to uncurl his tail, so most of the time he slept in a giant basket in the sewing room upstairs. He must have jumped awake at the sound of gunshots. He would have smelled what was wrong right away. Jenny had gotten him as a puppy during high school—Larry had been dating her then; he remembered sitting on the kitchen floor with her at her parents' house, the dog skidding happily back and forth between them. Kodiak had grown old loving Jenny. He must have stood on the landing and growled and barked at Wayne, before Wayne shot him. Larry had seen dogs driven vicious by bloodshed; it turned on switches in their heads. He hoped Kodiak had at least made a lunge for Wayne, before getting shot.

Larry walked into Wayne and Jenny's bedroom. He'd been in it before. Just once. Wayne had gone to Chicago on business, and the kids were at a friend's, and Jenny called Larry—at the station. She told dispatch she thought she saw someone in the woods, maybe a hunter, and would the sheriff swing by and run him off? That was smart of her. That way Larry could go in broad daylight and smoke in the living room and drink a cup of coffee, and no one would say boo.

And, as it turned out, Jenny could set his coffee down on the dining-room table, and then waggle her fingers at him from the foot of the stairs. And he could get hard just at the sight of her doing it, Jenny Sullivan smiling at him in sweatpants and an old T-shirt.

And upstairs she could say, *Not the bed.*

They'd stood together in front of the mirror over the low bureau, Jenny bent forward, both of them with their pants pulled down mid-thigh, and Larry gritting his teeth just to last a few minutes. Halfway through he took his hat from the bureau top—he'd brought it upstairs with them and couldn't remember why—and set it on her head, and she'd looked up and met his eyes in the mirror, and both of them were laugh-

ing when they started to come. Jenny's laugh turned into
something like a shriek. He said, *I never heard you sound like that
before,* and Jenny said, *I've never sounded like that before. Not in this
room.* She said, *This house has never heard anything like it.* And
when she said it, it was like the house was Wayne, like somehow he'd walked in. They both turned serious and sheepish—
Jenny's mouth got small and grim—and they'd separated,
pulled their clothes up, pulled themselves together.

Now Larry went through the drawers of the bureau, trying to remember what Jenny wore that day. The blue sweatpants. The Butler Bulldogs shirt. Bright pink socks—he
remembered her feet, going up the stairs ahead of him. He
found a pair that seemed right, rolled tight together. Silk
panties, robin's-egg blue. He found a fluffy red thing that she
used to keep her ponytail together. Little fake-ruby earrings in
a ceramic seashell. He smelled through the perfumes next to
her vanity and found one he liked and remembered, and
sprayed it on the clothes, heavily . . . it would fade over time,
and if it was too strong now, in ten years it wouldn't be.

He packed all of it into the plastic bag from the kitchen.

Then he sat at the foot of the bed, eyes closed, for a long
few minutes. He could hear his own breath. His eyes stung.
He looked at the backs of his hands and concentrated on
keeping steady. He thought about the sound of Wayne's voice
when he called. *I left her sexy for you, Larry.*

That made him feel like something other than weeping.

When he was composed he looked through the desks in
the bedroom and the drawers of all the bed tables. He glanced
at his watch: it was only eight.

He walked down the hall into the sewing room, and sat
at Jenny's sewing table. The room smelled like Kodiak—an

old-dog smell, a mixture of the animal and the drops he had to have in his ears. Pictures of the children and Jenny's parents dotted the walls. Wayne's bespectacled head peeped out of a few, too—but not very many, when you looked hard.

Larry rooted through a drawer under the table. Then he opened Jenny's sewing basket.

He hadn't known what he was looking for, but in the sewing basket he found it. He opened a little pillowed silk box full of spare buttons, and inside, pinned to the lid, was a slip of paper. He knew it right away from the green emboss-ment—it was from a stationery pad he'd found, at the motel he and Jenny had sometimes used in Westover. He unfolded it. His hands shook, and he was crying now—she'd kept it, she'd kept something.

This was from a year ago, on a Thursday afternoon; Wayne had taken the boys to see his folks. Larry met Jenny at the motel after she was done at the school. Jenny wanted to sleep for an hour or two after they made love, but Larry was due home, and it was better for them to come and go sepa-rately anyway, so he dressed quietly while she dozed. He'd looked at her asleep for a long time, and then he'd written a note. He remembered thinking at the time: *evidence*. But he couldn't help it. Some things needed to be put down in writ-ing; some things you had to sign your name to, if they were going to mean anything at all.

So Larry found the stationery pad, and wrote, *My sweet Jenny,* and got teary when he did. He sat on the bed next to her, and leaned over and kissed her warm ear. She stirred and murmured without opening her eyes. He finished the note and left it by her hand.

A week later he asked her, *Did you get my note?*

She said, *No.* But then she kissed him, and smiled, and put her small hands on his cheeks. *Of course I did, you dummy.*

He'd been able to remember the words on the note—he'd run them over and over in his head—but now he opened the folded paper and read them again: *My sweet Jenny, I have trouble with these things but I wouldn't do this if I didn't love you.*

And then he read on. He dropped the note onto the table-top and stared at it, his hand clamped over his mouth.

He'd signed it *Yours, Larry*—but his name had been crossed out. And over it had been written, in shaky block letters: *Wayne.*

December 24, 1975

If Jenny ever had to tell someone—a stranger, the sympathetic man she imagined coming to the door sometimes, kind of a traveling psychologist and granter of divorces all wrapped up in one—about what it was like to be married to Wayne Sullivan, she would have told him about tonight. She'd say, *Wayne called me at six, after my parents got here for dinner, after I'd gotten the boys into their good clothes for the Christmas picture, to tell me he wouldn't be home for another couple of hours. He had some last-minute shopping, he said.*

Jenny was washing dishes. The leftovers from the turkey had already been sealed in Tupperware and put into the refrigerator. From the living room she could hear Danny with her mother; her father was with Alex in the playroom—she could hear Alex squealing every few minutes, or shouting nonsense in his two-year-old singsong. It was 8:40. *Almost three hours later,* she told the man in her head, *and no sign of him.*

And that's Wayne. There's a living room full of presents. All anyone wants of him now is his presence at the table. And he thinks he hasn't done enough, and so our dinner is ruined. It couldn't be more typical.

Her mother was reading to Danny; she was a school-teacher, too, and Jenny could hear the careful cadences, the little emphases that meant she was acting out the story with her voice. Her mother had been heroic tonight. She was a master of keeping up appearances, and here, by God, was a time when her gifts were needed. Jenny's father had started to bluster when Jenny announced Wayne was going to be late — *Jennifer, I swear to you I think that man does this on purpose* — but her mother had gotten up on her cane and gone to her father, and put a hand on his shoulder, and said, *He's being sweet, dear, he's buying presents. He's doing the best he knows.*

Danny, of course, had asked after his father, and she told him *Daddy will be a little late,* and he whined, and Alex picked up on it, and then her mother called both of them over to the couch and let them pick the channel on the television, and for the most part they forgot. Just before dinner was served her mother hobbled into the kitchen, and Jenny kissed her on the forehead. *Thank you,* she said.

He's an odd man, her mother said.

You're not telling me anything new.

But loving. He is loving.

Her mother stirred the gravy, a firm smile on her face.

They'd eaten slowly, eyes on the clock—Jenny waited a long time to announce dessert—and at eight she gave up and cleared the dishes. She put a plate of turkey and potatoes— Wayne wouldn't eat anything else—into the oven.

Jenny scrubbed at the dishes—the same china they'd had since their wedding, even the plates they'd glued together after their first anniversary dinner. She thought, for the hundredth time, what her life would be like if she was in Larry's kitchen now, instead of Wayne's.

Larry and Emily had bought a new house the previous spring, on the other side of the county, to celebrate Larry's election as sheriff. Of course Jenny had gone to see it with Wayne and the boys, but she'd been by on her own a couple of times, too—Emily saw her grandmother twice a month, at a nursing home in Michigan, staying away for the weekends. Jenny had made her visits in summer, when she didn't teach, while Wayne was at work. She dropped the boys at her folks', and parked her car out of sight from the road. It was a nice house, big and bright, with beautiful bay windows that let in the evening sun, filtering it through the leaves of two huge maples in the front yard. Larry wouldn't use his and Emily's bed—*God, it wouldn't be right, even if I don't love her*—so they made love on the guest bed, narrow and squeaky. It was the same bed Larry had slept on in high school, which gave things a nice nostalgic feel; this was the bed in which Larry had first touched her breasts, way back in the mists of time, when she was sixteen. Now she and Larry lay in the guest room all afternoon. They laughed and chattered; when Larry came (with a bellow she would have found funny, if it didn't turn her on so much), it was like a cork popped out from his throat, and he'd talk for hours about the misadventures of the citizens of Kinslow. All the while he'd touch her with his big hands.

I should have slept with you in high school, she told him, during one of those afternoons. *I would never have gone on to anyone else.*

Well, I told you so.

She laughed. But sometimes this was because she was trying very hard not to cry—not in front of Larry, not when they had so few hours together. He worried after her constantly, and she wanted him to think as many good thoughts about her as he could.

I married the wrong guy, was what she wanted to tell him, but she couldn't. They had just, in a shy way, admitted they were in love, but neither one had been brave enough to bring up what they were going to do about it. Larry had just been elected; even though he was doing what his father had done, he was the youngest sheriff anyone had ever heard of, and a scandal and a divorce would probably torpedo future terms. And being sheriff was a job Larry wanted—the only job he'd wanted, why he'd gone into the police force instead of off to college, like her and Wayne. If only he had! She and Wayne had never been friends in high school, but in college they got to know each other because they had Larry in common—because she pined for Larry, and Wayne was good at making her laugh, at making her feel not so lonely. At being gentle and kind—not like every other boozed-up asshole trying for a grope.

And, back home, Larry met Emily at church—he called Jenny one night during her sophomore year, to tell her he was in love, that he was happy and he hoped Jenny would be happy for him, too.

I'm seeing Wayne, she said, blurting it out, relieved she could finally say it.

Really? Larry had paused. *Our Wayne?*

But as much as Jenny now daydreamed about being Larry's wife (which, these days, was a lot) she knew such a thing was unlikely at best. She could only stand here waiting for the husband she did have—who might as well be a third son—to figure out it was family time, and think of Larry sitting in his living room with Emily. They probably weren't talking, either—Emily would be watching television, with Larry sitting in his den, his nose buried in a Civil War book. Or thinking of her. Jenny's stomach thrilled.

But what was she thinking? It was Christmas Eve at the Thompkins's house, too, and Larry's parents were over; Jenny's mother was good friends with Mrs. Thompkins and had said something about it earlier. Larry's house would be a lot like hers was, except maybe even happier. Larry and his father and brother would be knocking back a special eggnog recipe, and Emily and Mrs. Thompkins got along better than Emily and Larry did; they'd be gossiping over cookie dough in the kitchen. The thought of all that activity and noise made Jenny's throat tighten. It was better, somehow, to think of Larry's house as unhappy; better to think of it as an empty place, too big for Larry, needing her and the children—

She was drying her hands when she heard the car grumbling in the trees. Wayne had been putting off getting a new muffler. She sighed, then called out, Daddy's home!

Daddy! Danny called. Gramma, finally!

She wished Wayne could hear that.

She looked out the kitchen window and saw Wayne's car pull up in front of the garage, the wide white glow of his headlights getting smaller and more specific on the garage door. He parked too close to the door. Jenny had asked him time and time again to give her room to back the Vega out of the garage if she needed to. She could see Wayne behind the wheel, his Impala's orange dashboard lights shining onto his face. He had his glasses on; she could see the reflections, little match lights.

She imagined Larry coming home, outside a different kitchen window, climbing out of his cruiser. She imagined her

sons calling him Daddy. The fantasy was almost blasphe-
mous—but it made her tingle, at the same time. Larry loved
the boys, and they loved him; she sometimes stopped at the
station house, and Larry would take them for a ride in his
cruiser. His marriage to Emily might be different if they
could have children of their own. Jenny wasn't supposed to
know—no one did—but Emily was infertile. They'd found
out just before moving into the new house.

Wayne shut off the engine. The light was out over the
garage, and Jenny couldn't see him any longer; the image of the
car was replaced by a curved piece of her own reflection in
the window. She turned again to putting away the dishes. I think
he's bringing presents, she heard her mother say. Danny answered this with shouts, and Alex answered him with a yodel.

Jenny thought about Wayne coming in the front door, forgetting to stamp the snow from his boots. She was going to
have to go up and kiss him, pretend she didn't taste the cigarettes on his breath. He would sulk if she didn't.

This was what infuriated her most: she could explain and
explain (later, when they put the kids to bed), but Wayne
wouldn't understand what he'd done wrong. He'd brought the
kids presents—he'd probably bought her a present. He'd
been moody lately, working long hours, and—she knew—
this was his apology for it. In his head he'd worked it all out;
he would make a gesture that far outshone any grumpiness,
any silence at the dinner table. He'd come through the door
like Santa Claus. She could tell him, *The only gift I wanted was a
normal family dinner,* and he'd look hurt, he'd look like she
slapped him. *But,* he'd say, and the corners of his mouth
would turn down, *I was just trying to*—and then he'd launch
into the same story he'd be telling himself right now—

They had done this before, a number of times. Too many times. This was how the rest of the night was going to go. And the thought of it all playing out, so predictably—

Jenny set a plate down on the counter. She blinked; her nose stung. The thought of Wayne made her feel ill. Her husband was coming into his house on Christmas Eve, and she couldn't bear it.

About a month ago she'd called in a trespasser, while Wayne was away in Chicago. This was risky, she knew, but she had gotten weepy—just like this—knowing she and Larry wouldn't be able to see each other again for weeks. She'd asked if the sheriff could come out to the house, and the sheriff came. He looked so happy when she opened the door to him, when he realized Wayne was gone. She took him upstairs, and they did it, and then afterward she said, *Now you surprise me,* and so he took her out in the cruiser, to a nearby stretch of road, empty for a mile ahead and behind, and he said *Hang on,* and floored it. The cruiser seemed almost happy to oblige him. She had her hands on the dashboard, and the road—slightly hilly—lifted her up off the seat, dropped her down again, made her feel like a girl. *You're doing one-twenty,* Larry said, calm as ever, in between her shrieks. *Unfortunately, we're out of road.*

At the house she hugged him, kissed his chin. He'd already told her, in a way, but now she told him, *I love you.* He'd blushed to his ears.

She was going to leave Wayne.

Of course she'd thought about it; she'd been over the possibilities, idly, on and off for the last four years, and certainly since taking up with Larry. But now she knew; she'd crossed some point of balance. She'd been waiting for something to happen with Larry, but she would have to act even sooner. The planning would take a few months, at most. She'd have to have a place lined up somewhere else. A job—maybe in Indy, but certainly out of Kinslow. And then she would tell Larry—she'd have to break it to him gently, but she would tell him, once and for all—that she was his for the taking, if he could manage it.

This was it: she didn't love her husband—in fact she didn't much like him—and was never going to feel anything for him again. It had to be done. Larry or no Larry, it had to be done.

Something out the window caught her eye. Wayne had the passenger door of the Impala open, and was bent inside; she could see his back under the dome lamp. What was he doing? Maybe he'd spilled his ashtray. She went to the window and put her face close to the glass.

He backed out of the car, and stood straight. He saw her, and stood looking at her for a moment in front of the open car door. He wiped his nose with his gloved hand. Was he crying? She felt a flicker of guilt, as though somehow he'd heard her thoughts. But then he smiled, and lifted a finger: *Just a second.*

She did a quick beckon with her hand—*Get your ass in here*—and made a face, eyeballs rolled toward the rest of the house. *Now.*

He shook his head, held the finger up again.

Jenny crossed her arms. She'd see Larry next week; Emily was going to Michigan. She could begin to tell him then.

Wayne bent into the car, then straightened up again. He grinned.

She held her hands out at her sides, palms up: *What? I'm waiting.*

1970

When Wayne had first told her he wanted to blindfold her, Jenny's fear was that he was trying out some kind of sex game, some spice-up-your-love-life idea he'd gotten out of the advice column in *Playboy*. But he promised her otherwise, and led her to the car. After fifteen minutes there, arms folded across her chest, and then the discovery that he was serious about guiding her, still blindfolded, through waist-high weeds and clinging spiderwebs, she began to wish it had been sex on his mind after all.

Wayne, she said, either tell me where we're going or I'm taking this thing off.

It's not far, honey, he said; she could tell from his voice he was grinning. Just bear with me. I'm watching your feet for you.

They were in a woods; that was easy enough to guess. She heard the leaves overhead, and birdcalls; she smelled the thick and cloying undergrowth. Twice she stumbled and her hands scraped across tree trunks, furred vines, before Wayne tightened his grip on her arm. They were probably on a path; even blind she knew the going was too easy for them to be headed directly through the bushes. So they were in Wayne's woods, the one his parents owned. Simple enough to figure out; he talked about this place constantly. He'd driven her past it a number of times, but to her it looked like any other stand of trees out in this part of the country: solid green in summertime and dull gray-brown in winter, so thick you couldn't see light shining through from the other side.

I know where we are, she told him.

He gripped her hand and laughed. Maybe, he said, But you don't know *why*.

He had her there. She snagged her skirt on a bush and was tugged briefly between its thorns and Wayne's hand. The skirt ripped and gave. She cursed.

Sorry! Wayne said. Sorry, sorry—not much longer now.

Sunlight flickered over the top of the blindfold, and the sounds around her opened up, became more expansive. She was willing to bet they were in a clearing. A breeze blew past them, smelling of country springtime: budding leaves and manure fertilizer.

Okay, Wayne said. Are you ready?

I'm not sure, she said.

Do you love me?

Of course I love you, she said. She reached a hand out in front of her—and found he was suddenly absent. Okay, she said, enough. Give me your hand or the blindfold's off.

She heard odd sounds—was that metal? Glass?

All right, almost there, he said. Sit down.

On the ground?

No. Just sit.

She sat, his hands on her shoulders, and found, shockingly, a chair underneath her behind. A smooth metal folding chair.

Wayne then unknotted the blindfold. He whipped it away. Happy Anniversary! he said.

Jenny squinted in the revealed light, but only for a moment. She opened her eyes wide, and then saw she was sitting, as she'd thought, in a meadow, maybe fifty yards across, surrounded by tall green trees, all of them rippling in the wind. In front of her was a card table, covered with a red-and-white-checked tablecloth. The table was set with dishes—their good china, the plates at least—and two wineglasses, all wedding presents they'd only used once, on her birthday. Wayne sat in a chair opposite her, grinning, eyebrows arched. The wind blew his hair straight up off his head.

A picnic, she said. Wayne, that's lovely—thank you.

She reached her hand across the table and grasped his. He was exasperating sometimes, but no other man she'd met could reach this level of sweetness. He'd lugged this stuff out into the middle of nowhere for her—*that's* where he must have been all afternoon.

You're welcome, he said. The red spots on his cheeks spread and deepened. He lifted her hand and kissed her knuckles, then her wedding ring. He rubbed the places he'd kissed with his thumb.

He said, I'm sorry that dinner won't be as fancy as the plates, but I really couldn't get anything but sandwiches out here.

She laughed. I've eaten your cooking. We're better off with the sandwiches.

Ouch, he said. He faked a French accent: This kitten, she has the claws. But I have the milk that will tame her.

He bent and rummaged through a paper bag near his chair, then produced a bottle of red wine with a flourish and a cocked eyebrow. She couldn't help but laugh.

He uncorked the bottle and poured her a glass.

A toast.

To what?

To the first part of the surprise.

There's more?

He smiled, slyly, and lifted his glass, then said, After dinner.

He'd won her over; she didn't question it. Jenny lifted her glass, clinked rims with her husband's, and sat back with her legs crossed at the knee. Wayne bent and dug in the bag again, and then came up with wheat bread and cheese, and a package of carved roast beef in deli paper. He made her a sandwich, even slicing up a fresh tomato. They ate in the pleasant breeze.

After dinner he leaned back in his chair and rubbed his stomach. When they first started dating she thought he did this to be funny; but soon she realized he did it without thinking, after eating anything larger than a candy bar. It meant all was well in the land of Wayne. The gesture made her smile, and she looked away. Since they'd married he'd developed a small wedge of belly; she wondered—not unhappily, not here—if in twenty years he'd have a giant stomach to rub, like his father's.

So I was right? she asked. This is your parents' woods?

Nope, he said, smiling.

It's not?

It was. They don't own it any more.

They sold it? When? To who?

Yesterday. He was grinning broadly now. To me, he said. To us.

She sat forward, then back. Wayne glanced around at the trees, his hair tufting in a sudden pickup of the wind.

You're serious, she said. Her stomach tightened. This was a feeling she'd had a few times since their wedding—she was learning that the more complicated Wayne's ideas were, the less likely they were to be good ones. A picnic in the woods? Fine. But this?

I'm serious, Wayne said. This is my favorite place in the world—second-favorite, I mean. He winked at her, then went on. But either way. Both of my favorite places are mine now. Ours.

She touched a napkin to her lips. So, she said, how much did—did *we* pay for our woods?

A dollar. He laughed, and said, Can you believe it? Dad wanted to give it to us, but I told him, No, Pop, I want to *buy* it. We ended up compromising.

She could only stare at him. He squeezed her hand, and said, We're landowners now, honey. One square mile.

That's—

Wayne said, Dad wanted to sell it off, and I couldn't bear the thought of it going to somebody who was going to plow it all under.

We need to pay your parents more than a dollar, Wayne. That's absurd.

That's what *I* told them. But Dad said no, we needed the money more. But honey—there's something else. That's only part of the surprise.

Jenny twined her fingers together in front of her mouth. A suspicion had formed, and she hoped he wasn't about to do what she guessed. Wayne was digging beside his chair again. He came up with a long roll of paper—blueprint paper, held with a rubber band. He put it on the table between them.

Our paper anniversary, he said.

What is this?

Go ahead. Look at it.

Jenny knew what the plans would show. She rolled the rubber band off the blueprints, her mouth dry. Wayne stood, his hands quick and eager, and spread the prints flat on the table-top. They were upside down; she went around the table and stood next to him. He put a hand on the small of her back.

The blueprints were for a house. A simple two-story house—the ugliest thing she had ever seen.

I didn't want to tell you too soon, he said, but I got a raise at the bank. Plus, now that I've been there three years, I get a terrific deal on home loans. I got approval a few days ago.

A house, she said.

They were living in an apartment in Kinslow, nice enough, but bland, sharing a wall with an old woman who complained if they spoke above a whisper, or if they played rock-and-roll records. Jenny put a hand to her hair. Wayne, she said, where is this house going to be?

Here, he said, and grinned again. He held his arms out. Right here. The table is on the exact spot. The contractors start digging on Monday. The timing's perfect. It'll be done by the end of summer.

Here . . . in the woods.

Yep.

He laughed, watching her face, and said, We're only three miles from town. The interstate's just on the other side of the field to the south. The county road is paved. All we have to do is have them expand the path in and we'll have a driveway. It'll be our hideaway. Honey?

She sat down in the chair he'd been sitting in. She could barely speak. They had talked about buying a house soon—but one in town. They'd also talked about moving to Indianapolis, about leaving Kinslow—maybe not right away, but within five years.

Wayne, she said. Doesn't this all feel kind of . . . permanent?

Well, he said, it's a house. It's supposed to.

We just talked last month. You wanted to get a job in the city. I want to live in the city. A five-year plan, remember?

Yeah. I do.

He knelt next to her chair and put his arm across her shoulders.

But I've been thinking, he said. The bank is nice, really nice, and the money just got better, and then Dad was talking about getting rid of the land, and I couldn't bear to hear it, and—

And so you went ahead and did it without asking me.

Um, Wayne said, it seemed like such a great deal that—

Okay, she told him. Okay. It *is* a great deal. If it was just buying the woods, that would be wonderful. But the house is different. What it means is that you're building your dream house right in the spot I want to move away from. I hate to break it to you, but that means it's not quite my dream house.

Wayne removed his hand from her shoulders, and clasped his fingers in front of his mouth. She knew that gesture, too.

Wayne—

I really thought this would make you happy, he said.

A house *does* make me happy. But one in Kinslow. One we can sell later and not feel bad about, when we move—

She wasn't sure what happened next. Wayne told her it was an accident, that he stood up too fast and hit his shoulder on the table. And it looked that way, sometimes, when she thought back on it. But when it happened, she was sure he flung his arm out, that he knocked the table aside. That he did it on purpose. The wineglasses and china plates flew out and disappeared into the clumps of yellow grass. The blueprints caught in a tangle with the tablecloth and the other folding chair.

Goddamnit! Wayne shouted. He walked a quick circle, holding his hand close to his chest.

Jenny was too stunned to move, but then, after a minute, she said Wayne's name.

He shook his head and kept walking the circle. Jenny saw he was crying, and when he saw her looking, he turned his face away. She sat still in her chair, not certain what to say or do. Finally she knelt and tried to assemble the pieces of a broken dish.

After a minute he said, I think I'm bleeding.

She stood and walked to him and saw that he was. He'd torn a gash in his hand, on the meaty outside of his palm. A big one; it would need stitches. His shirt was soaked with blood where he'd cradled his hand.

Come on, she said. We need to get you to the hospital.

No, he said. His voice was low and miserable.

Wayne, don't be silly. This isn't a time to sulk. You're hurt.

No. Hear me out. Okay? You always say what you want, and you make me sound stupid for saying what I want. This time I just want to *say* it.

She grabbed some napkins and pressed them against his hand. Jesus, Wayne, she said, seeing blood from the cut well up across her fingers. Okay, okay, say what you need to.

This is my favorite place, he said. I've loved it since I was a kid. I used to come out here with Larry. He and I used to imagine we had a house here. A hideaway.

Well—

Be quiet. I'm not done yet. His lip quivered, and he said, I know we talked, I know you want to go to Indy. Well, we can. But it looks like we're going to be successful. It looks like I'm going to do well and you can get a job teaching anywhere. I'll just work hard and in five years maybe we can have two houses—

Oh, Wayne—

Listen! We can have a house in Indy and then this—this can be our getaway. He sniffled, and said, But I want to keep it. Besides you, this is the only thing I want. This house, right out here.

We can talk about it later. You're going to bleed to death if we don't get you to the emergency room.

I wanted you to love it, he said. I wanted you to love it because *I* love it. Is that too much to ask from your wife? I wanted to give you something *special.* I—

It was awful, watching him try to explain. The spots of red in his cheeks were burning now, and the rims of his eyes were almost the same color. The corners of his mouth turned down in little curls.

Don't worry, she said. We'll talk about it. Okay? Wayne? We'll talk. We'll take the blueprints with us to the emergency room. But you need stitches. Let's go.

I love you, he said.

She stopped fussing around his hand. He was looking down at her, tilting his head.

Jenny, just tell me you love me and none of it will matter.

She laughed in spite of herself, shaking her head. Of course, she said. Of course I do.

Say it. I need to hear it.

She kissed his cheek. Wayne, I love you with all my heart. You're my husband. Now move your behind, okay?

He kissed her, dipping his head. Jenny was bending away to pick up the blueprints, and his lips, wet, just grazed her cheek. She smiled at him and gathered their things; Wayne stood and watched her, moist-eyed.

She finally took his good hand, and they walked back

toward the car, and his kiss, dried slowly by the breeze, felt cool on her cheek. It lingered for a while, and—despite everything—she was glad for it.

Then

The boys were first audible only as distant shrieks between the trees.

They were young enough that any time they raised their voices—and they were chasing each other, their only sounds loud calls, denials, laughter—they sounded as though they were in terror. When they appeared in the meadow—one charging out from a break in a dense thicket of thorny shrubs, the other close behind—they were almost indistinguishable from one another in their squeals, in their red jackets and caps. Late afternoon was shifting into dusky evening. Earlier they had hunted squirrels, unaware of how the sounds of their voices and the pops of their BB guns had traveled ahead of them, sending hundreds of beasts into their dens.

In the center of the meadow the trailing boy caught up with the fleeing first; he pounced and they wrestled. Caps came off. One boy was blond, the other—the smaller one— mousy brown. Stop it, he called, from the bottom of the pile. Larry! Stop it! I mean it!

Larry laughed, and said with a shudder, Wayne, you pussy.

Don't call me that!

Don't be one, pussy!

They flailed and punched until they lay squirming and helpless with laughter.

Later they pitched a tent in the center of the meadow. They had done this before. Near their tent was an old circle of charred stones, ringing a pile of damp ashes and cinders. Wayne wandered out of the meadow and gathered armfuls of deadwood while Larry secured the tent into the soft and unstable earth. They squatted down around the piled wood and worked at setting it alight. Darkness was coming; beneath the gray, overcast sky, light was diffuse anyway, and now it seemed that the shadows came not from above, but from below, pooling and deepening as though they welled up from underground springs. Larry was the first to look nervously into the shadowed trees, while Wayne threw matches into the wood. Wayne worked at the fire with his face twisted, mouth pursed. When the fire caught at last, the boys grinned at each other.

I wouldn't want to be out here when it's dark, Larry said, experimentally.

It's dark now.

No, I mean with no fire. Pitch dark.

I have, Wayne said.

No you haven't.

Sure I have. Sometimes I forget what time it is and get back to my bike late. Once it got totally dark. If I wasn't on the path I would have got lost.

Wayne poked at the fire with a long stick. His parents owned the woods, but their house was two miles away. Larry looked around him, impressed.

Were you scared?

Shit, yeah. Wayne giggled. It was dark. I'm not *dumb*.

Larry looked at him for a while, then said, Sorry I called you a pussy.

Wayne shrugged, and said, I should have shot that squirrel.

They'd seen one in a tree, somehow oblivious to them. Wayne was the better shot, and they'd crouched together behind a nearby log, Wayne's BB gun steadied in the crotch of a dead branch. He'd looked at the squirrel for a long time, before finally lifting his cheek from the gun. I can't, he'd said.

What do you mean, you can't?

I can't. That's all.

He handed the gun to Larry, and Larry took aim, too fast, and missed.

It's all right, Larry said now, at the fire. Squirrel tastes like shit.

So does baloney, Wayne said, grim.

They pulled sandwiches from their packs. Both took the meat from between the bread, speared it with sticks, and held it over the fire until it charred and sizzled. Then they put it back into the sandwiches. Wayne took a bite first, then squealed and held a hand to his mouth. He spit a hot chunk of meat into his hand, then fumbled it into the fire.

It's *hot,* he said.

Larry looked at him for a long time. Pussy, he said, and couldn't hold in his laughter.

Wayne ducked his eyes and felt inside his mouth with his fingers.

Later, the fire dimmed. They sat sleepily beside it, talking in low voices. Wayne rubbed his stomach. Things unseen moved in the trees—mostly small animals, from the sound of it, but once or twice larger things.

Deer, probably, Wayne said.

What about wildcats?

No wildcats live around here. I've seen foxes, though.

Foxes aren't that big.

They spread out their sleeping bags inside the tent and opened the flap a bit so they could see the fire.

This is my favorite place, Wayne said, when they zipped into the bags.

The tent?

No. The meadow. I've been thinking about it. I want to have a house here someday.

A house?

Yeah.

What kind of house?

I don't know. Like mine, I guess, but out here. I could walk onto the porch at night and it would be just like this. But you wouldn't have to pitch a tent. You know what? We could both have it. We'd each get half of the house to do whatever we want in. We wouldn't have to go home before it gets dark, because we'd already be there.

Larry smiled, but said, That's dumb. We'll both be married by then. You won't want me in your house all the time.

That's not true.

You won't get married?

No—I mean, yeah, I will. Sure. But you can always come over.

It's not like that, Larry said, laughing.

How do you know?

Because it isn't. Jesus Christ, Wayne. Sometimes I wonder what planet you live on.

You always make my ideas sound dumb.

So don't have dumb ideas.

It isn't a dumb idea to have my friends in my house.

Larry sighed, and said, No, it isn't. But marriage is different. You get married and then the girl you marry is your best friend. That's what being in love is.

My dad has best friends.

Mine, too. But who does your dad spend more time with—them or your mom?

Wayne thought for a minute. Oh.

They looked out the tent flap at the fire.

Wayne said, You'll come over when you can, though, right?

Sure, Larry said. You bet.

They lay on their stomachs and Wayne talked about the house he wanted to build. It would have a tower. It would have a secret hallway built into the walls. It would have a pool table in the basement, better than the one at Vic's Pizza King in town. It would have a garage big enough for three cars.

Four, Larry said. We'll each have two. A sports car and a truck.

Four, Wayne said, a four-car garage. And a pinball machine. I'll have one in the living room, rigged so you don't have to put money in it.

After a while, Wayne heard Larry's breathing soften. He looked out the tent flap at the orange coals of the fire. He was sleepy, but he didn't want to sleep, not yet. He thought about his house and watched the fire fade.

He wished for the house to be here in the meadow now. Larry could have half, and he could have the other. He imagined empty rooms, then rooms packed with toys. But that wasn't the way it would be. They'd be grown-ups. He imagined a long mirror in the bedroom and tried to see himself in it: older, as a man. He'd have rifles, not BB guns. He tried to imagine things that a man would have, that a boy wouldn't: bookshelves, closets full of suits and ties.

Then he saw a woman at the kitchen table, wearing a blue dress. Her face kept changing—he couldn't quite see it. But he knew she was pretty. He saw himself opening the kitchen door, swinging a briefcase which he put down at his feet, and he held out his arms, and the woman stood to welcome him, making a happy girlish sound, and held out her arms, too. Then she was close. He smelled her perfume, and she said— in a woman's voice, warm and honeyed—*Wayne,* and he a felt a leaping excitement, like he'd just been scared—but better, much better—and he laughed and squeezed her and said, into her soft neck and hair, his voice deep: *I'm home.*

ACKNOWLEDGMENTS

This is my first book, so please forgive the indulgence of a long list of thank-yous.

I'm the product of two graduate programs in creative writing, and the people I met in each need to be mentioned, not only as teachers and colleagues, but as friends and family. So thanks to the good folks at Miami University of Ohio: the fine professor/writers Steven Bauer, Constance Pierce, Eric Goodman, Kay Sloan, and Laura Mandell; and my esteemed fellow workshoppers and friends—especially Scott Berg, Peirce Johnston, Beth Slattery, Kathleen Riggs, Greg Kaufmann, Bill Willard, Tom Hyland, Kathy Wise, and Michael Parker.

My MFA is from Ohio State University, and most of this book was written while I was a student there. Primary thanks go to Michelle Herman, writer and mentor extraordinaire; much of my current life wouldn't be happening without her insistence that I buckle down and get one. And thanks, too, to the extraordinary OSU faculty who've taught me personally—Lee K. Abbott, Erin McGraw, Lee Martin, and Kathy Fagan—and to those who've always offered advice and encouragement: Stephanie Grant, Steve Kuusisto, David Citino, and Andrew Hudgins. And thanks to my classmates who workshopped these pieces—a more talented and good-hearted bunch I could not have dreamed up for myself: Rebecca Barry, Erica Beeney, Jeff Butler, Akhim Cabey, Keith Cooper, Cameron Filipour, Bill Fowler, Nancy Ginzer, Holly Goddard-Jones, Teline Guerra, Charles Harmon, Buddy Harris, Matt Healy, Donna Jarrell, Cecilia Johnson, Joanna Kalafarsky, E. J. Levy, Bob Loss, Bill Lamp, Danielle Lavaque-Manty, Jolie Lewis, Kelly Magee, Amanda Scheiderer, Nick Scorza, Amy Thorne, Kristina Torres, and Star Zagofsky. Thanks also go to Jenny James Robinson, Heather Sebring, Joshua Jay, Adam Cole, Eddie Lushbaugh, Scott Black, Kathleen Gagel, Christopher Griffin, Preston Pickett, Susan Wittstock, Jack Nasar, Judith Mayne, and Terry Moore.

Here are a few more teachers. At Western Boone: Janet Dingman, Margaret Keene, Denise Beck, Virginia Smith, and Lloyd Tiffany. At Ball State University: Marjorie Smelstor (how I hope this book finds you!), Dennis Hoilman, William Miller, David Upchurch, William Liston, Richard Whitworth, and especially Margaret Kingery, a terrific writer and teacher to whom I attached myself, barnaclelike, during my final two years as a Cardinal. (And I can't mention Ball State without thanking Mike McCauley, Frank Eikenberry, and all the good folks at OPASSS, who for three years listened to me explain my writer fantasies in excruciating detail.)

I worked for several years for Half Price Books, a wonderful company that provided me with unblinking support when I badly needed it. Many, many thanks—with an understanding that they're inadequate—to John Wiley. And I have to mention a few of the great folks I've worked for and with: Marie Wiley, Doug Gurney, Mark Maxwell, Rob Zapol, Christine Rohweder, Mark Eppich, Shannon Rampe, Jeff Mathys, Timmy Schmidt, Tracy Nesbitt, and Karen Graham. And special thanks to Ed Morrow, for the pep talk.

Thanks to Stacy at Caribou Coffee and Anton at Caffé Apropos, for time and space and fuel and, in Stacy's case, employment.

I don't know how to begin thanking Larry Weis and Terry Hartley for going far above and beyond the call of duty.

Big thanks go, of course, to my agent, Marian Young, and my editor, Ann Patty, who conspired in giving me the best present ever. And thanks as well to Nat Sobel, Lindsay Sagnette, Otto Penzler, and especially Nick Hornby, who has been unflagging in support of my writing.

I've gone through a lot in the last few years, and I could not have done it—could not have imagined getting out of bed, let alone writing a single word—without the support of the following group of friends and adopted family:

Taylor, Heidi, and Michael Snodgrass; Greg Harris (and his wonderful parents, Charlie and Victoria); Pat and Gina Kanouse; Doug Bowers; Wes and Tory Herron (and the whole wacky Herron clan); Michael P. Kardos and Catherine Pierce; Linda Bevington; Rodney and Dawn Fontana; Kelly Bahmer-Brouse and Andrew Brouse; Sean Apple; James Michael Taylor; Lori Rader Day; Beth Giles; Gail Bartlett; Rob and Elizabeth Trupp; Kristina Chilian; Chad Hill; Ariane Bolduc; Shari Goldhagen; the Lauers (Steve, Gretchen, John, and Liz), and the Thomases (Maryellen, Kenny, and Jennifer).

I'll end with thanks to four extraordinary women, all of whom I love without measure:

My mother, Jan Coake—who, when I was five, wrote down the stories I dictated to her (we've come a long way, haven't we?), and who has been my biggest fan ever since.

My sister, Whitney Coake, who's younger, but who has always tried to protect me (or, failing that, to dress me).

My late wife Joellen, who showed me what it takes to be courageous and happy, all at once.

And, at last, Stephanie Lauer, whose love continues to surprise me. I didn't expect to find her—but every day I consider myself lucky I did.